He kissed her— angrily and violently

The gentleness Cal had shown her earlier was gone. He wanted her, and he wanted her to know it.

Rebecca felt his body shudder against her. He was asking her to trust him—she felt it keenly, and she did trust him, completely, though he had lied to her.

"Tomorrow," he said, pulling away from her. "Can you come to me tomorrow?"

"I'll come."

He smiled then, grimly, but he smiled. "Your roommate—I get the feeling she's not very discreet. If she asks..."

"I'll lie. If necessary."

He gave her a strange look, a second of doubt, a moment of admiration. "I believe you would," he said as he climbed back into his Jeep. Then the headlights came on, dazzling her for an instant.

VANESSA JAMES

give me this night

Harlequin Books

TORONTO • NEW YORK • LONDON
AMSTERDAM • PARIS • SYDNEY • HAMBURG
STOCKHOLM • ATHENS • TOKYO • MILAN

Harlequin Presents first edition January 1986
ISBN 0-373-10849-4

Original hardcover edition published in 1985
by Mills & Boon Limited

CHAPTER ONE

The first time Rebecca set eyes on Cal Ryder, she took a dislike to him. It was early morning, the week before Easter, and a thin mist still hung over the harbour and the sea, although later, she knew, it would be hot.

The ferry-boat, delayed at Corfu the previous night, must have set off this morning at dawn, because Corfu was a good three hours off from the tiny and more remote Ionian island of Paxos, and it was still only eight in the morning when she saw its bows rounding the headland, heard its warning horn as it started to negotiate the narrow channel to the harbour.

She and Nicky, summoned half an hour before by telephone, now stood on the quayside together. Rebecca, the taller of the two might have been taken for a Greek: slender, her almost black hair falling straight to her shoulders, her skin already tanned by weeks of exceptionally warm spring weather, she stood now staring out across the water, shivering slightly, drawing her jacket more tightly around her, for—until the sun was fully up—the air was chilled.

Nicky, her friend, could only have been English; no one would have mistaken her for any other nationality. Shorter than Rebecca by half a head, plump, her fluffy fair hair blowing around her face with its pink-and-white English rose complexion, she was, as often, flustered. While Rebecca gazed out to sea, and appeared to Nicky to day-dream, she herself feverishly consulted lists. Pieces of paper flapped in the breeze; ineffectively she smoothed them down again, tried to check the names of the passengers on the ferry-boat, and muttered to herself.

'Three,' she said at last, making Rebecca jump. 'Only three groups, thank goodness. The real rush won't start for a few more days. One lot are staying here in Gaios; the family with the children and the baby are going on to Lakka, and there's a honeymoon couple staying in the little cottage on Anti-Paxos ... Now. The baby—did we remember to get the cot

5

put in for them? Oh, and the Lakka family have hired a boat—God. I hope Nico remembered to service it—I forgot to check. Oh damn . . .' She swore as the papers fluttered out of her grasp again. 'Goodness, I'd love some coffee, wouldn't you? I still feel half asleep. It's all right for you, you're always up with the lark, but I feel ghastly. I was sound asleep when the 'phone went—they could have given us a bit more warning, don't you think? I thought we'd have until eleven at least before the ferry got in and then . . .' She broke off, and looked up. '*Rebecca*,' she cried in exasperation, 'you're not listening to a word! You do day-dream, you know. Half the time I think you . . .'

At that point she broke off once more, following Rebecca's gaze. The ferry was now quite close, manoeuvring in the narrow channel so that it could tie up at the quay. Through the thin morning haze the passengers were now clearly visible, leaning over the rails, peering in the direction of the island.

Rebecca could make out two children, calling excitedly to one another; a woman wearing a headscarf and carrying a baby in a canvas sling; a man and a woman, their arms wrapped around one another—the honeymoon couple, she guessed; two others, young men with rucksacks who looked like students; and then, right up in the bows of the boat, leaning over the rail, and looking down into the water . . . She tensed slightly, and Nicky following her gaze, gave a peculiar muffled squeak and nearly dropped her clipboard. She then poked Rebecca in the ribs, very hard, with one sharp elbow.

'It's *him*,' she hissed. 'Look, up in the front, leaning on the rail. The writer. You remember. I told you. Oh God—It's *him*. Becky, it's him . . .'

'Cal Ryder?' Rebecca screwed up her eyes, although she could already see the man in question quite distinctly. He was tall, and dark, with severe, slightly narrow features; and wearing crumpled but expensive clothes. Nicky had started jabbering again, apparently quite forgetting that the mist and the water amplified her words as effectively as a microphone.

'Oh God, oh God, oh God! What are we going to do, Becky? He shouldn't be here—not yet. He's not on the list. Check the list, quick, I can't, my hand's shaking. I'm sure I'm right. I *know* I'm right. Next week—he's not supposed to be coming until the very end of next week—Easter Saturday. He moves into the villa then, Michael said, I remember distinctly. "Don't worry," Michael said, "I'll be over by then, if there's any problems I'll handle it" ...' She gave a long-drawn out wail of despair. 'Becky, what can we *do*? He's in the Villa Circe, he won't stay anywhere else, and the roof's still not fixed. Oh God ...'

Rebecca looked down at the trembling list, which indeed did not include Cal Ryder's name, and back up again at the ferry. The wail of distress must have attracted his attention, because the dark man had straightened up, and was looking directly at them. Rebecca, seeing his features for a second across the water, seeing the darkness of his eyes and the strong harsh line of his mouth, instinctively shrank back behind Nicky. She felt thrown, jarred, somehow ...

He was extremely good-looking, of course, but then she had known that from seeing photographs of him, and from Nicky's gossip, and she had always distrusted very handsome men. He also managed to convey—though he stood quite still—a certain haughtiness, a disregard for his fellow passengers that she instantly branded snobbish. They, seeing the island of Paxos for the first time, and, as the ferry lined up along the quay, having their first full glimpse of its harbour— one of the loveliest in the Greek islands—were crying out with enthusiasm and excitement. Rebecca saw the two honey-mooners stare in the direction of the central village square, which opened out off the harbour: the little domed white church; the oleander trees shading the café tables; the huddle of houses—white, and ochre, faded pink ... The honey-mooners turned back to each other with expressions of delight. The family with children called out to one another in excitement; one of the two students angled his camera— everyone on board, in fact, was displaying precisely the same disbelieving joy and elation that she herself had felt when she first arrived here a few weeks before, and thought that she had never, ever, seen a place more beautiful. Everyone, that was, except the tall dark man in the bows. He simply straightened up, his expression bored and irritable, as if he found such enthusiasm tediously naive and silly. With an impatient gesture he bent and picked up a solitary case, and made for the side where the gangplank was being lowered, with no more emotion than if he had just pulled in at Paddington station and was getting off the train.

Nicky stared and moaned and fluttered her list, and Rebecca thought: *So—that's the great Cal Ryder. I thought I wouldn't like him, and I was quite right* ...

Nicky and Rebecca had been friends since they were children; they had been at school together, and their friendship had survived the period when Nicky, who was two years older, left to work in London, and Rebecca stayed on at school, though, as they grew older, the differences between them became more marked. Each could exasperate the other; each retained an obstinate and unshakable fondness for the other. Nicky, who took the fact that she was the elder very seriously, enjoyed bossing Rebecca about, and attempting to organise her life, and Rebecca good-humouredly allowed her to do so—up to a point.

It was Nicky, who had worked for Michael Hamilton for several years, who had suggested that Rebecca should come out to Paxos to work with her—a suggestion that, at the time, Rebecca had had good reason to accept quickly and gratefully. So, although Rebecca was learning fast about the travel agency business in general, and the villa rental business in particular, it was still Nicky who was, very much, the senior partner. There were times when Rebecca felt extremely grateful for that fact, and this morning was one of them. For now, collecting herself, smoothing her hair into place, and assuming the head-girl demeanour that Rebecca remembered of old, Nicky prepared to do battle with Cal Ryder, and Rebecca, silently rejoicing, was spared. She was deputed to help the family with the children and the baby—the Templar family, Nicky said their name was—who had rented a villa in the smaller fishing village of Lakka, further up the coast.

'You take the car and drive them up there, would you, Becky?' Nicky had pulled herself together. Her eyes were scanning the passengers as they filed down the gangplank, and Rebecca saw them focus for a moment on the two tall young students. 'I'll try and sort out Cal Ryder, and then I'll deal with the honeymoon couple, and those two . . .' She gestured to the students, her cheeks deepening slightly in colour, and Rebecca smiled to herself. Then Nicky was off, pushing her way through the crowd that had gradually assembled on the quay.

Rebecca went up and introduced herself to the Templar family. Mrs Templar was looking exhausted, she thought, so she found a place for her to sit down, parked the children firmly with her husband, and then went back on board the ferry to search out their luggage.

It did not take long, and while she searched among the welter of packages to be delivered to the island, fragments of conversation drifted up to her from the quay below.

'. . . I'm most awfully sorry, Mr Ryder, but there must be some mistake. I was expecting you on the fifteenth, Easter Saturday . . . You see, the repairs to the villa aren't complete yet and . . .'

'I know all that. Please.' Cal Ryder interrupted Nicky irritably. His voice was cold, and clipped. 'I've made my own arrangements—you have no need to worry.'

'Your own arrangements?' Nicky's voice rose in dismay, and Rebecca paused. Poor Nicky: she never knew when to leave well alone . . . 'Oh, but I thought . . . Does that mean you won't be staying at the Villa Circe as usual then? I thought that . . .'

'Excuse me.' Again Cal Ryder cut Nicky off in mid-sentence. This time, Rebecca saw, peering cautiously over the ship's side, he also pushed past her, not in a rude manner exactly, although it was so brusque that you certainly couldn't have called it polite either, but in a way that made it clear he found this conversation a waste of his time, and Nicky an irritation. Rebecca felt sympathy for her friend, and a wave of indignation at Ryder: after all, Nicky was only doing her job . . .

'As I said. I have made my own arrangements. As of the fifteenth I shall be moving into the Villa Circe as planned. Until then you have no need to concern yourself on my behalf. And now—if you'll forgive me—the Jeep over there is mine, and I'm pressed for time. Good morning . . .'

With that he was gone. Rebecca saw Nicky pull a face at

his retreating back, and then turn away to what was clearly
the more pleasurable job of greeting the two young students.

'Hello,' she said gaily, her cheeks still a little flushed from
the encounter with Cal Ryder. 'You must be the Sullivans—is
that right? I'm Nicola Thomas, Michael Hamilton's repre-
sentative on the island. I hope you had a good journey—I'm
sorry the ferry was delayed. You're in Pan Cottage, I think,
aren't you? Good—well, actually, it's very near. If you could
wait a moment I could show you to the door . . .'

She moved off towards the square with the two students,
and as she did so, Rebecca, looking up, heard the Jeep's
engine fire. Cal Ryder revved it impatiently, let out the brake,
swerved round in a tight expert circle that set every dog on the
quay barking, and accelerated out of sight. Rebecca, watching
the clouds of white dust settle in his tracks, felt only relief.
There goes trouble, she thought to herself, and, finding the last
of the Templars' bags, rejoined them on the quay.

'It's a tiring journey, isn't it?' Rebecca met Mrs Templar's
eyes in the driving mirror, and gave her an encouraging smile.
'And it can't have helped, the ferry's being delayed like that.
But don't worry . . .' She let in the clutch of the large Volvo.
'It's worth it—I'm sure you'll think that. You'll be in one of
our loveliest villas—it's only about twenty minutes from here,
and everything is ready for you . . .'

Mrs Templar smiled a little wanly, and leaned back in her
seat. The two children, Rebecca saw, were nearly asleep, and
the baby, after a few fretful cries, also seemed to settle.
Rebecca negotiated the narrow village streets of Gaios with
care, and then urged the laden car up the hill that led out of
the village.

Mrs Templar looked frail, she thought, as if she were
recovering from an illness, and her husband, sitting next to
Rebecca in the front, looked harassed; she saw to her relief,
though, that the mist was lifting, and the sun was getting up
strength: she hoped fervently that the island would quickly
begin to work its magic. They drove for a little while in
silence, Rebecca pointing out a few landmarks occasionally,
and allowing the Templars time to unwind. Then, as they
rounded the bend of the hill above Gaios, and she turned

on to the narrow, rutted, coastal road, she heard Christopher Templar give an exclamation of pleasure, saw his wife turn to the window and stare out, and she relaxed a little. The magic was beginning to work . . .

To their right the ground sloped down steeply to the sea. On either side of the road were groves of silvery grey olives, their trunks gnarled, twisted and bent with age; nearer the sea on the narrow headlands that jutted out and created such beautiful bays of still blue water, grew cypress trees, their tall dark shapes, pencil thin, outlined against the clear sky. The ground, and the outcrops of rock, were reddish, and among them could be seen the spring flowers for which the island was so famous: drifts of the palest pink cyclamen, delicate groups of tiny narcissus, ferns and purple orchis. And beyond them the sea, the colour of lapis in the morning light, stretching still calm and dazzling, to the wide horizon.

'Oh, Chris, you were right, it's *beautiful*,' Mrs Templar sighed, and, catching her eye in the mirror again, Rebecca saw that animation had returned to her pale face; she smiled at Rebecca with sudden gaiety.

'We're driving north,' Rebecca explained, 'along the east coast of the island. There are only three villages of any size— Gaios, where your ferry came in, is the largest. It's about eight miles from there to Lakka, where you'll be staying. Lakka is a tiny fishing village, in a very sheltered bay. Your villa is on the edge of an olive grove, you can practically walk straight out on to the beach, and the bathing is absolutely safe . . .' She paused, and gestured ahead. 'This road goes on, beyond Lakka, to the third village, Logos, which is at the northeastern tip—and then it stops! There are good tavernas in all three villages, and shops—you'll find they stock almost everything. Even disposable nappies now . . .' Again she caught Mrs Templar's eyes in the mirror, and smiled. 'In your villa you'll find a map of the island, and information on where all the shops and tavernas are. There's no bank on the island, but the grocer in Gaios will change travellers' cheques. He has a siesta, but apart from that he's open from about seven in the morning to about ten at night. And there's a baker, about two minutes' walk from your villa, who bakes fresh bread every day . . . You have a maid—her name is Agape, and she will come in every morning and clean the villa, and you'll find she'll be more than delighted to baby-sit. She has eight children and five grand-children, so I think you'll find she's pretty expert. And—' she drew breath, 'if there's anything else you need—anything at all—just contact me at the office. I'm there to help.'

'You're very kind. And it sounds great.' Chris Templar turned and patted his wife's hand. 'You see, Pamela? I told you it would all be fine . . .' He turned back to Rebecca with a shy smile. 'I'm a teacher,' he said. 'I first came to Greece when I was a student, and I'm afraid I've been banging on to Pamela about it ever since. She hasn't been terribly well, since the baby, you know, and so—well, we decided, blow the expense, we'd come. But we were a bit apprehensive . . .' He hesitated. 'You know, it's such a tiny place, and difficult to get to, and so on . . .'

'I don't think you need have any worries,' Rebecca tried to sound as encouraging as she could. 'The island is so restful, so quiet, I'm sure it will do your wife good. And there's an excellent doctor on the island—you need have no worries on that score.' She paused. 'You can be as quiet or as energetic as you like, really. There's a sailing school the other side of Gaios—you could sail or windsurf there if you wanted. You can fish. At this time of the year—when it's not too hot—there are wonderful walks. Or, if you prefer, you can just lie on the beach and get brown . . .'

'I might settle for that, quite happily!' Pamela Templar laughed. 'And all the children will want to do is swim—I can predict that!'

'What about the west coast of the island?' Christopher Templar gestured off to their left through the olive groves. 'Are there villages there?'

'No, none.' Rebecca changed gear as the incline grew steeper. 'No—the west coast of the island is very different. The cliffs that side are very high; there are no beaches, no villages—very few houses, just a few old farms, and most of those are uninhabited now. It's spectacularly beautiful there, much wilder than here, but too dangerous to swim, and we generally advise parents with children to stick to the east coast . . .'

'We'll certainly be doing that,' Mrs Templar said firmly. 'Tom and Francie *will* climb everything in sight . . .'

'What about by boat?' Christopher Templar said. 'We've hired a little boat from you—you know, not a sailing boat, just one with an outboard. Are there any rules about that?'

'Very few.' Rebecca smiled at him reassuringly. 'I think you'll find it all explained in your brochure, and Nico, he's the man who looks after all the boats for us—well, Nico will explain the finer details. There's only one strict rule. You can take the boat quite safely anywhere along the east coast between Logos and Gaios, but you must not attempt to round either end of the island, or explore the west coast. The tides that side are very strong, and it gets rough very frequently. But apart from that . . .'

She left the rest of the sentence uncompleted. They had just crested the top of the hill, and had reached the point where the road divided. To their right was the turning to Lakka; straight ahead the road continued on to Logos. Rebecca liked to pause at this point, before taking the steep winding turning down to the village, for the views to the east were spectacular. She slowed now, and the Templars exclaimed with delight; at the same moment she heard the engine of another car, a car going fast. The roar of its engine startled her for a second; she looked up and saw it was a Jeep, coming from the north end of the island, travelling fast, and coming straight towards them. She was about to change gear, and pull off to the side of the road to let it pass, when, to her surprise, the Jeep slowed, swerved, and then, about two or three hundred yards ahead of her, turned off the road and into the olive groves. There was a track there, she knew, though she had never explored it. It was deeply rutted and steep, and it led—presumably—to the west coast.

The Jeep slowed; one wheel spun then held; she heard the grind of its gears, then it bucked its way up the path and out of sight. Rebecca frowned, listening to the sound of its departing engine. Her glimpse of it had been brief, but long enough to recognise both the vehicle and its solitary occupant: Cal Ryder. Now, where could he be going? As far as she knew that track led nowhere in particular. Come to that, where was

Cal Ryder staying? He had said he was making his own arrangements until he could move into the Villa Circe, and Rebecca suddenly found herself curious as to what those could be. There was no hotel on the island—not even of the simplest kind. She was familiar with all the houses Michael Hamilton had to rent, but clearly he wasn't staying in one of those . . .

She sat still, staring in the direction the Jeep had taken, and then, hearing that the two children were waking up, collected herself with a start. She turned the nose of the Volvo in the direction of Lakka, and let in the gears.

After all, what did it matter where Cal Ryder was staying, or where he was going in such a hurry? It was not her business or—luckily, she thought with a wry smile—her concern.

The villa where the Templars were staying was really not a villa at all—not in the sense of a brash new house, anyway. It was a long, low building, and very old: once it had been a store house, and had contained an olive press: the two huge pitted stone wheels that had been used to crush the olives for oil now lay in the pretty courtyard garden. Like all the houses Michael had renovated on the island, it was both beautiful, and practical: it might have all the charm of an old Greek dwelling but it also boasted modern plumbing, and a small but efficient kitchen and bathroom. As she showed the Templars around the house, and heard them exclaim with pleasure, she felt again an admiration for Michael Hamilton who had, in the last six years, achieved so much on this island.

Paxos was poor; its only industries were the olives, fishing, and the tiny smallholdings with goats and chickens. The visitors who came there thanks to Michael's enterprise, brought an income to the islanders, and yet had changed the character of the place mercifully little. It was not spoiled, she thought with relief, as Corfu was so rapidly being spoiled, with its huge vulgar hotels insensitively placed on its most lovely beaches: here there were no crowds, no tourist razzmatazz to destroy the peace and tranquillity of centuries. It was a perfect compromise—as perfect as one could get, perhaps—between a way of life unchanged for hundreds of years, and the exigencies of the twentieth century.

She said goodbye to Mrs Templar and the children, leaving them to unpack, and crossed out from the cool interior of the house to the courtyard. There Agape lovingly tended a tiny garden: bougainvillaea climbed the pale stone walls; old cans and containers, white-washed, had been turned into ingenious flower-pots; they burgeoned with leaves and flowers; even now, brought on by the mildness of the weather, the first white gardenias filled the little space with a scent like cloves.

Christopher Templar had come out with her to see her off. Rebecca turned to him with a smile, and shook his hand. 'You have everything you need? Is there anything else I can do? I don't think I need to direct you to the beach really, do I?'

Christopher Templar laughed. 'Hardly. I don't think we can exactly miss it! We'll be able to hear it when we're indoors at night, shan't we? And first thing in the morning. I love that. No—everything's perfect. Thank you, Miss Farrell.'

'Please—call me Rebecca. It's much simpler. And remember—I'll look in from time to time to check, but if any problem comes up just telephone me at the office, yes? Enjoy your stay . . .'

She climbed back into the Volvo, and then, with a wave of her hand to Pamela Templar, and to the children, who had come out into the courtyard and were obviously raring to explore, she started the engine and pulled away.

At the top of the hill, where she rejoined the main road, she pulled up. She was ahead of schedule: she had an hour to kill at least before she needed to be back in Gaios, where she was having lunch with Nicky. She stretched luxuriously, and drew in deep breaths of the soft scented air. For the millionth time since she had come to the island she thought how incredibly lucky she had been. It was just so beautiful: though the view below her was now familiar, it still made her catch her breath: that wide arc of sea; the cluster of terracotta-tiled roofs below; the grey of the olives that shimmered silver when the breeze caught their leaves. It was so lovely, she thought, that the island was wooded; it added to its enchantment. Many of the islands in the Cyclades, she knew, were treeless and bare, unprotected from the fierce sun in mid-summer. But here, in the gentler Ionian islands, the woods were thick and mysterious. Even in August, she thought, you would be able to escape the sun, take refuge in the cool shade of the groves with their tiny brooks and still pools. In August . . .

She frowned a little. She didn't want to think ahead too far. August was all right—she would still be here then. But after August, when the holiday season came to a close, and one by one the visitors departed, and the villas were shuttered up for the winter—Michael closed down his operation then, until February or March at least. So what would she do then? She didn't want to leave, she realised. She loved this place; she had felt it draw her from the first; often she thought she never wanted to leave it.

And she didn't want to go back to London, did she?

She sighed, and tapped her fingers irritably on the steering wheel. It was so unfair. There had been a time when she had loved London. When she had left school she had had two clear ambitions: one was to train as a cook, which she had done, including six glorious and inspiring months in France. The other ambition was to go to London.

She had done that too, three years ago, a few months after her twenty-first birthday. Her key-to-the-door had been the key of a small bedsitter studio flat which had seemed to Rebecca like a kingdom. With a friend she had started by cooking special meals in other people's houses. That had expanded to include executive lunches in the City, which was where she had met Conrad, and it was from that moment, she realised now, that everything had started to go wrong.

Imperceptibly at first, then gradually more blatantly, Conrad had taken her over. He persuaded her to stop working freelance; to cook full time at his highly successful advertising agency instead. First lunches, for his clients, then more and more often, dinners. And after the dinners, Conrad, who lived in Hertfordshire with his wife and three children, would insist on driving her home in his large black BMW.

'A taxi?' he had said, laughing, when Rebecca had suggested it. 'Don't be ridiculous, child. It's five minutes out of my way. Less. I practically pass the door. Now. Get in.'

Conrad was Irish. He was very tall, with pale skin and bright red hair, and a great deal of charm. He could out-talk anyone Rebecca had ever met, and when he advised her to do this or do that he always made it seem so reasonable, that whatever her misgivings might have been at first she ended up agreeing. Besides, if she didn't, Conrad sulked, and when he sulked he was intolerable. So, she agreed to stop being freelance; she agreed to work for his agency; she agreed to lay on sumptuous dinners for his clients, and she agreed to the lifts home. She liked Conrad, and he amused her, and that, as far as she was concerned, was that.

That there was a great deal more to it as far as Conrad was concerned had, quite simply, never occurred to her. This was partly because Conrad himself gave no obvious indication that there was. He never touched her, never so much as put an arm around her, even when he drove her home. He flirted with her, she supposed, in a way: he'd say 'Rebecca, you slay me. You've gone too far. Today you look too beautiful,' or something like that, and Rebecca would giggle and take no notice. He said much the same to the secretaries who worked for him. Of course she hadn't believed him; she'd forgotten what he'd said the very next minute.

And besides, Conrad was a lot older than she was—well over forty, her own father's age had he lived. She looked on him as a friend, and an employer; her boyfriends, who were numerous, and about whom Conrad occasionally quizzed her, were all more or less her own age.

'When are you going to fall in love, then, Becky?' he had said to her once. 'Has it happened yet then?'

'No, Conrad. It hasn't,' she had answered firmly, disregarding deliberately any double meaning there might have been in his question, which, with Conrad, was usually the best course. This was just before he went away, with his family, to the West Indies. And it was when he came back that the trouble really started.

For, when he returned, Conrad had been different. Bad-tempered, on a short fuse, making everyone in the agency's life a misery. Rebecca, used to his unpredictable moods, had shrugged them off: he ought to have taken a longer holiday, not come back after two weeks, cutting his stay short.

And then there had been the Christmas party. Just to think of that party now, made Rebecca blush with embarrassment and shame. To start with, Conrad had got drunk, very drunk, and made an absolute exhibition of himself, kissing all the secretaries under the mistletoe, and falling over a waste-paper basket. Rebecca had crept away to the cloakroom, ashamed for him, not wanting to watch any longer.

'Rebecca? Rebecca Farrell?' The woman had spoken so suddenly that Rebecca had jumped. She swung round. A small woman, of about forty, in a chic and expensive black dress; Conrad's wife.

'Mrs O'Hara. I'm so sorry. I was miles away. I . . .'

'I was looking for you.' She had spoken quite quietly, and the speech had obviously been rehearsed. 'I came to ask you. What exactly are you after? Is it marriage? Because, if so, I think you ought to know—I shan't let him go, you know. Not without a fight. We've been married twenty years, you see, and I've put up with a lot. I don't intend to give in now . . .'

Rebecca had stared at her, speechless. As the sense of her words slowly registered, she knew she had blushed, a slow deep scarlet. 'I know you haven't been to bed with him,' Conrad's wife had continued imperturbably, only the skin drawn tight over her knuckles as she clasped her hands together betraying her tension. 'I suppose you thought that was a rather clever move on your part. And it was. It's unusual, you see. Normally Conrad persuades them to jump into bed very quickly, and then of course, he gets bored with them, and sooner or later it's all over. In your case . . .' She had paused. 'In your case I'm afraid it's rather more serious. Conrad's persuaded himself he's in love with you. I took him off to the West Indies to try and make him see sense, and it made things much worse. He now thinks he can't live without you. Apparently you're essential to him—like food; like oxygen. You know how he talks . . .' She had smiled a tight little smile. 'So—I just came to say—go to bed with him. Do. Let him get it out of his system. But don't imagine anything is going to come of it, that's all. I put the money in to start Conrad's business—he hadn't a penny, you know, when he started. If Conrad persists in this idiocy, I shall pull that money out. It'll be the end of the agency. I don't think Conrad would risk that, even for you. What do you think?' She had looked up, her face cold, her eyes watering slightly, though she fought to keep back the tears.

Finding her voice, Rebecca had stepped forward impulsively. 'Please,' she had begun desperately. 'Please, Mrs O'Hara—you're wrong. You're terribly wrong. I . . . I don't love your husband. There's nothing between us, nothing . . .'

'I'd like to believe you.' The other woman cut her short. 'But I'm afraid I don't. Think about what I've said, will you?' Then she had walked out. And Rebecca had thought about what she had said. She'd thought about it every day, ever since. Even here on the island she still thought of it, and the memory still pained her. She had been, she realised it now, incredibly naive, and incredibly stupid, and as a result she had caused a number of people considerable pain. Though she was technically innocent, she still couldn't forgive herself.

'Don't blame yourself so much, darling,' her mother had said, that Christmas, when Rebecca had told her. 'It was his fault, not yours.' She had paused, thoughtfully. 'If you were a bit vainer, Becky, a bit more conscious of yourself as a woman, you'd probably have realised. As it was, you didn't, and you've left the agency. You've done the right thing. Now all you can do is forget it. The world is full of Conrads darling. Just be a bit more wary, next time . . .'

There wouldn't be a next time, Rebecca had thought silently then, and thought again now. It was too painful, and too humiliating. When she had resigned from her job, Conrad had seemed so stunned that he'd said virtually nothing. But the night she left, he had turned up at her flat, very drunk, and the scene that had then ensued, of pathos compounded with black farce, was one she preferred not to remember. Conrad had wept; but the moment she betrayed her sympathy and tried to be gentle with him, he had cunningly misinterpreted her gestures, tried to kiss her, tried to convince her that she might as well be honest, might as well own up . . .

'Face it,' he had said, trying to hold her in his arms, and breathing whisky all over her. 'You love me, Becky. You do. You don't want to admit it maybe, but you do. I'm crazy about you, Becky. I'd do anything for you . . .'

'Conrad.' Somehow she had stopped him. 'I don't love you. I never have loved you. I'm not going to love you. If I'd had any idea what you felt I'd have left long ago . . .'

He hadn't believed her, of course. It had gone on and on,

the cajoling, the arguing, the pleading, the bursts of temper. It had shaken Rebecca to the roots of her being, because at some point, quite when she couldn't have said, she had realised that Conrad was serious. He believed what he was saying.

It was then, when she had finally bundled him out of the flat and into a cab, that she had resolved to leave London for a while. She'd been confirmed in the decision by a sleepless night, punctuated with increasingly distraught calls from an increasingly drunken Conrad. The next day, completely by chance, she had bumped into Nicky, and Nicky had thrown her a life-line.

'You've left the agency? No! But I thought you were enjoying it so much—and you were doing terribly well, too. What are you going to do, go freelance again? Well, you'll have no problem. My boss, Michael, was having lunch in the City the other day, and he said they were all talking about you and how terrific your cooking was, and how efficient you were and . . . Hey!' She had broken off, and clutched Rebecca's arm. 'I've just had *the* most incredible idea. You wouldn't like to come out to Greece, would you, with me, for the spring and the summer? I was going to take my assistant, but it would be much more fun with you, and Michael would be delighted. It's not exactly your line, I know, oh, Rebecca. What a wonderful idea! Say yes—go on. Come and talk to Michael about it. No—now. Why not? It would cheer you up. You look really miserable. What's the matter—is it a man? It always is, isn't it? Well, Greece will cure that for you. Come on . . .'

Nicky hadn't stopped talking all the way back to the office, and Rebecca, bemused, had let her rattle on. In fact, she hadn't needed much persuasion; the instant Nicky made her suggestion she had known, instinctively, that she wanted to do it.

And now, here she was, safe on her island, she thought to herself, ruefully, straightening up, and starting the Volvo's engine once more. She should forget all that—why should she think of it now? She was here, she was free, and—thank goodness—there was no danger on Paxos of any entanglements.

Then, on impulse, knowing she still had time in hand, she turned the car, not back towards Gaios, but on, along the road to Logos.

CHAPTER TWO

A LITTLE way along the road, in a place where the olives were so old and so tall that they met in a roofed arch overhead, she saw on the left the turning that the Jeep had taken earlier. She drove past it, turning her head curiously, to peer up between the trees where the track disappeared out of sight, and then, a little further along the road, she stopped, and pulled in on the verge.

She locked the car, and walked back to the track, and stood looking at it thoughtfully. She still hadn't been to the west side of the island; she had more than half an hour in hand, and she was curious. She hesitated, glancing at her watch, kicking idly at the white dust of the road with the toe of her sandals. Then suddenly decisive, she crossed, and began to walk up the track.

She hadn't thought she could get the Volvo up here, and she quickly saw she had been right. Only a Jeep could get through here, and a Jeep with a bold driver at that, for within a few hundred yards the track narrowed and began to climb very steeply. It was only just wide enough for a vehicle, its surface crazily rutted, strewn with boulders and stones.

Rebecca paused, panting and out of breath, thinking perhaps she ought to turn back, for she had no idea where the track led, and she had no wish to round a corner and run slap-bang into Cal Ryder. Nicky had said he was a man who guarded his privacy ferociously, and he would be bound to think she was snooping—which she was, she thought to herself with a grin. Or, if not snooping, curious. She got her breath back and decided to go on. If there were a house up here, she would like to see it.

She pushed on for another ten minutes or so, until she saw ahead of her that the trees were thinning, and the slope grew less steep. Glimpsing sunlight and flowers, she gave an involuntary cry of pleasure, and began to run. A second later she crested the rise, and stopped.

She had been right. The island was narrow, she must have walked about a mile, and she was now, she realised, on the open ground above its western cliffs. In front of her was the dazzling sea and a verdant natural meadow of sweet grass. It stretched away on either side, and Rebecca, coming out of the shadows of the olive groves into the warmth of the sun, felt a sudden quick elation. She stopped, looking ahead of her, and then, realising that here the track went no further, swung round. Sure enough, almost hidden from sight, there was a house, a tiny house, probably once belonging to a shepherd. It was tucked away to the right of the track she had come up, almost obscured by the olives that grew close to it and arched over its roof. Under one of the olives, pulled well into the shade, was the Jeep. She hesitated, shrinking back for a second instinctively, for the windows of the house faced in her direction.

Then, telling herself not to be stupid, she had every right to be here after all, she braced herself, and turning her back to the house and those windows, began to walk across the grass towards the sea.

Moments later she forgot all about the house, the Jeep, and its occupant, for the view that opened out before her almost took her breath away. Now she could see the cliffs themselves, pale ivory, falling sheer down to the sea. Just to her right was a famous landmark, one she had seen before only in photographs: a great arch of rock, now isolated by water, almost as tall as the cliffs of which it must once have been part, and, on the cliff face, a dark recess, blank, and slightly forbidding—the Cave of Aphrodite, it was called, Rebecca knew. Like many other places in these islands, it was claimed as the birthplace of the goddess, and championed as such with great fervour by the local fishermen, who dismissed all the other, equally unlikely claims with patriotic disgust. It was possible to go into that cave by boat, Rebecca had heard, though the waters there were treacherous, and it was dangerous. Looking at it now, the only darkness in a place of glittering light, she felt a rising excitement, a determination that, whatever else she did, she should visit that cave before she left the island.

She stayed there a while, looking out to sea, lulled by the crash of the waves on the rocks below and the wild cries of the gulls, then, reluctantly, she turned back. She had slipped off the sandals she wore, so that she could feel the coolness of the grass against her bare feet, and she left them off as she walked back towards the track. She bent her head back, feeling the sun on her face, and swung along happily, her toes curling luxuriantly in the grass, all the nervousness she had felt earlier quite dispelled.

She was alone, she felt quite certain of that; she didn't even glance in the direction of the little farmhouse. Pausing only to pull on her sandals again, she ducked under the branches of an olive, down a bank thick with tiny ferns, and on to the path. There she stopped. Cal Ryder was blocking her way.

He meant to do so, that much was clear. Obviously he had been watching her, and had waited here. Now he stood full-square, in the middle of the path, and looked down at her from his considerable height. His narrow and rather beautiful features were dark with displeasure; his fists were clenched. He looked her up and down, dismissively; then seemed to hesitate, then said something, in Greek, a question, obviously, and roughly put, which Rebecca, whose Greek was minimal, did not understand.

She stared back at him for a second, not answering, and puzzled, and then suddenly, she realised. She was wearing a plain dark cotton frock which she had bought in Gaios; her sandals came from the village also. She was so dark, her hair thick and straight, now caught back carelessly from her face; her skin, which tanned easily, was already quite brown. Her dark eyes glinted, and a smile lifted the corner of her lips. If he had seen her in some of her London clothes, or even at the wheel of the car, for none of the island women drove, he would not have made that mistake. But now he had; he thought she was Greek.

He spoke again, obviously repeating his question, and then stepped forward, looking down into her face.

Rebecca met his gaze coolly; she waited, and then smiled. 'I'm so sorry. I'm English. I don't understand. *Kalimera . . .*' With that, she attempted to push past him, as haughtily as she could, but to her surprise, and alarm, he caught her wrist, none too gently, and held her.

'I said, what are you doing here? This is private land.'

'It is?' As coolly as she could, though she was fuming with anger, Rebecca released herself from his grip. She looked around them. 'It doesn't say so. I saw no notice.'

'There is no notice.' His eyes flashed. 'No one comes up here—there's no need of a notice. But it's private land, just the same.'

'Oh, really? Your land?' Rebecca tilted her chin and met his eyes. They were dark, and deep set, and their expression was coldly hostile. He didn't answer, and, very deliberately, she gave him another sweet smile. 'Oh well, if it's your land I'll make a point of staying away from it . . . Excuse me.' She moved past him, with the rudest most arrogant sideways glance she could summon up, and was glad to note that his lips tightened at her jibe, and a slight colour mounted in his cheeks.

He made no attempt to stop her this time, but simply moved to one side. Then he stood there and watched her as she swung off down the path. When she reached the bend that would take her out of his sight, Rebecca turned back. She was so angry, at his arrogance, his unneccessary rudeness, at the way he had cast a blot on a beautiful place and a beautiful moment, that she knew she was shaking. She looked him up and down deliberately, the way he had done her.

'Do tell me,' she called back, 'do you own the sea and the sky as well, or just the land? Just so I know another time, you understand . . .'

Her sarcasm was a bit overdone, she knew it and was irritated by it. She'd liked to have thought of a really cutting rejoinder, and this one was not cutting enough; its feebleness amused him; she saw his lips lift.

'No no,' he called after her, his voice now icily polite. 'You needn't worry. I don't own the sea or the sky—avail yourself of them any time you like. Just stay off the land . . . *Kalimera* . . .'

He lifted his hand, too, in a graceful and ironic gesture of farewell. Then he turned and disappeared through the trees. Rebecca, who had gone red, and who felt undignified and rather stupid, and who wished she'd resisted the temptation of the parting shot, resisted now the temptation to run after him and shout something even more unsubtle and even more rude. It would have made her feel a whole lot better, she thought ruefully, as she walked back down the track. How un-Greek! How typically English! How inhospitable and arrogant and . . . She climbed into the Volvo and slammed the door savagely. Why, given the opportunity, at that moment, she'd cheerfully have pushed him off the cliff!

'Goodness, wasn't that delicious!' Nicky laid down her knife and fork and leaned back in her chair. 'Shall we have some coffee? Then you can tell me all the juicy details.'

Rebecca smiled. They were sitting outside their favourite taverna, the one nearest the harbour in Gaios, where they could watch the coming and going of the boats as they ate. The sea air always made them hungry, and they had feasted on a simple but delicious meal—a salad of Mediterranean tomatoes sprinkled with white feta cheese and fresh oregano, followed by grilled red mullet caught that morning. Since coming to the island she had acquired a taste for retsina; in London she had always disliked its slightly sour taste of resin, but here it seemed to go with the food and the sun. She and Nicky had drunk half a bottle, and now she felt warm and contented, very relaxed.

'There are no details,' she said, when Andros, the owner of the taverna, had brought them two little metal pots of strong black Turkish coffee, and a tiny saucer with pink and sugary Turkish delight. 'No details—juicy or otherwise. I've told you everything. He told me to get off his land, pronto, and that was that.'

'Pity.' Nicky wrinkled her eyes against the sun, and laughed. 'I mean, it's pretty romantic. There you are, slipping through the trees like a nereid, and out pops the celebrated Cal Ryder. Like Apollo, or Pan or something . . .'

'More like the god of the underworld. I felt like Persephone, I can tell you. If he'd had Cerberus on a leash I wouldn't have been surprised . . .' Rebecca paused. 'I'd never been up there before. I had no idea there was a house there. Who does it belong to, do you know?'

Nicky shrugged. 'If it's the one I think it is, and it must be, from your description, it belongs to someone called Grey Jameson. I've never met him. He's a painter.'

'Grey Jameson? I've never heard of him. And what an odd name, it doesn't sound real—especially if he's a painter...'

Nicky giggled. 'It probably isn't. And he's a pretty odd man, too, according to Michael. Ex-patriot, been living in Greece for years. Gay. In fact, Michael says, as camp as a row of tents, but then Michael would say that, you know what's he's like.' She shrugged. 'He's not here at the moment anyway, I know that. So Cal Ryder must know him, and he must have been lent the house ... Gosh.' She broke off, her eyes rounding. 'You don't think Ryder's gay, do you? Could that explain it?'

Rebecca thought back, and an image of Cal Ryder, tall, his face shadowed, his eyes mocking, sprang clear into her memory. She shifted a little in her seat.

'I wouldn't have said so,' she replied dryly, and Nicky at once relaxed, laughing conspiratorially.

'Me neither,' she said. 'No, it can't be that. I expect he just wanted to be here longer that's all, and the villa he always rents from us still isn't fixed, so he borrowed Jameson's. He's probably finishing another of those creepy books of his. He comes here to write, you know. It seems odd to me. I mean have you *read* any of his books?'

'One or two,' Rebecca looked away. 'On a 'plane or something. I'm not that keen on who-dunnits.'

'Oh, they're not just who-dunnits—they're better than that. Cleverer. I mean there's always a murder, and so on, but—well, you ought to read some more. I've probably got some here in paperback, I'll lend you one if you like ...' She paused. 'No, what I meant was—it's odd. After all, he's very successful. Each book a best-seller and all that—he could go anywhere in the world he wanted to write, and yet he always comes back here. To this lovely peaceful beautiful island, where there's no crime, no violence—it's the exact opposite of everything he writes about. I'd have thought it would've made it harder, that's all.'

'Oh, I don't know.' Rebecca shrugged. 'You've seen him close to—more than a little frightening. That man could conjure up evils wherever he was, I'd say . . . Anyway, don't let's talk about him any more. Let's forget him. I'll just pay Andros, and then . . .'

She bent to pick up her shoulder bag and reach for her purse as she spoke, so it was not until she had found her money and looked up that she saw Nicky's face, and the change in her expression.

'Not as easy as you might think,' Nicky said lightly. 'Talk of the devil and there he is. Look—by the Jeep. Just the other side of the square . . .'

'Did you tell him you were working for Michael?'

'No, no, I didn't.' Rebecca hurriedly counted out some drachmas, and left them in the little saucer on the table. 'I told you. Hail and farewell, that was about it . . .'

'Well, you can tell him now. Look, he's coming over . . .'

Glancing up, Rebecca saw that Nicky was right. Cal Ryder had been staring in their direction; now he was moving purposefully across the square. Quickly, she stood up.

'You can have that pleasure. Twice in one day is too much. I'm off . . .'

Nicky grinned. The prospect of an interview with Cal Ryder seemed not to dismay her, and she made no attempt to persuade Rebecca to stay. Every afternoon, taking it in turns, either she or Rebecca would make the rounds of Michael's properties on the island, checking that all was in order; that afternoon it was Rebecca's turn: Nicky had already announced her intention to go swimming. Now she raised a hand languidly.

'See you back at the flat then—this evening?'

'Fine—see you then . . .'

Rebecca darted away without a backward glance. With a bit of luck, she thought, as she wove her way between the tables, Cal Ryder would not have realised that she had seen him, and so her summary departure might not look overtly rude. If he had realised—well, it was too bad; offending him was hardly high on her list of anxieties.

At the far side of the square a network of narrow streets

opened up; turning quickly off to the left Rebecca knew she could be hidden from sight. As she turned she allowed herself one quick discreet glance backward. Cal Ryder had reached Nicky's table; she saw Nicky smile up at him, he hesitated, and then drew back a chair, as if to join her. She smiled to herself triumphantly. That was him out of the way! Nicky could have the pleasure of his company, and meanwhile she herself could get back to their flat and pick up her moped without danger of bumping into him again. For the trouble with Gaios, indeed with the whole island, she realised, was that it was so small it was extremely difficult to avoid meeting people. Before, that had always seemed to her one of the island's charms: the briefest walk, a visit to a shop—all activities were punctuated by greetings, by wonderful unhurried invitations to stop, to talk, to have some coffee, or simply to pass the time of day. It was very Greek, and one of the aspects of being here which she had most loved after the impersonality of a large city like London—but now she was not so sure. She didn't want to feel that she might meet Cal Ryder every time she turned a corner: she hoped heartily that he had merely come down to Gaios to stock up on food, and that he would then depart back to his west coast eyrie and stay there . . .

She and Nicky shared a marvellous flat, overlooking the water on the far side of Gaios. It was in an old pink-washed house with shuttered windows; the ground floor was taken up by the island's post office, a sleepy place adorned with racks of old-fashioned picture postcards. She and Nicky had the upper floors: three marvellous rooms with wooden floors and sloping ceilings, and window seats, so—in the evenings—they could sit and watch the world go past.

'This is the Oxford Street of Gaios,' Nicky had said, their first evening, gesturing out to the little harbour street, and the few tiny shops. 'You may not realise it, but we're well placed. The world and his wife goes past here, you know . . .'

Hurrying upstairs, Rebecca quickly changed into shorts and a T-shirt, grabbed the satchel with the lists of houses she had to visit that afternoon, and then went out to the little courtyard at the back where she and Nicky kept the mopeds they generally used for getting around the island. Rebecca loved the moped: she'd never ridden a motorbike of any kind in her life, and had at first been doubtful as to her ability to do so—but the mopeds, top speed about twenty miles an hour, with a following wind downhill, had presented few problems. There was little traffic on the island, and the only hazard was avoiding chickens and goats.

Within seconds she was off, weaving her way through the narrow alleyways and streets. She stopped to check that two of Michael's houses which were as yet unoccupied, and which had needed repairs, were now ready for the visitors who would arrive in Easter week. She called in at Pan Cottage, a tiny yellow-painted fisherman's house which had been rented by the two students who had arrived that morning: they were out, but she saw their maid, checked all was well, and left the agency's card reminding them of the number to call if they had any problems.

Then, wheeling the bike round and keeping her fingers crossed that the gears would work for once—they were very temperamental—she set off up the steep hill that led out of Gaios and along the coast road. She had a couple of properties to check in Lakka, both due to be occupied the following week, then she had to find Nico and check that the Templars' boat was ready for them, and that the rest of Michael's small fleet was ready and serviced for the new arrivals.

It took much longer to reach Lakka on the moped than it had done by car that morning, and half way up the hilly part of the coastal road the moped spluttered rebelliously to a halt and she had to push it the rest of the way up. But it was worth it, she thought, as, the cool wind on her face, she coasted down to Lakka once more. She checked the two properties, and then went in search of Nico: he lived near the harbour, but was a law unto himself. He might be at home, he might be fishing; he had a very Greek interpretation of time, and although Rebecca had an appointment with him, there was no certainty he would keep it.

Sure enough, Nico was not at home, not in the harbour, and not at either of the tavernas. She saw the Templars, looking relaxed, happy and replete, obviously just finishing what had been a very successful lunch: Christopher and

Pamela Templar sang the praises of the lobster they had just eaten, and Rebecca stopped to admire the sea-urchin shells which Tom and Francie had collected on the beach. Of Nico, though, there was no sign: the Templars were planning to take their little boat out the next day, and although Rebecca was certain that Nico would have it ready for them, she knew she must check.

It was now very hot, the tavernas were closing, the shops were already shut; there was no sign of Nico anywhere. Rebecca had just decided to go back and try his house once more, when, just off the harbour, she met Agape. Agape was married to Nico's wife's brother; she was also blessed with that particular telegraphic gift which is the mark of people who live on small islands: by some magic of her own, and without apparent effort, Agape always knew exactly where anyone on the island was, at any time of the day or night. Rebecca greeted her with relief, in bad Greek, and Agape smiled. Her face was deeply lined, her eyes astonishingly sharp; she possessed three teeth, two of them gold. In response to Rebecca's halting enquiries, she smiled widely, displaying the teeth, of which she was very proud, and— taking Rebecca by the arm—began to point and gesture. The explanation took some time, because Rebecca's Greek had not made as much progress as she had hoped in the last few weeks, but eventually, after much laughter and repetition it became clear that Nico was most certainly not in Lakka: he had gone up to the Villa Circe to assist Agape's husband who was working on the repairs there.

Rebecca frowned. The Villa Circe was the house Cal Ryder had rented, and into which he was due to move at Easter. Its roof had been damaged by winter storms, and needed extensive work; but that work was nearing completion—she'd been up there the previous week—and she couldn't think why Nico should be there. However, Agape seemed quite certain, and also seemed to think that Nico would still be there, so, resignedly Rebecca climbed on the moped again, and set off.

The Villa Circe was particularly beautiful—her favourite house on the island—and yet it was the least popular of the villas Michael owned and rented. The reason many visitors shied away from it were clear enough: spectacularly sited, it was difficult to reach. A narrow track skirting the cliffs at the northern end of the island led up to it, a track with some terrifying hair-pin bends and sheer drops. You could drive up it—if you kept a cool head—and you could walk up it, but it was a long, exhausting trek, without benefit of shade. It had no telephone; it was remote from other houses, shops or beaches; it had a glorious view, straight out across the Ionian sea towards Corfu and the distant shores of Albania, but it was exposed, in bad weather, to prevailing winds of considerable force.

The moped took one look at the steep track and gave up the ghost. Rebecca, getting hotter and hotter by the second, climbed off and, puffing and panting, and occasionally swearing, began to push it up. It took a long time, and she had plenty of leisure to reflect on Cal Ryder, who always stayed here and had done so for years, and who obviously had such a taste for seclusion.

It was her mother who had first introduced Rebecca to his books. Her mother read, constantly and voraciously—a habit acquired, Rebecca thought, in the early years of her widowhood, when she must often have been lonely, stuck in that house in the wilds of Suffolk, the older girls at boarding school and with only Rebecca for company. Her mother's taste was catholic: one day she'd be reading Jane Austen, the next an Agatha Christie. But she had a particular weakness for murder and mystery, and it was Rebecca who, one Christmas some years before, had bought her her first Calvin Ryder. Not that Rebecca had heard of him: she'd just been struck by the book's title and jacket—it had been called *Dying Fall*, she remembered it still—and also, if she were honest, by the photograph of the author on the fly-leaf. Rebecca had been then about eighteen—and impressionable, she thought to herself now, with a wry smile, as she dragged the wretched moped over the stones. Calvin Ryder, winner of this award and that, had looked startlingly handsome. The present had been a marked success: her mother had hardly taken her nose out of the book for two days, and had then, in quick succession, borrowed the complete works of Calvin Ryder from the library. And, as Rebecca had told Nicky, quite truthfully, she had herself read a couple of them, and—while admiring their ingenuity—had disliked them. Quite why she couldn't have said: certainly they were gripping, terse, and well-written. But they had seemed to her then very cynical: Rebecca, aged eighteen, liked books with heroes. Calvin Ryder clearly didn't believe in the existence of such a species. All his characters had seemed to Rebecca so profoundly unsympathetic, so uniformly evil in their intentions and malicious in their behaviour, that she had abandoned Ryder's books after two tries, and with relief. She had not given the man a second thought from that day until her arrival on Paxos, when Nicky had mentioned him first as one of the agency's most regular—and difficult—clients.

'Michael likes him,' Nicky had said. 'I think he knows him from way back. But then Michael's impressed because he's so famous. He doesn't have to deal with him on a day-to-day basis. The last girl Michael had out here supervising things—well, to be honest, I think she may have been a bit keen on Ryder—she said she went up to the Villa Circe once, unannounced, just to check everything was OK, you know, and he practically bit her head off. Told her to go away and stay away, in no uncertain terms. And when I had to fix his booking this time—I rang him up, and—God, I've never known anyone so terse. He was furious the house wasn't going to be ready earlier. I did the full charm routine, you know, smooth the ruffled feathers and all that, never known to fail . . .'

'And it failed?' Rebecca had asked, with amusement. Nicky had pulled a face.

'And how!'

Well, once bitten, twice shy, Rebecca thought to herself grimly as she toiled up the final slope. Cal Ryder wouldn't be getting any unannounced visits from her! His damn roof could fall in before she'd drag herself up here again.

It was at this point, as she neared the house, that Rebecca began to have the sensation that she was being watched. It was an odd feeling, which came to her quite suddenly, as she paused to get her breath back, and to wipe her brow. A sudden sense of unease, a prickling of the skin at the back of the neck. She wheeled round, but there was no one behind her, just the stony track winding through dry scrub and boulders back down the hill. No one there, no one at all, yet the sensation was acute. The house was well-placed, she realised, for a man who wished to avoid visitors: why, from the terrace above you could see anyone coming, by sea or by land, for miles . . .

She gave the wheel of the moped an irritable kick, set off again, and came to the high wall that surrounded the terrace. There she leaned the moped in the shade, and hearing voices above her, speaking Greek, toiled up the last few yards and on to the terrace. There she came to an abrupt halt. Nico was there all right, just as Agape had promised; and so was Cal Ryder!

She stopped dead in her tracks. The two men had their backs to her and were standing looking out to sea, talking rapidly in Greek, their voices slightly lowered—not that she could have understood what they were saying anyway. Nico was gesturing as he spoke, and seemed worried about something; Cal Ryder interjected something, a question, Rebecca thought, for Nico shook his head, and began again on a rapid flood of Greek. He stopped when he realised he no longer had Ryder's attention, for Ryder had looked up, and registered Rebecca's presence. Her arrival seemed not to surprise him, and for a second she wondered if she had been right, and that they could have been watching her from the terrace as she came up the slope, but the next moment she rejected that idea. Nico swung round, as if startled; for an instant she saw an odd alarm on his features, then it was replaced with a broad smile. He stepped forward, a small swarthy man, whom she had liked instinctively from the first.

'Rebecca! *Kalimera-sas*—you got my message? But no . . .' He paused, taking in her flushed face, and then laughed. 'I see you did not. Who told you I was here? Agape?'

Rebecca nodded, still trying to get her breath back, aware that Nico was not entirely pleased Agape should have sent her here, but that he was trying to disguise that fact—and not doing it very well, for he was a man of transparent honesty.

'I left a message—at my house—that I would be a little late. I told my eldest, Dimitrios, you met him, you remember? Rebecca will be coming, and you will sit her down in the shade, and give her some ouzo and a *meze*, and entertain her, and then I shall be back . . .' He paused. 'That boy. He is in love, I think. He forgets everything. Everything. And now you have had this terrible walk. Here, come and sit down in the shade. You have not met Mr Ryder, I think, who will be staying here? He's thinking of doing some fishing this time . . .' Nico hesitated, glancing at Cal Ryder. 'I came up to talk to him about hiring my boat . . .'

'Oh . . .' Rebecca allowed herself to be drawn into the shade. Cal Ryder had not moved. 'I must have misunderstood Agape then. I thought she'd said you came up here to help her husband, you know, with the roof . . .'

Nico smiled widely, with a flash of gold teeth. 'Agape said that? I think you did not understand perhaps? I should help with a roof? I know only about boats . . .'

'Please, it doesn't matter . . .' Rebecca felt embarrassed. She didn't want Nico to feel she had been checking up on him, for she liked him, and knew he worked hard and well. And she didn't like the way Cal Ryder was looking at her either; it made her feel dreadfully self-conscious, bitterly aware of the fact that she was hot and tousled and must look a mess—her hair all blown about, covered in dust and grime from the long haul up to the house.

'Please, sit down. You look exhausted.' He spoke suddenly, as if he read her thoughts, and moved across, drawing one of the terrace chairs into the shade. He glanced at Nico as he did so, and Rebecca saw a dart of amusement in his eyes. Nico saw it too, and seemed at once to relax.

'Miss Farrell and I have met, as it happens. This morning— by chance. And then, at lunch, in the taverna in the square— we just missed each other unfortunately . . .' Here he met Rebecca's eyes, and she blushed.

'Oh really?'

'Yes. I was coming across to your table just as you left. To apologise. You must have thought me very rude, this morning . . .'

'I did. Yes,' Rebecca said ungraciously, aware of the fact that he knew quite well she had deliberately avoided him.

'Well, I asked—Nicky, isn't it? Yes, Nicky—I asked her to pass on my apologies, and she explained you were working with them now. I hadn't realised. And I hadn't expected I'd have the chance to apologise in person. So soon.'

This last was said distinctly coldly, in tones that implied their encounter for the third time on the same day was three times too many. Nico shuffled his feet slightly and looked up at the sky.

'Please ...' Cal Ryder turned to her with a passable imitation of polite solicitude. 'It's a long climb up here. You must be very hot. Would you like something to drink? There's a bottle of ouzo somewhere, I think ...'

'I'd love a glass of water.' Rebecca looked away. 'Thank you. And then I must go back. I ... I didn't expect to find you here. I just came up to check with Nico about the hire-boats ...'

'Don't let me interrupt you.' He turned away quickly, and again Rebecca saw some glances pass between him and Nico which she did not understand. 'I'll fetch some water ...'

With that he disappeared into the house. He was away some time. Rebecca checked with Nico that the Templars' boat would be ready for them the next day, that the other hire boats were all serviced and ready for the Easter visitors—and hearing all was well, just as she had known it would be, cursed her own thoroughness, her refusal to give up, which was responsible for bringing her here and meeting Cal Ryder yet again.

Nico answered her questions readily enough, with his usual wide smiles and expressive gestures, but she could see that he was still not at his ease, and she had a vague sense that something was wrong, as if she had interrupted something, and should not have been there ... She was still puzzling at this sense of unease, of something being wrong, when Cal Ryder returned with a glass of cold water, and she sipped it gratefully. The two men stood and watched her solemnly as she drank, and she was certain both were anxious to get rid of her. It was not until she put down the glass and stood up that she realised what it was that was wrong. She looked around her; the terrace was silent. The house behind was silent. She met Nico's gaze, and his eyes slid away from hers. She cleared her throat.

'Isn't Leandros here?' she said. 'Agape's husband? I

thought he was working on the roof—we have to have it finished so Mr Ryder can move in . . .' She hesitated. 'If some problem has come up . . .' There was a discernible pause, and Rebecca looked at them uncertainly. Then she turned towards the dark doorway that led into the house. 'Perhaps I'd better check. Michael's due back from England soon and if there are any difficulties . . .'

With one swift movement Cal Ryder was blocking the doorway. 'No need for that, Miss Farrell,' he said smoothly. 'The roof's fine. In fact, it's nearly finished. I came up myself to see how Leandros was getting on.'

'Then where is Leandros? You mean he's finished and gone home?' Rebecca stared at him blankly. The move to the door had been quick, odd, and slightly threatening. She had the sensation that no matter what she did or said Cal Ryder didn't intend her to go into the house.

'No, no . . .' He took her arm, and led her away from the door and across the terrace. 'No, Leandros is down at the landing stage—it needed a bit of repair work, I gather, and as he was up here and had some wood and his tools and so on— he said he'd fix it . . .'

'The landing stage?' Rebecca gazed in the direction in which he was pointing, where a tiny path wound down the cliff. 'I thought that landing stage was never used . . .'

'I never used it,' Cal Ryder corrected her. 'I think it has been used though, in the past. And, as I thought I might be doing a bit of fishing with Nico here, it will be useful. I'm sure Michael will raise no objections—the repairs weren't too extensive . . .'

'Oh, I see . . .' Rebecca hesitated. She was thrown, and she knew it. Thrown by the way in which he had taken her arm, thrown by the information about the landing stage, and unsure what to do next. She could have made a fuss, she thought, and insisted on checking how the roof repairs were progressing . . . but she was already beginning to feel like an officious idiot for coming up here in the first place, and the last thing she wanted was to prolong her stay. So, straightening up, she stepped back. She held out her hand to Nico, and then, merely nodding in Cal Ryder's direction, she gestured back to the path.

'Fine,' she said. 'OK I'm glad the work's done . . . I'd better be getting back. Goodbye, Nico . . . Mr Ryder.'

She turned on her heel, but, to her surprise, escape was less easy than she had expected, for Cal Ryder came after her.

'You must let me drive you back,' he said coolly. 'My Jeep's parked round the back.'

'And my moped's parked round the front. I don't need a lift, thank you,' Rebecca answered sweetly.

'Oh—you didn't walk then?' He feigned surprise, but Rebecca felt quite certain he knew how she had come up the path, and knew perfectly well that, as she had transport, the offer of a lift could be safely made, and was certain to be refused. He fell into step beside her, and Rebecca felt irritated. Clearly he didn't intend to depart until he was certain she had left.

'Seeing me off your land?' she said sharply, as they reached the moped, and he lifted it upright for her. 'For the second time today?'

He said nothing; he had bent over the scooter and seemed to be fiddling with the stand mechanism. Then he straightened up, and gave her a cold smile.

'I have apologised,' he said.

'By proxy and in person. I know . . . Thanks, I can manage myself.' Rebecca took the handlebars of the moped from him rather roughly; he needn't think he could charm her into forgetting how rude he had been.

He stepped back, and, feeling self-conscious, Rebecca swung one long tanned leg over the saddle, balanced, and then, carefully ignoring Cal Ryder who was watching her manoeuvres with some attention, gave the starter throttle a rather savage kick. It would have been glorious, she thought, for the engine to have fired and to have accelerated away with impressive agility and speed—just then she'd have given practically anything to have been mounted on a loud and powerful Harley Davidson, just for the pleasure of roaring off in a cloud of dust—but in fact nothing happened at all. She kicked the throttle again; again nothing, not a whisper, not a cough, not the most flickering sound of life. She glowered at the bike, tried again: nothing.

'Oh dear.' Cal Ryder's voice was exquisitely polite. 'What could be wrong do you think?'

'I haven't the least idea,' Rebecca said, through gritted teeth. 'It's never done this before. Maybe some dust got in somewhere . . .'

'Maybe it did,' he replied gravely.

Rebecca tried a few more times, but the wretched machine was deader than a dodo. Eventually, her face scarlet with mortification, she got off. The second she had dismounted, and with startling ease and strength, Cal Ryder stepped forward and lifted the machine out of her hands and into the air, as if it weighed no more than a box of groceries.

'Fortunate I have the Jeep here, after all,' he said. 'You can hardly push that all the way back to Gaios, can you? Come on . . .'

Before Rebecca could say or do anything, he had moved off at a fast pace, and she was forced to follow. By the time she caught up with him, there was the moped, lying in the back of the Jeep, there was the passenger door, wide open, and there was Cal Ryder with an expression of such amusement on his face that she could have slapped him, holding back the door, and proffering his hand to help her into the seat.

Rebecca ignored the hand and climbed in. She stared straight ahead of her, trying not to look or to pay the slightest attention as, beside her, Cal Ryder swung into the driver's seat. The engine roared into life at the first pressure on the accelerator—it would do, Rebecca thought sourly; she'd have been delighted if it had stalled. But no: lean, muscular tanned arms, strong hands on the steering wheel: he backed the Jeep round expertly, threw it into gear, and then stopped.

'Belts,' he said, peremptorily. 'Especially on a slope like this one—you know, if we turned over . . .'

'You're not wearing your belt . . .'

'I am now.' He clicked the seat belt across and into place over his left hip. He then waited patiently while Rebecca, who was suddenly all fingers and thumbs, fumbled to fix her own.

'Allow me,' he said at last, and reached across. The back of one tanned hand brushed her breast, the other hand brushed her thigh, caught the strap, pressed against her hip, found the

fastening, and slipped the metal connecting piece home into
its slot. It took about thirty seconds; if he was aware of the
fact he touched her he did not betray it: the whole manoeuvre
was undertaken with swift efficient precision. He did not even
glance in her direction. Rebecca shivered: her skin felt as if it
were on fire.

'Right.' He turned to her; she caught for a second a dark
mocking glance. 'Hold tight. We're on our way.'

CHAPTER THREE

'HAVE you worked for Michael long?'

They had driven down the steep track from the Villa Circe in silence; he put the question now as they turned back on to the Gaios road, and Rebecca, who had been deep in her own thoughts, jumped.

'No, not long,' she answered mechanically. 'I've been out here for about three weeks, that's all. Nicky got me the job: she needed an assistant . . . She and I have known each other a long time, we were at school together.'

'I see.' There was a little pause. 'Have you been to these islands before?'

'No, never. I was working in London . . .'

'For a travel agency?' He glanced towards her, and Rebecca shook her head.

'No, no—nothing like that. I . . . I was a cook. I cooked, oh, you know, for executive lunches, that kind of thing. For an advertising agency.'

'Really?' He looked slightly surprised. 'Rather a dramatic change—is this just a temporary move? Are you going back to the agency?'

His questions unsettled Rebecca, and she turned away to look out of the window.

'No—I've left that job,' she said flatly. 'I'll go back to London, I suppose, when this job finishes. But not the agency . . .'

'You didn't like working there?'

'Yes, I did. I liked it very much, to begin with, but . . .'

'Then why leave?'

Rebecca shifted in her seat; she was beginning to feel trapped by these questions which were moving with unerring precision in a direction she disliked, as if Cal Ryder, with some horrible writer's instinct, scented the unease she felt. She shrugged. 'Oh, personal reasons, I suppose.'

He gave her a dark sideways glance, and Rebecca tensed,

but obviously he decided not to pursue the matter, because he did not press her further. He changed gear, and accelerated slightly.

'Well,' he said, in a neutral tone. 'Paxos is very lovely. I hope you enjoy your time here . . .'

His gaze was on the road ahead now, and Rebecca was able to steal a glance at him. He drove with concentration, a little tensely, she thought, his beautifully formed hands gripping the steering wheel tightly. In profile, his face was startlingly beautiful, strongly etched and classically formed; she realised she felt a great deal more relaxed when his eyes were averted, when she didn't have to meet the cold and penetrating gaze of dark eyes beneath straight dark brows. She hesitated, and then took the plunge: after all, if he could ask questions, why couldn't she?

'You've been coming to the island for many years, haven't you?' she said, imitating his tone of polite routine enquiry.

'Yes. Ten or eleven years now,' he answered shortly.

'You come here to write?' she went on, feeling daring.

He shrugged. There was no pretence at surprise that she should know he was a writer, and Rebecca found she liked the avoidance of all false modesty.

'Among other things. Yes.'

Rebecca expected him then to ask her if she had read his books—it seemed the next logical move in what was a stilted and difficult conversation, but he did not. Silence fell again, and they drove on a little further before Rebecca risked saying anything more.

'Why Paxos?' she said. She spoke only because the silence was beginning to weigh on her, and she couldn't think of anything else to say, and his reaction surprised her. He half swerved, and braked, and shot her a suddenly hostile cold glance, so she stammered. 'I . . . I mean, I just wondered if there was a particular reason for coming to this island. There are so many others, after all, and I . . . imagine you could go anywhere you wanted.'

'Oh, I see.' He straightened the wheel again, and stared straight ahead. 'Well, I like it I suppose.' He hesitated. 'It suits me. I'm used to it. That's all.'

Silence fell again, and Rebecca felt her cheeks burn. He had

resented the question, that was obvious. Somehow she had
stepped across that line he drew around his privacy, and she
could not understand why. The question was innocuous
enough surely? Glancing nervously at his dark profile she felt
again a second's unease, just as she had felt up at the house.
For an instant, she could not have said why, it was a purely
instinctual reaction, she sensed danger. This man was
dangerous. Odd irrational alarm prickled her skin; then the
sensation passed, and she told herself not to be stupid. Her
imagination was playing tricks on her, that was all ... But
still; she set her lips. She wouldn't risk another question. They
could drive all the way back to Gaios in awkward silence, if
that was what he preferred ...

It seemed indeed that it was, for he drove on, keeping his
eyes on the road, quite silent, and his manner abstracted, for
several miles. And so, when he did speak, his voice soft, and
thoughtful, tinged with an odd regret, it took Rebecca by
surprise. She listened the more carefully, and afterwards
almost word for word, she was to remember what he said.

'I first came here,' he began slowly, 'when I was in my
twenties. About your age now, I imagine. Twenty-one,
twenty-two, something like that. I'd just left Cambridge.' He
did not look at her, but paused, and then went on. 'I had not
begun to write then. It was just a holiday. Pure chance that
chose Paxos, out of all the other islands ... In those days
very few visitors came here. There were no villas to rent; one
ferry a week ... I meant to stay only a few days, and ended
up staying months. I was staying in Lakka, and I met Nico,
and one night—they still used to fish at night then, in the old
way, with naphtha lamps to attract the fish—one evening Nico
took me fishing. We stayed out all night. There was no moon,
no wind. The water was very still, and very black; once we
anchored it was totally silent ... Then Nico lit the flare. It
burns palely. Against the water it looks like moonshine. The
fish rise—hundreds of them, seeking the light. Nico caught
them—the old way, casting his net for the small ones,
spearing the large ones ...

'We came back at dawn. The boat was laden ...' He smiled
slightly. 'I expect we stank of fish, but I wasn't thinking of
that. We came back at dawn, and, as the light rose, the island

seemed to rise with it. It materialised, out of the waves, shimmering: there's almost always mist at dawn, and the mist and the angle of the light play tricks on your eyes ...' He hesitated. 'It was the most beautiful thing I've ever seen, like an apparition, but real. Neither of us spoke: I think it affected Nico too, though he's lived here all his life, and he must have seen the same thing, many times. Anyway ...' His tone lightened, and he glanced at her, as if to deflect the seriousness with which he had spoken. 'I fell in love with the island that night and that morning, and, being a constant man, I'm in love with it still. So I come back. There—does that answer your question?'

'Yes.' Rebecca, looking up, met his eyes, and was held by their darkness. Then she looked away. 'Yes,' she said again, softly. 'Yes, it does.'

As he had been speaking the light had begun to fade, with the suddenness of spring in the Mediterranean. Turning back to the window, Rebecca saw dusk had softened and transformed the trees and the land; colour had seeped out of it. It was a world now composed of greys and greens, softness and shadow, with beyond them the dark of the sea, and a line of lights.

'We're in Gaios ...'

'Yes. We're in Gaios,' he answered.

Rebecca felt an instant of disassociation, of dislocation, as if his words had taken her to some other place, from which it was difficult to return to the exactitude of streets and directions. She shivered, for it was suddenly cold, and indicated the way to her flat through the warren of streets and alleyways. Something has changed, she thought to herself, groping after a sensation she sensed but could not pin down. Something has shifted, altered ...

By the time he drew up outside the flat, on the edge of the harbour, she could still not have said what it was. All she knew was that the hostility she had felt towards him had left her, departed with the light, and with his speech. It was as if, quite deliberately, he had allowed her to glimpse something of himself, and the revelation left her both tranquil and on edge.

He behaved, though, as if nothing had happened. He braked, then jumped down and lifted the moped out of the

back of the Jeep. Feeling cold in her shorts and T-shirt, and
stiff from the drive, Rebecca climbed down also, and joined
him.

'I wonder...' He glanced up at her, and she caught the
ghost of a smile on his lips. 'Do you think there's any point in
trying this thing again? It might start now, you never know.
They can be very temperamental...'

Rebecca shrugged. 'I'll try if you like,' she said. 'But I don't
have much hope. It seemed completely dead...'

'Just give it a try...'

He held the scooter out, Rebecca mounted it. He put out a
hand to steady her, and—expecting nothing to happen—she
kicked the starter pedal. Instantly and without hesitation, the
engine roared into life. Rebecca stared down at it in
stupefaction.

'I don't *believe* it...' she began. 'How on earth...?'

She stopped; he was regarding her intently, his gaze
mocking, and for a second she felt a needle of suspicion at
the back of her mind. Had Cal Ryder fixed the scooter in
some way—up at the Villa Circe—done something to its
mechanism so it wouldn't start, and she would be forced to
accept a lift? But instantly she dismissed that thought; it
made no sense. She couldn't think how he could do it, or
why he should do it, because she couldn't believe he'd been
very anxious for her company back to Gaios. And now
anyway, he seemed anxious to depart, for he was already
moving away, had opened the Jeep door. Hurriedly Rebecca
cut the engine, climbed off, and went after him. He turned
and she held out her hand awkwardly, feeling suddenly shy
of him.

'I've inconvenienced you twice today,' she began shyly.
'I'm sorry—and thank you for the lift...'

'Only once,' he corrected her, and then—seeing she did not
understand—pressed her hand lightly and climbed into the
Jeep. 'It's of no account. Glad to have been of assistance.
Goodbye.'

And with that he slammed the door, wheeled the Jeep
round in a sharp arc, and with a quick lift of the hand, a
passing salute, accelerated up the hill, round the corner, and
out of sight. Rebecca watched him go. His departure had been

abrupt, his greeting minimal; except perhaps in passing she would not be seeing him again, that much was obvious. She felt an instant's sharp regret and a confusion; then she turned, and went slowly upstairs to her flat.

She was late returning, Nicky had heard the Jeep, and was consumed with curiosity. They went out, and ate dinner together near the harbour, and there Rebecca answered Nicky's questions honestly enough. But she did not tell Nicky of the strange way both Nico and Cal Ryder had behaved at the Villa Circe, and she made no mention of Cal's long speech on their return home. Nicky noticed no gaps in her narrative; she listened, looking thoughtful.

'Well,' she said, waving her fork in the air reflectively, when Rebecca had finished. 'It's very odd—I mean that business with the scooter. I wonder if he did fix it? You can do it—didn't you know that? It's quite simple. There's a little switch, under the front axle thing—it cuts off the petrol supply. It's a safety device or something. Switch that off and of course the engine won't fire. Not a dicky-bird. Just the way you described . . .' She pushed her plate away, and looked at Rebecca curiously, and also—Rebecca thought—with a certain envy. 'Maybe he fancies you,' she went on at last. 'Stranger things have happened . . .'

'Thanks a lot.'

Nicky giggled. 'No, you know what I mean. You're pretty good-looking—to someone who doesn't remember you in a gym-slip, with braces on your teeth, the way I do. Thin, and all that, which, considering you eat like a horse always seems unfair to me . . . Maybe he does. Maybe you've cracked the celebrated reserve . . .'

'I shouldn't think so for a minute. He gave me a lift, and then he left. That's it. End of story.'

'He was asking a lot of questions about you at lunchtime . . .' Nicky looked up, and met Rebecca's eyes candidly. 'Who you were, how you came to be here—all that. I didn't think much of it at the time, but I did tell him—and then he asked you the same questions. That's odd.'

'He asked you about me?' Rebecca looked up sharply. 'Oh God—Nicky, what did you say?'

Nicky blushed, and Rebecca gave a groan. Nicky was not famous for her discretion.

'If you told him anything about Conrad I'll kill you. Honestly, Nicky . . .'

'I didn't!' Nicky looked at her indignantly. 'Well, not much. You hadn't told me much, so I couldn't, could I? I mean, I might have mentioned Conrad's name—he asked which agency you'd worked at for God's sake, I had to say something . . . and I might have sort of hinted that you'd had good reasons for leaving—after all, I didn't want him to think you'd been fired, that there was anything wrong, I mean you're on our staff now, and . . .' She broke off, seeing Rebecca's expression. 'What *did* happen with Conrad anyway, Becky? You've been awfully close about it. You can tell me, you know, I'd understand. He was married, wasn't he? Well, it can happen, I know, you don't need to feel guilty—I'd understand . . .'

'Oh, Nicky, do shut up.' Rebecca turned away irritably. 'Nothing happened with Conrad. I . . . I just didn't want to go on working for him, that's all. And I do wish you'd be a bit more discreet . . .'

Nicky looked offended. 'There's no need to be so huffy,' she said defensively. 'I didn't say anything wrong, and I can't see what you're getting het up about anyway. According to you, you don't like Cal Ryder, and you're unlikely to see him again unless he happens to bump into you in the baker's or something, so why should you care?'

'I don't.' Rebecca stood up. 'Let's forget it, shall we?'

But Nicky wouldn't forget it; she kept harking back to the subject of Cal Ryder, past and present, all evening, until Rebecca felt she could have screamed with tension. Eventually, when they were sitting over coffee, there was at last a diversion. The two students staying at Pan cottage appeared, and Nicky asked them to join them: Rebecca saw she had a chance of escape, and promptly took it. Pleading a headache, she left Nicky to the two young men, and fled back to their flat.

There she took a shower, pulled on a thin nightdress, and then retired to the safety of her bedroom. But even here, it seemed there was no escape. Nicky, true to her word, had hunted out a paperback copy of one of Cal Ryder's novels, by an odd chance the same one Rebecca had given her mother all those years before: *Dying Fall*. Nicky had placed it on her bedside table, and, pulling a blanket around her for warmth, Rebecca opened it curiously. She'd just glance at it, she thought, before she lay down. She couldn't remember the plot, or the characters, or indeed anything about it; it might while away half an hour before she went to sleep.

The plot involved murder, and love—or murderous love, that much she learned from the back of the jacket. It was set in New York.

Settling herself comfortably against the pillows, Rebecca opened it, and began to read:

> It was her lover who, knowing how much she liked islands, persuaded her to go to New York.
> 'Manhattan is an island,' he said, trying to persuade her.
> 'Too large,' she answered, laughing. 'It doesn't count.'
> But she went anyway. . . .

Half an hour later, an hour later, Rebecca was still reading. Her light was still on when, past midnight, Nicky returned. But Nicky did not disturb her—perhaps she was still offended—and Rebecca was glad, for it meant she could go on reading. In the early hours, when the village and the harbour outside were silent, and all lights except hers had been long extinguished, she finally closed the book.

Then, and only then—she had finished it—did she put it down. It was a while after before she felt able to switch off the light, and when she finally did and lay in the dark, it was even longer before she could free her mind of Cal Ryder's imaginings. Towards dawn, she did so; then, his story and his voice overlapped in her tired mind; she tossed and turned in her bed, pursued by inchoate but threatening dreams.

The next morning she gave the book back to Nicky. And borrowed another one.

For the next few days Rebecca was kept very busy. As Easter approached, and English school holidays began, there was an increasing number of new arrivals and, as always, a few last-minute hitches, so Rebecca was constantly chasing back and

forth across the island, and looked back ruefully to the quiet
days, when she and Nicky had first arrived, and there had
been time for the odd leisurely lunch, or swim. Now there was
no time for such diversions: she and Nicky were up early each
morning to meet the ferry, and were both hard at work all
day: it was only in the evenings that they had much chance to
talk, or to unwind.

Nicky, meanwhile, had become very friendly with the
Sullivan students at Pan cottage. They were cousins, both up
at Oxford, and she and Nicky met up with them quite often in
the evenings. But although Rebecca liked them well enough,
she didn't want to spend every night in their company, though
Nicky seemed quite happy to do so. The first few invitations
she accepted; after that she avoided them, or left them
immediately after dinner—and so she found, by the time a
week had passed, that she was spending an increasing amount
of her time alone, and that this suited her.

In that time she had hardly seen Cal Ryder. Once or twice
she had glimpsed him in the distance in Gaios. On one
occasion she saw his Jeep parked outside Nico's house in
Lakka. Another time, seeing Nico's boat a little way to sea,
she had waved to him and then realised that he was not alone,
that Cal Ryder was with him. She couldn't see him clearly,
but, as she waved, she had suddenly seen the glint of sun on
binoculars, and realised that the tall dark figure in Nico's boat
had his glasses trained on her; he had not answered her wave,
as Nico had done, but she had known at once that it was he.

He had made no attempt to contact her again. Once, it was
true, when she was sitting in the square at Gaios after supper,
drinking the strange Greek brandy, Metaxa, that tasted like
talcum powder, she had seen him across the square, seen him
start in the direction of her table. But she had been with
Nicky and the Sullivan cousins, and he must have changed his
mind, because when she looked up again, he had disappeared,
melted away into the dusk, so quickly that she wondered if
she had been mistaken.

He had spoken to her just once, an afternoon when she had
volunteered to look after the Templars' children so that
Christopher and Pamela could go out in their little boat alone
for once. It had been a beautiful day, and she had spent most

of the time on the beach at Lakka with the children, helping Tom and Francie with their swimming, and keeping a watchful eye on the baby, who liked nothing better than eating sand. Towards tea-time, when they were sitting in a group together, the baby was happily asleep in her arms, and she was telling Tom and Francie a story, she had gradually become aware that Tom's attention was wandering. He kept glancing up, over her shoulder, and just as Rebecca resolved to cut the story short, he interrupted her.

'Who's that man, Becka?' he said, in a low voice. 'I don't know him, and he's been just standing there, watching us, for *hours . . .*'

Rebecca swung round. Behind them, at the edge of the beach, was a low stone wall. And leaning against it, indeed watching them, was Cal Ryder. As she turned he straightened up, and lifted his hand in a casual greeting.

'Don't move,' he called, and before Rebecca could speak, 'You make a charming picture. Finish the story—I was just passing. I didn't mean to interrupt . . .'

Rebecca, embarrassed, unsure what to do, took him at his word. She continued the story in a low monotone, cutting it as short as she could, wanting all the while to turn round and see if Cal Ryder had gone. He had not, and, as she finished, he strolled towards them. The two children looked up at him, open-mouthed, perhaps sensing the tension in Rebecca. To her surprise, Cal Ryder bent down to them with an easy smile.

'That's a fine collection of shells . . .' He gestured to the little pile on the sand. 'Did you collect all those?'

His tone, easy, direct, evoked an immediate response.

Tom looked up at him seriously.

'That's just the ones we got today,' he said firmly. 'At home we've got *millions . . .*'

'And Becka helped find these.' Francie looked up at the tall man and smiled. She plucked one of the shells from the pile. 'She found this one, the speckled one. It's my favourite . . .'

She held it out to Cal Ryder, and he examined it solemnly. Then he raised his head slowly, and looked Rebecca straight in the eyes. 'It's very beautiful,' he said.

Francie hesitated. She looked at Tom, then back at Cal.

'Would you like to keep it?' she said.

'I should like to very much.' Cal regarded her solemnly.
'But I don't think I'd better, do you? Not when it's your
favourite . . .'

'It's all right. It's only my favourite *today*.' Francie put out
one plump hand and patted his. 'You keep it.'

Cal looked at the little girl, and Rebecca saw his features
soften. He gave her a smile of great gentleness and warmth.

'Thank you very much,' he said. 'I shall keep it always. I'll
put it on my desk, so I look at it first thing every morning. All
right?' This appeared to content Francie, and Cal straightened
up. He looked at Rebecca, and Rebecca raised her face to his.

'You're well?' he said formally. 'Not working too hard?
How's the bike—no more trouble, I hope?'

Rebecca saw the hint of a smile at the corners of his lips.

'No. No more trouble at all,' she said, evenly. 'Amazing,
isn't it? I can't think what went wrong with it.'

'Temperament.' He smiled. 'Bad temper most probably.
Machines are like that . . .' He hesitated for a second, and
Rebecca saw his gaze fall from her face, flushed a pink-gold
from the sun, to the baby whose head lolled sleepily against
her breast. For a moment she thought he might stay, and
realised she would have been happy if he had done so, but
then he turned away.

'I've an appointment with Nico . . .' He glanced down at his
watch. 'I'll have to go, I'm afraid. Nice to run into you . . .
Goodbye . . . Oh, and thank you for the shell again, young
lady . . .'

Then he left them, strolling away across the sand, his figure
tall and lithe against the light. There was a little silence.

'How he stared at you, Becka,' Tom said.

'He's *nice*,' said Francie. 'I'm glad I gave him that shell. You
don't mind, do you, Becka?'

'No, no, of course not . . .' Rebecca gently put the baby
down and began to gather up their things.

'Why does he sit at a desk every morning?' said Francie
pensively. 'That can't be very nice. Specially on holiday . . .'

'He's a writer . . .'

'Does he write stories we'd like?' Francie persisted.

'No—not really,' Rebecca answered patiently. 'When
you're grown-up you might like them, though . . .'

Tom looked at her with renewed interest.

'When we're grown-up? You mean lots of bad things happen in them? Murders and that?'

Rebecca smiled. 'Oh, lots.'

'*Ace* . . .' Tom looked in the direction of Cal's tall figure as he rounded the trees at the edge of the beach and disappeared from sight. He was obviously full of approval. This approval re-doubled the following day when, via Nico, Cal Ryder sent down two small parcels to the children: in Tom's a Swiss Army pen-knife; in Francie's a necklace of tiny shells. When she heard this, Rebecca was touched, both by the childrens' wild excitement and by Cal's thoughtfulness, but she also felt an odd sad little ache settle in her heart. She would have liked to have seen him again, she thought; yes, she would have liked that.

She could have forced an opportunity—it would have been easy enough and in fact she knew that she ought to contact Cal about the Villa Circe, to assure him the repairs were almost finished and that he could move in on schedule. But she shied away from this, and put it off. It might look pushy; after all, if he wanted to contact her, he would have done so, wouldn't he?

A few days after the encounter on the beach, Rebecca at last had a day off. She looked forward to the free time eagerly, for she and Nicky had been working exceptionally hard. Nicky was going off on a boat-trip with the Sullivans, and they asked Rebecca to go with them, but Rebecca refused. She wanted to be on her own.

She went in early to the office to check there were no emergencies, and, finding the tape on the answering machine blissfully free of all calls, she stretched happily. The day was her own—gloriously free. She began to make plans. She would buy some food for a picnic, she decided, and then take one of the little agency boats up the coast. Between Lakka and Logos there were many tiny little beaches and coves accessible only by sea, and almost always deserted. She would go to one of those, and sun bathe, and swim, and read, and be for once thoroughly, gloriously, lazy.

Carefully she locked up the office, went back to the flat and packed her swimming things and another Cal Ryder novel which she had found among the rack of English paperbacks at the village store.

It was still early, not yet nine, when she returned to the main square to buy the food for her picnic. The sun slanted across the paving, and glinted on the white walls of the little church; the air felt light and clear, and Rebecca knew that, by mid-day, it would be very hot. She bought some freshly baked bread, still warm from the ovens, some cheese and some fruit, and then, swinging the string bag that held her purchases, she set off down to the harbour where the boat was moored. She was waylaid several times, by Nico, Leandros and Agape, and then by the Templars, who hailed her from Andros's taverna, and persuaded them to have coffee with them before she set off.

Tom and Francie were already tanned; their parents looked happy and relaxed, and Rebecca was glad to see that Pamela Templar seemed gay, and in high spirits.

'Come and sit with us, Rebecca,' she called, patting the chair beside her. 'Isn't it the most glorious day? We're going to walk down through the olive groves, and have a picnic . . .'

Rebecca smiled. 'I don't think I need to ask if you're enjoying yourselves,' she said, sitting down. 'You look marvellous. Is everything working out?'

'Everything. I just don't want ever to leave, that's the only problem . . .' Pamela laughed. 'This is the holiday of a lifetime for us, you know. I'm afraid we're being spoiled. Devon and Cornwall just won't seem the same after this, will they, Chris?' She turned to Rebecca impulsively. 'Tom and Francie have been swimming every day—even the baby's been in the water. We went fishing with Nico yesterday—and Agape has been babysitting for us, just the way you said, so Chris and I have been able to go out and have dinner on our own—I can't tell you what a treat it is. My appetite's come back—I've been sleeping like a log. It's just perfect . . .'

She paused, as her husband got up to pay the bill, and when he was out of ear-shot, she turned to Rebecca confidentially. 'Chris doesn't make that much money, you know,' she said, 'And with the three children—well, we've never been able to be extravagant. So this is a big thing for us; we had to save for ages, and I know Chris was worried about it, whether it would work out and everything—especially as I'd been ill.' She hesitated shyly, looking down. 'I expect a lot of the people who come on your holidays—well, it's probably not so special for them. But for us—we'll never forget it. I wanted you to know—how grateful we are. It's the most perfect place, isn't it? A little bit magical, I think.' She looked up at Rebecca with a quick shy smile. 'I felt better the first day we got here, and it's wonderful for Chris, too. He works awfully hard—the parents never realise, I think, what a strain it is, teaching small children, day in day out. So, it's good for him too. He can fish and swim—and read ...' She leant across and picked up the book her husband had left on her chair.

'Look at that,' she went on, with a laugh. 'Jane Austen! His favourite author. At home he doesn't get much chance for reading any more, but here! Well, he's making up for lost time, I can tell you. It's lovely for me to see him relaxed ...' She dropped her voice slightly, seeing her husband return. 'He worries so, you see,' she said softly. 'Especially about me. I wish he wouldn't sometimes, but ...'

'I don't think you should mind.' Rebecca smiled at her, seeing the sudden concern in her eyes as she looked up to her husband, 'He cares for you—it's only natural that he should worry a little bit, when you'd been ill and so on ...' She paused. 'After all—you'd mind much more if he didn't, wouldn't you?'

Pamela laughed, and her husband came to a halt, looking down at them.

'You two look very conspiratorial,' he said, with mock-sternness. 'What are you whispering about?'

'About you!' His wife laughed. She flicked the book in the table before her. 'I was telling Rebecca about all the reading you've been doing. Jane Austen! Do you know, Rebecca, when I first met Chris, I used to be quite jealous of her? He used to say she was the only other woman he could fall in love with!'

Rebecca smiled, and stretched, 'Oh, I don't think I'd worry too much about that if I were you,' she said easily. 'The nicest possible kind of rival, I'd say ...'

But, she realised, Pamela and Christopher Templar weren't

listening. They were looking at each other with an expression of great warmth and happiness; Christopher reached down and took his wife's arm, drawing her to her feet.

'I said no such thing,' he murmured. 'Her mind attracted me—I won't deny that. I think it's quite possible to fall in love with a writer's imagination—or a musician's or an artist's for that matter. What happened when I met you was of a rather different order, however . . .'

'You mean it wasn't my imagination that attracted you?' His wife smiled up at him flirtatiously, her tone mockingly belligerent.

Her husband patted her bottom. 'Let's just say other qualities came first . . .'

They laughed together softly, and Rebecca, turning away, felt a sudden loneliness, a sense of exclusion. Just then, for one weak instant, she would have given a great deal to have shared such easy intimacy, such assured happiness, with someone else. And Christopher Templar's words, although teasing, had perturbed her. Was that true? she thought. Could you fall in love with someone through their work—through looking at a picture they had painted . . . or reading a book that they had written?

'Rebecca—goodbye! Have a lovely day . . . Come and have a meal with us at the villa one night, will you do that?' Pamela pressed her arm warmly as they turned away, and at her obvious happiness and in the face of her warm friendliness, Rebecca felt the shaft of sudden melancholy leave her.

'I'd love to do that—yes, soon, I promise . . . 'Bye Tom, 'bye Francie—don't swim too far . . .'

She raised her hand to wave as, the children skipping and weaving around their parents, they rounded the corner of the harbour. Christopher had his arm around his wife's waist; she was looking up at him, and laughing. Again Rebecca felt that sharp painful tug at her heart. She sighed. What was wrong with her today? For some reason she was being stupid and maudlin; she must snap out of it. It was a glorious day; she was going out in the boat and . . .

She felt a shadow fall across her back; someone had come up behind her, quite silently, and now stood between her and the sun. She knew who it was instantly, without having to turn around.

'Hello,' Cal Ryder said pleasantly, as if he had expected to meet her, as if they had last met a few hours, and not nearly a week before. 'It's your day off, isn't it? Had you made plans?'

Rebecca swung round. Her eyes were instantly dazzled by the sun, and she had to shield them with her hand. Cal Ryder was looking down into her face, and smiling at her. He was wearing old and very faded denims, the shirt undone, and tucked loosely into the belt around his waist, and old, scuffed blue espadrilles. The light breeze from the sea blew one strand of dark hair across his forehead.

'I was going out in the boat . . .' Rebecca hesitated, then smiled, and indicated her string bag. 'With a picnic . . .'

'On your own?' He frowned, and Rebecca smiled at him wickedly.

'With a good book for company . . .'

He glanced down; the jacket of the book could be seen clearly through the string bag, and he grimaced.

'I'd thought you might like to come out in my boat—but maybe you'd prefer my prose to my presence . . .'

'I don't think so.'

'We could go up the coast. I brought a picnic too . . .'

He met her eyes, and to her surprise Rebecca realised he expected her to refuse.

'I'd like that,' she said quickly. 'I'd like it very much. Thank you.'

He seemed pleased, she thought, but he bent to take the picnic bag from her, so she could not see his face. Then, taking her arm, he led her down towards the quay.

'How well do you swim?' he said, as they passed along the rows of boats.

Rebecca glanced at him in surprise. 'Pretty well. I'm quite a strong swimmer. Why?'

He stopped, and looked down into her face. 'Because I thought we might do something a bit risky, that's why. And I wouldn't attempt it if you couldn't swim.'

'Something risky?' She stared at him.

He had come to a halt beside a large black inflatable sea-skimmer, on which was mounted a powerful outboard engine. He bent to its ropes.

'Go round to the west coast.' He glanced up at her. 'If you're willing . . .'

CHAPTER FOUR

'I'VE always wanted to go in one of these...' Rebecca climbed into the inflatable, and watched as Cal Ryder untied the painter ropes, and then stepped in beside her. She took the rope, and began to coil it, as, barefooted now, balancing surely, he moved to the stern, and lowered the outboard.

'Yes, well, they have certain advantages...' He glanced up at her.

'They go very fast—I know that. I've seen them...'

'Very fast. And they're extremely stable, practically impossible to sink...'

'That's good to know...'

'And—because they have no keel—you can take them into very shallow water, places you'd never reach in a boat...' He pulled the starter string, and the engine roared into life. He settled himself on a low cross-bar seat, one tanned hand grasping the tiller, and began carefully to edge them away from the harbour's edge.

'On the other hand,' Rebecca said dryly, glancing down at the thin skin of rubber beneath her feet, 'if you misjudge, if there should be rocks...' She gave a little involuntary shiver; she had seen what happened to one of these that had ventured incautiously close to rocks; no one, luckily, had been hurt, but the inflatable had been ripped to shreds in seconds.

Cal Ryder shrugged; out in the channel now, and clear of the other harbour boats, he paused. 'You're sure you want to come? You sound nervous. If it's any help, I'm not a novice. I've been sailing since I was a boy, and I've had one of these— oh, two, three years now...'

There was a gleam of amusement in his eyes as he looked at her, and Rebecca felt a dart of irritation. If she sounded nervous it was not because of the boat, she thought. She tilted her chin.

'Not nervous at all. I'm sure I'm in safe hands...'

He raised an eyebrow at this, as if to indicate that she was not exactly in his hands, but he wouldn't have minded if she had been, and Rebecca blushed. But he said nothing, merely adjusted the throttle, and set the course northwards. Rebecca, grateful that for a while at least his concentration was elsewhere, settled back in the bows. She stretched her arms across the taut wide rim of the inflatable, and let her fingers trail in the water. Gradually, Cal Ryder increased their speed.

It felt glorious, Rebecca thought, tilting her head back and luxuriating in the sun. There was virtually no wind; the water was still and almost without ripples; they seemed to fly over its surface effortlessly. Turning her head, she watched the coast go past—they had cleared Gaios now, there were no houses to be seen—the island, a secret place of groves and coves, might have been uninhabited.

'Like it?' Cal cut the engine back a little, and called to her.

She lifted her head and smiled at him happily. 'Like it? It's wonderful—I feel like a bird . . .'

He laughed, and gestured ahead of them. 'I thought we might stop first a little way further on, on this coast. We could swim here, and have our lunch, and then decide whether to risk the west coat or not. All right by you?'

'Anything you say—you're the captain!'

They went on further, for about another fifteen or twenty minutes, until they reached a part of the coast Rebecca had not visited before, somewhere between Lakka and Logos—about midway, she calculated. On a headland above them she saw the ruins of a farmhouse; then Cal adjusted the tiller, and began to move into the bay beyond it. It opened out before them, a wide arc of sand, the olive groves stretching almost down to the edge of the beach. It was deserted, its boundaries marked by two arms of rock, flat-topped, gleaming silver in the sunlight. Cal called to her over the purr of the engine:

'I've brought her in here before—I don't think we've any problems with rocks. But just to be on the safe side—can you keep a lookout?'

'Sure . . .' Rebecca turned, and knelt, leaning over the edge of the inflatable, and peering into the water below. It was clear; she could see right to the bottom.

'It's clear,' she called over her shoulder. 'I can see sand—oh, and fishes, little tiny ones. But no rocks. . . .'

'Fine . . . Hang on. You stay where you are . . .'

He cut the engine, and stood up. In the sudden silence, as they drifted towards the beach, Rebecca glanced back at him. He had pulled off his shirt; she saw the wide muscles of his shoulders glint gold in the sunlight. He had already kicked off his shoes; now, without a trace of self-consciousness, he pulled off his jeans. He was wearing brief black trunks: silhouetted against the sun, she saw him for an instant, very tall, perfectly formed, a figure from a Greek vase come to life. Then, with one swift graceful move, he dived over the side, and surfaced at the bows in front of her.

'Toss me the rope, can you?' He tossed back his wet hair; water ran in rivulets, like diamonds, over his skin. Wordlessly, Rebecca tossed him the rope. He caught it, and began to tow the inflatable the last few yards to the beach. Rebecca, feeling rather useless, and also knowing that she wouldn't be able to undress with his easy aplomb, seized her opportunity. She had her swimming costume on under her dress; in a second, she had kicked off her sandals, pulled the dress over her head, and slipped over the side into the water.

The sudden coldness after the heat of the sun made her catch her breath. She surfaced, gasped, tossed back the long strands of wet dark hair, and found herself face to face with him. They were about fifteen yards from the shore, in the shadow of the boat. For an instant she saw his eyes darken; he moved towards her slightly, and instinctively, treading water, then starting to swim, she moved out of his reach.

'I don't see why you should tow me, as well as the boat,' she called lightly, and, resting one arm over the side, she helped him guide it in to the shore. They lifted and pulled it as far up the beach as they could—which was hard work, and hot and then, once it was safe above the water-line, without speaking, and as if by common consent, they both dived like fishes back into the blue of the sea. Rebecca swam out a little way, fast, her arms cleaving through the water. He followed her more slowly, lazily, taking his time, but swimming with such controlled power that she knew he could catch her up, and overtake her easily if he wished.

At last, out of breath, she stopped, and let herself float in the silk of the water. She looked back to the beach, the rocks,

the bay: powered by the sun, by the water, by the beauty of
the place and by the fact of his presence, she felt suddenly an
intoxicating and exultant happiness. It surged through her;
she felt it course through her veins; she wanted to do
something mad—to sing or to shout—because, just then, the
world felt perfect.

The water beside her parted; Cal surfaced at her side, the
water rippling from his skin and hair. Their eyes met for a
second, and Rebecca knew he felt as she did. He touched her
arm, very lightly, the most glancing of touches, and Rebecca
froze. Every nerve-ending in her body felt suddenly electric
with anticipation. His hand tightened around her wrist. For
an instant the grip was almost painful; then he released her.
Confused, alarmed by the suddenness and intensity of her
own feelings, Rebecca tore her eyes away from his face. She
looked back to the shore.

'Does it have a name, this place?' she said, softly. 'If it does,
I should like to know it . . .'

'I don't think so. No one lives here. Hardly anyone comes
here . . .' He moved off again, ahead of her, in a quick surge
through the water. Then he turned, and looked back at her,
and smiled.

'We can christen it *i paralia mas*—we could call it that.'

'What does that mean?' she called after him.

'It means, "our beach",' he called, laughing. 'Come on—
let's have lunch, shall we?'

The lunch was delicious; Rebecca noted with interest that
the food Cal had brought had been carefully chosen, carefully
packed up, and had clearly been intended for two people.
Two helpings of cold chicken, two hard-boiled eggs, two
freshly baked rolls, two apples, two nectarines—even, she
noted with a smile to herself—two glasses for the wine. It was
a bachelor's picnic, she thought; and a bachelor who'd been
quite certain he'd have company, despite that anxious look at
the harbour earlier. She glanced up at him teasingly, when he
offered her the nectarines.

'You knew I'd come today, then, I see . . .' She paused. 'Or
did you intend to picnic with someone else if you missed me?'

'Not at all.' He stretched lazily, apparently unpreturbed by
her accusation. 'I hoped you would come, obviously. I went to

a great deal of trouble with this picnic on your behalf. Preparing lunch for a professional cook—even a picnic lunch—well, it's very nerve-racking. I hope you observe the eggs are perfectly hard-boiled? Not squidgy, and not like grey bullets either . . .'

'I most certainly did observe,' Rebecca looked at him solemnly.

'And the chicken . . . I had the devil of a job with the chicken. I've never had to cut one up before. It was quite extraordinarily difficult, bones where you'd never expect them . . . And the wine. I chose the wine with care . . .'

'Yes. And you're not answering my question. What would you have done if I hadn't come? Who was going to be my understudy?'

'No one.' He looked injured at the suggestion. 'You don't imagine I'd waste a cordon bleu picnic on someone who lacked your professional expertise? Certainly not. I should have eaten it myself, that's all. I should have had a rather sad, lonely little picnic, all by myself, in this beautiful bay, and . . .'

Rebecca laughed. 'What a sob story! I don't believe a word of it.'

'Quite right. You shouldn't.' He rolled over on to his stomach, and rested his face on his hands. His eyes met hers with a mocking glint. 'The question didn't arise. I knew you'd come with me. I had a premonition. And if you'd refused . . .'

'Ah yes! Refused! I might have done. What then?'

'Then I should have kidnapped you. Main force. I should have picked you up in the market square, to the astonishment and delectation of Andros and all his customers at the taverna, put you over my shoulder, like a sack of potatoes . . .'

'Thank you very much . . .'

'All right, like a very *light* sack of potatoes, I'd say slender but I don't think you can have a slender sack, do you? Anyway, where was I? Ah yes—over my shoulder. Then I should have dumped you unceremoniously in the boat, started the engine, hijacked you here, and forced you to eat. How about that?'

'Oh, I don't know . . .' Rebecca met his gaze, which was now openly flirtatious. She smiled teasingly. 'It sounds rather fun as a matter of fact. If you ask me out for a picnic again I shall certainly say no. I've always wanted to be kidnapped . . .'

He laughed, breaking what had been, for a second, a slight sense of tension between them, and Rebecca was grateful. Whatever was happening to her seemed to be happening alarmingly fast, and she felt as if she needed time. Time for what she couldn't quite have said, but time to be quiet, to consider—yes, she needed that, because she still felt an edge of anticipation in herself, of expectation partly sensual, partly emotional.

Everything about Cal Ryder—his closeness, the scent of his skin, the brush of his hand as he gave her a glass of wine, the sound of his voice—all these things seemed to conspire with the perfection of the place, the peace and warmth of the sun, to throw her off balance. She felt drawn to him, attracted by him—intensely so. And that attraction unnerved her—the more so because she suspected he sensed it. Another man, seeing how she felt, might have pressed home his advantage— become more openly flirtatious, touched her, or kissed her. Cal Ryder did not: one moment she thought he too felt attraction, the next he treated her brusquely, in a matter-of-fact manner, as if the tension between them existed in her imagination only. That changeability of his both relieved her—this is all happening too fast! she wanted to cry—and also confused her. She could not read him at all, she thought to herself, as she helped him pack up the picnic things; not at all.

Cal had brought a rug with them, and, when the picnic things were stowed in the boat again, he suggested they should rest for a little in the shade before they set off again. Rebecca agreed gratefully, it was mid-day, the sun was nearly vertical above their heads, and it was very hot. The wine she had drunk had left her feeling sleepy, and, though they talked for a little while, she lying on the rug, Cal leaning with his back against the trunk of an old olive, her replies to his questions grew slower, and her eyelids heavier. Eventually their conversation dwindled companionably; Cal opened a book and began to read; Rebecca gave up the struggle and allowed her mind to drift lazily into a dream-state, half sleep, half waking.

At least she thought she remained half awake, lapped pleasurably in the sound of the waves on the beach. But she must have slept more deeply than she realised, for when she did finally open her eyes, Cal knelt beside her, looking down into her face. He had been in the water again for it gleamed against his skin, and glittered on his dark lashes.

'You've been asleep,' he said. 'For ages. I've been watching you. Then it became rather too much for my self-control so I went for a swim . . .' He paused, looking deep into her eyes, and in the depths of his she saw something kindle, darken, become intent. She sat up hurriedly, her hands moving instinctively to her breast, covering the low neckline, the place where pale skin could be glimpsed, beyond the golden tan. He smiled sardonically.

'It's a little late for that . . .'

Very gently he lifted his hand, and moved hers away. Lips parted, her veins still pulsing with the images of her dreams, Rebecca did not speak. Delicately he lifted his hand to her throat; he ran just the tips of his fingers very slightly and caressingly over her skin, along the line of her lips, over her chin, down the curve of her throat to the hollow at its base. The touch, so light, so delicate, fired her blood; she heard herself catch her breath, then expel it in a sigh as, very gently, his fingers moved lower. They followed the edge of her neckline, tracing it over the swell of her breast; for a second they rested there, while he looked into her eyes, then he eased one of the shoulder straps just a very little to one side, and lowered his mouth very deliberately into the bare curve of her shoulder. He pressed his lips against her skin; Rebecca felt their warmth, and trembled.

He drew back, and gently, courteously, helped her to her feet. 'Your skin tastes of the sea . . .' He smiled at her, and then, as if nothing had happened, as if that too had been an extension of her dream, he took her by the hand, and led her back to the boat.

'Right.'

The engine fired, and Cal held out a hand to her. 'Shall we try the west coast? What do you think? Do you feel up to it?'

'Certainly!' Rebecca smiled back at him challengingly. 'I

haven't been round there yet, and I've wanted to ever since I came to the island—let's!'

'OK. But sit up in the stern beside me, will you? Once we round the headland at the north it gets rough: I want all the weight in the back of the boat—here . . .'

Carefully Rebecca eased herself upright, and balancing carefully, made her way to his side. He drew her down beside him, putting his arm around her waist. He glanced at her sideways, his lips curving with amusement.

'You're not going to burn? It's very hot. You could borrow my shirt if you like—and we're going to get drenched, you know.'

'I'm fine.' Rebecca leaned back against the strong curve of his arm. 'I don't burn too easily, and I think I'm used to the sun now . . .'

'Right then. Hold tight. We're off . . .'

He opened the throttle, and the inflatable surged forward at a speed that alarmed Rebecca momentarily. She realised how much he had been holding it in earlier; now they must be going at fifty or sixty miles an hour. The boat tilted in the water as its speed increased, so that the bows rose up before them at an angle and they sped over the water like an arrow. Looking to their left, realising Cal had steered away from the land and that they were much further out to sea than they had been, she saw that they were passing Logos, that the last headland at the end of the east coast was already just ahead of them.

There was a breeze now, she could feel it, and, looking out over the water she saw why he steered this course: the sea seemed calm enough, but away to their left, closer in to the land, she could see white, the telltale breakers that hinted at the rocks beneath their surface. Even as she looked she felt the whole boat shudder and begin to buck: Cal's hand tightened on the tiller, his arm increased its pressure against her waist, and Rebecca, exhilarated, startled, clung to her seat and to him as best she could. They had reached the northern tip of the island: as they rounded it and came out into the open sea she realised for the first time the realities of all the warnings.

Suddenly the water around them was translated: behind them it was still unruffled, smooth, tranquil and without threat: in the lea of the island, it was as calm as a lake. Ahead of them—even though the day was so warm and so calm with no suggestion of storm—the breakers rolled in high and crashed against the shore. She heard them pound against the rocks away to their left; she saw the spray rise glittering in the air, and she felt the pliant framework of the boat respond to their power, bucking, surging, swooping across the crest of the breakers, so the water hit its underside like a series of great slaps from an unseen hand. She caught her breath, and shouted over the sound.

'It's amazing! Not like being in a boat at all—more like a hovercraft or something . . .'

'Just hold tight—we're OK, but I need to concentrate . . .' Look, could you do something for me? Can you get my wristwatch off? I need one hand on the tiller and I can't manage it. Can you?'

Rebecca looked at him in surprise, then did as he asked. He moved the arm around her waist so it lay across her lap, pinning her safely between it and the rounded gunnels. Carefully, her hands shaking with the effort of balancing and of not dropping it, she eased the heavy watch off his wrist. It was more than a watch, she saw, looking at it more closely, when it lay in the palm of her hand. She thought it was what they called a chronometer, anyway, it was clearly waterproof, the kind of watch divers wore.

'It's got a stopwatch mechanism . . .' Cal shouted to her through the spray that was now full in their faces. 'The button at the top on the right hand side. When I tell you, I want you to press it, OK?'

'OK!' Rebecca shouted back, not having the least idea why he should want her to do this. She saw him glance up to their left, and, following his gaze she saw they were passing the Villa Circe. The boat bucked under them, the engine roared, and she saw the house, and its terrace for a second quite clearly. She also saw, or thought she saw, the glint of light on glass, as if someone with binoculars watched them from that terrace as they passed.

'Now!' Cal yelled. She pressed the stopwatch button, a huge breaker slammed the underside of the boat, and Rebecca was thrown heavily against Cal's side. When she righted herself again and peered through the mist of spray the Villa Circe was already out of sight, and Cal was steering them round in a wide pitched arc. Suddenly the sun was in her eyes, the breakers were catching the boat at an angle, and she realised they had rounded the further headland and were going south, down the west coast of the island.

Here the water was rough, and in places she could see patterns rippling on its surface crossing and counter-crossing, indicating currents. But it was not quite as rough as it had been on the north coast, and the noise of waves and spray lessened a little. She felt Cal relax slightly; now he risked moving his arm, putting it around her waist again. He glanced at her and smiled, and Rebecca thought how marvellous he looked, and how transformed, when he did smile. It softened and lit his whole face, giving him an aspect of sudden gentleness that she found disarming.

'Well done! It's exciting, isn't it? And today it's calm.'

'Calm?' Rebecca laughed. 'You call this calm . . .'

'It's true. I've been round here in a storm once—in a boat on that occasion. It's not an experience I'm anxious to repeat . . .' She saw his mouth tighten slightly, and he looked away to the cliffs that now rose up sheer to their left.

Following his gaze she saw through the shimmering spray an arch of white rock rising up out of the sea before them, and in her excitement, in the moment of recognition, she forgot everything else.

'The arch!' she cried. 'Why, that's the one I saw—from the cliffs, the day we met . . . It is, isn't it? We must be below the cliffs where you live . . .'

He smiled at her excitement. 'That's right. Now listen. I'm going to take the boat in close. I've done it before and there's nothing to worry about, you just have to time it right because of the way the water moves between the arch and the cliff . . .'

'We're going *between* the arch and the cliff?' Rebecca turned to him with a cry. 'No, Cal, don't—you can't—it's too narrow . . .'

He laughed; he had already moved the tiller. 'It looks too narrow. I promise you it isn't. It's the only way into the bay beyond. If you try and go into the mouth of the bay, the other side of the arch, you get caught in the undercurrent, and you get smashed on the rocks. This way it's quite safe: it just looks dangerous, you have to do it and do it fast, on the surge of the water—like this—hold tight . . .'

As he spoke he suddenly opened the throttle full; Rebecca gave a cry as the boat surged forward. She felt the water lift them and carry them then, on its own power, as if they had no engine, lifting them up and travelling them like a surfer on a perfect wave up and forward, close, very close to the sharp white rock of the arch to their right, close, very close to the more jagged rocks of the cliff to their left, up and through. She shut her eyes against the iridescent haze of water and light. She opened them again and all was quiet; they idled on still water in the bay. Impulsively she turned to Cal, her eyes alight with relief and with excitement, but before she could speak he reached across and took the stopwatch from her, pressed it, read the dial, then smiled. Rebecca stared at him.

'You were timing us?'

He nodded.

'To here? But why?'

He shrugged, looking up at the cliffs. 'Just for a book. It's something I thought of using in a book. That's all.'

'And how long did we take?'

'Four minutes, thirty-two point five seconds. That's the fastest I've ever done it . . .' He turned to her as he spoke, and Rebecca suddenly began to laugh.

'The fastest? You mean you do this often and you time yourself? And all for a book? You go through that . . . that . . . Scylla and Charybdis back there, and . . .' She broke off. He was regarding her intently, his eyes dark, his mouth lifting a little as if he were amused, but with something in his expression that puzzled her, so that, for an instant, she felt he was not telling her the truth.

'Well, anyway . . . we broke your record. That's good. I suppose. And it was exciting, when we came through, so fast, a bit like shooting the rapids . . .'

'You thought so?' He spoke evenly, his eyes never leaving her face, and Rebecca grew still and silent under that gaze. Her somewhat nervous outpouring of words stopped; she was conscious suddenly of the silence around them. The boat drifted gently with the lap of the waves; beyond the shelter of the bay the surf pounded, but distantly. Here it was quiet, the water was still and it was deep, and Rebecca was suddenly reminded of the kind of books he wrote. She swallowed.

'When you say timing—for a book—you mean the timing's important for the plot? Because it's something to do with . . . with a murder? A killing?'

'What?' He frowned, as if his thoughts had been elsewhere. 'Oh—yes. Something like that . . .'

His arm tightened around her waist; Rebecca tensed.

'Do you always work things out so thoroughly for your books? The timing? The clues?' She looked at him curiously, puzzled by something in his manner, and he shrugged.

'But of course. I like to get the details exactly right. And this is complicated . . .' He hesitated, his voice becoming purposefully vague, she thought. 'The timing of the journey— it's affected by different factors—the time of day, the weather, the state of the tides, the number of people in the boat, the kind of boat you use, of course . . .'

'You mean you can get through that gap in an ordinary boat?' Rebecca stared back at the arch of rock in disbelief, and Cal laughed.

'Oh sure. A very small boat. *If* the tide's exactly right, and you know what you're doing. It's easier in an inflatable, obviously. Anyway . . .' He slipped the heavy watch around his wrist again, and buckled it. 'Thanks for your help . . . Shall we swim here? We can, if you like. It's quite safe in the bay. Then we can go back . . .'

'OK. Fine . . .'

Rebecca watched as he slipped over the side of the inflatable and into the water. Clearly he intended to say nothing more about his book or its plot, and she knew him well enough now not to risk further questions. She felt for a moment a fractional unease, wondering if she should mention to him the flash of light on glass she had seen as they passed the Villa Circe, wondering if he had noticed it, too. Someone had been watching them, someone with binoculars, she was certain of that, and that was odd. The Villa Circe should have been deserted. Leandros would not have been working there that day, and anyway, she'd never seen any of the islanders use field glasses . . . She looked down at Cal Ryder's dark head, at the wide powerful shoulders rippling through the water as he towed the inflatable into the shallows. And she decided to say nothing. She might have been mistaken; if someone had been there it might have been a tourist, someone who'd ventured up to the north of the island to explore, who'd happened to be looking out across that beautiful expanse of water, who'd been trying, perhaps, to make out the distant shoreline of Albania, that beautiful mysterious purplish haze that lay along the northern horizon. It wasn't important . . .

She slipped into the water beside him, helped him tether the inflatable in a tranquil and safe neck of water where it bobbed gently and did not brush against the rocks, and then, luxuriating in the cool freedom of the water, in the sun against her skin, she swam back out into the bay, looking up at the cliffs before them.

Cal swam idly back and forth for a while at a distance from her, occasionally disappearing beneath the water, and then surfacing again in a fountain of diamond spray. Rebecca swam and floated, floated and swam, and eventually— choosing her site with care, knowing the rocks harboured sea urchin, and that their spines were difficult and painful to remove if stepped on incautiously—she hauled herself out on to a flat jutting of rock from where she could see the full width of the bay. Almost opposite her was the black cleft in the cliffs which she had glimpsed on her walk: the cave of Aphrodite! She turned lazily on to her stomach, resting her chin on her hands, and stared at the cave across the water. If it were true the cave could be reached by boat she could not see how. From here its entrance seemed to her quite inaccessible, guarded by serried ranks of ferocious-looking rocks. It might, she thought, be possible to swim to those rocks, and then clamber across them to the cave mouth, and, of course, it was low tide now. At high tide those rocks must be covered—they were black and shiny with seaweed. Perhaps then, if the tide rose high enough over them. But it would be perilous; she gave a little shiver.

Cal, at that moment, reached the water below her, and with practised ease, pulled himself up and on to the rock beside her. He smiled a greeting, but said nothing. With a sigh of contentment he lay back, stretching out in the sun, pillowing his dark head on his hands. He closed his eyes, and they lay there, side by side, the sun warm on their skin, the only sound the suck and lap of the water and the occasional cry of a sea-bird. Cal did not move; Rebecca did not move. She felt at peace, completely so, yet, as the minutes slipped by she realised she also felt watchful. She had turned her face away from the man beside her, was letting her gaze slide again over the sea and the rocks and the cliffs towards the opening of the cave. But although she did not look at him her very skin seemed to sense his nearness, to register his tiniest shift or movement. Warmth crept through her body and through her veins; she felt as if some force pulsed across the few inches that separated their bodies. She stole a glance at him, seeing grains of salt glitter at the edge of his dark lashes. He appeared to be asleep; he lay in an attitude of complete relaxation, as if oblivious of her presence. Quickly she looked away again; involuntarily she sighed.

With a quick movement—he had not slept, after all—he rolled over. His body glanced against hers; instantly he edged aside. She could not bring herself to look up at him, though she sensed his gaze, burning into her skin. He lay, propped up on his elbow, half on his side, and she knew he watched her. After a little while he bent and very gently lifted one of her hands in his. He held it lightly. Turning her head, narrowing her eyes against the sun, she saw he examined it closely, her ringless fingers, her nails pale from the sea, the pale gold of her skin frosted like his with salt.

'Sea creature . . .' he said softly, his voice teasing. The sun and the sound of the sea beat in on her; he drew her up to him, gently but strongly, saying nothing, so she knelt beside him. Then, so surely and gently she was hardly aware of what was happening, it was like being lifted by the tide, he gathered her in his arms, drew her against the bare damp skin of his chest, and bent his mouth to her lips. She shut her eyes, felt her breasts jut and harden against him, felt herself drift, shimmer, dissolve in the cool power of his embrace. He parted her lips; she sighed; his mouth tasted of the sea. He held her face between his hands, tilted her head back, deepened his kiss as if he would drink from her mouth. His fingers laced themselves in the loose strands of her wet hair, pulled her back, so her body was arched against him and her breasts and throat were offered up to him. Then he pressed his lips against the pulse that hammered in her throat, and with a sudden swift angry movement moved his hands, down the arch of her spine, across her shoulderblades, forward and under the thrust of her breasts so his cool firm fingers pressed for an instant against her hardening nipples, against the curve of her flesh in the thin cups of the bikini.

He sighed then, a deep sigh that seemed to break from his throat; a sigh of urgency and impatience as if he would prefer to deny his own arousal but could not. She opened her eyes, feeling her own body tremble, feeling heat and a maddening insane urgency which she could not control spark from nowhere, and shoot through every nerve-ending in her body. For an instant she saw his face, looking down into hers; the eyes dark, half-lidded, languorous and yet intent. The desire she saw in them was so naked, and so fierce that she felt her breath catch in her throat. She moaned, closing her eyes, lifting her mouth blindly to his, reaching her arms up to him. As they tightened around his neck, his lips met hers. They sucked her down instantly into some dark sweet secret place, where her mind had no sovereignty, and her senses sang. Place and time slipped away; she felt as if he took her down, under the water and into the dark recesses of the sea, where they were bound only by the tides of their own bodies, now full and in flood, now, as he kissed her more gently, in sweet ebb.

At last, she felt him grow still. Her hands fluttered against him. He caught her wrists, held her tight; though he did not speak she sensed the strength of his will. Inexorably he calmed himself; his calm calmed her. At last, very gently, they drew apart. Rebecca opened her eyes. The sea, the sunlight, the bay—all was as it had been; a day might have gone past, or a minute. She looked up into his face; he looked down into her eyes. For the first time since she had met him she felt no shyness, and no nervousness, but a curious calm and trust. For an instant, in the darkness of his eyes she thought she saw a wry taciturn acknowledgement of what she herself had felt. Then it was gone, and he smiled at her gently.

'I have thought of you . . .' he said. 'Every day and every night this last week. Since we met. Did you think of me?'

'Yes.'

'I knew . . .' He hesitated. 'I imagined . . .' He broke off, and then smiled again, with a wry gaiety that did not quite mask a seriousness and gravity in his eyes. He picked up her hand, held it an instant, and then let it fall. 'I think you cast some spell on me, that must be it. That day. Up at the Villa Circe. Sorceress . . .'

His lips curved, and Rebecca laughed.

'When you cast a spell—on my moped.'

He gave her a quick dry glance, then rose to his feet and pulled her up beside him.

'Nonsense,' he said briskly. 'What gave you that idea? Mechanical failure. Convenient, I admit, but purely mechanical. And now—before you tempt me any further, we'd better go back. The tide's turning. It's slack water now. If we stay here too long we'll be trapped . . .'

'I'm not sure I'd care . . .' Rebecca said recklessly.

'Yes, you would. We'd drown. And a watery death isn't what I have in mind for us just at present . . .'

'What do you have in mind for us?' She looked up at him teasingly, and he bent his head and gave her mouth a kiss designed to quell such insubordination.

'Wait and see . . .' he said darkly, holding her face up to his, his eyes burning dark into her own. 'We'll make plans if you like. Over dinner. But not here. Understand? Now come on— siren . . .'

He drew her back into the water, swam beside her and helped her back into the inflatable. Loosing it, turning it, firing its engine, his movements were quick and sure, businesslike and efficient, as if nothing had happened. Rebecca watched him; she felt lulled and yet exultant; as if her whole life had changed, as if it were just beginning.

As he turned the bows of the boat back towards the narrow gap between rock-arch and cliff, she gestured to the dark shadow to their right that marked the entrance to the cave.

'That cave,' she said. 'The cave of Aphrodite, isn't that what they call it?'

'I believe so . . .' He appeared to be only half-listening; his eyes were on their course ahead, he did not turn his head.

'Can you go into it? By boat?' Rebecca lifted her face to him. 'I'm sure I heard somewhere that you could. And I saw it—that day when I walked on the cliff—and I thought then . . .'

'What did you think?' His voice was suddenly sharp, and Rebecca looked at him in surprise, narrowing her eyes against the sun and trying to see the expression on his face.

'That it would be exciting to do that—to go into the cave . . .' She heard her own voice falter slightly. 'It . . . it looks so beautiful, and so mysterious . . .'

'And so dangerous.' He cut her off.

'Can one go in there?' She persisted, feeling suddenly obstinate, sensing some resistance from him which she could not understand.

'I don't think so. No. Once perhaps, but not now. There's been a cliff-fall. There are rocks right across the entrance . . .'

'Have you been in there?'

'No. I haven't.' His voice was suddenly cold. 'I told you. The entrance is blocked. It's been blocked for years—certainly for as long as I've been coming to the island . . .' They were passing under the shadow of the cliff as he spoke, and, no longer dazzled by light, Rebecca could see his face clearly. Its expression was closed, his mouth was tight. For an instant, glancing back at the dark opening in the cliffs and then at his dark shuttered face, she felt again that alarm, that sudden irrational dart of fear she had felt in his presence before. Looking down she saw the water boil around them; she gasped. Then they were between arch and cliff, then out in the sun and the open sea. Exhilaration lifted her heart again. He glanced at her, smiling, turned the bow of the boat for home, and the instant of unease passed and dissolved as if it had never been.

I imagined, he had said. What had he imagined? She had kept her own imagination under a tight rein for a whole week. Now, enfranchised, she gave it free rein, and that, and the memory of his kisses, filled her with happiness. She felt as if the little boat carried them on wings over the water, water that was tinted red gold as the sun declined towards the west.

When they rounded the north coast she glanced up at the Villa Circe; this time there was no glint of light on glasses, no sense of being watched. She relaxed into the curve of Cal's arm; he too glanced up at the villa, and then smiled at her, as if they shared a memory.

'Come back to my house,' he said softly. 'Will you do that? We can eat dinner outside, and watch the sun go down. We can go to a taverna if you prefer, but it's so beautiful there. Rebecca—say yes.'

Rebecca looked into his eyes. She felt as if there were no cares in the world. She said yes.

CHAPTER FIVE

By the time they reached the tiny house where Cal was staying the sun was almost setting; its dying radiance lit the house, the grove of olives behind it, and the cliff-top meadow; the sun itself, a huge disc of bright copper hung just above the dark line of the sea's horizon, and sent a path of golden light across the water, directly, it seemed, to where they stood.

Cal smiled at Rebecca, and gave her a little push. 'You stay here. Watch the sunset. I see it every night—I'll cook the dinner. No, really . . .' He cut off her protests. 'It's a selfish request. I cook very badly; it'll be even worse if I know you're watching . . .'

So Rebecca sat on the terrace outside the house, and watched the sun go down, watched the colours of the sky turn, watched the fire flies come out beneath the trees. Then, when the light had almost completely gone, she got up and went back into the cottage. Cal shouted instructions from the kitchen, and one by one Rebecca lit the oil lamps, for the house had no electricity. She laid the table for their meal, and looked around her with pleasure.

The whole of the ground floor of the house was taken up with one very large room, which was basically a studio, and presumably used as such by Grey Jameson, though more for storage of paintings than anything else, Rebecca thought, for the windows were too small and the light too poor to have allowed him to paint inside. Its furnishings were odd, beautiful and shabby, a collection of random objects from different countries and of different periods, which, in this room, worked perfectly, as if they had been meant from the first to be alongside one another. A Victorian chaise longue, covered in threadbare but beautiful silk velvet; a kelim rug from the Caucassus; a carved wooden statue which Rebecca thought was Italian, and which was certainly very old; a narrow bed, covered with a hand woven Greek rug; shelves and shelves of books; an old wind-up gramophone and a collection of 78 rpm records of opera, stacks of paintings everywhere, most of them water colours and of landscapes ... She looked around her curiously. It was a simple room, the walls rough plaster distempered white; the dining table had obviously been made by a local craftsman, and was rough pine. But the cutlery she laid out was solid silver, and crested; the china, though cracked and mended, was Derby; the books on the shelves, piled higgledy piggledy, and crammed in on one another, were in several languages—French, she saw, and Russian, and German, as well as English and Greek.

She was looking at the books when Cal reappeared from the kitchen. He smiled at her.

'Nearly ready. I think I deserve a drink, don't you? I'll open a bottle of one of Grey's French wines. This is a special occasion and he won't mind—hang on a minute. I'll just have to go down to his cellar ...'

He disappeared outside on to the terrace; Rebecca heard the sound of a lock, the clang of a metal door. A few minutes later Cal reappeared dusting off a couple of bottles.

'There's a cellar here?' Rebecca looked at him in surprise and he grinned.

'You bet. Grey wouldn't live anywhere without one—not with his collection of wines. And this one is perfect—a natural hollow in the rock almost under the house. It keeps the wine at a perfect temperature, winter and summer. I should think that's why Grey chose the house actually ...'

Rebecca smiled. He brushed past her and began carefully and with respect to open one of the bottles.

'He's obviously very erudite ...' She gestured at the books behind her. 'Such an amazing library—to have that here ... does he speak all those languages?'

Cal looked up at her.' Grey? Oh yes. He's a very gifted linguist. In fact that's how we met. He used to teach Classics. And he taught me—for his sins. He's one of those people who can learn almost any language with amazing speed ... He must speak at least nine or ten languages fluently, and then there are others which he reads but claims not to have mastered ...' Cal looked up with satisfaction as expertly and quietly he drew the cork from the bottle. 'But Grey has been and has done so many different things it's rather difficult to define him.' He paused. 'He was a great oarsman at Eton; he won the Newdigate poetry prize at Oxford; he took a first in Greats . . . he was in the Foreign Service between the wars I believe, and with his linguistic gifts that would make sense of course. But he drank—So he was kicked out.' He shrugged. 'Will you have a glass of wine now? And then we might risk eating . . .'

Rebecca nodded, and Cal very carefully poured some of the pale honey-coloured liquid into a glass and handed it to her. When he had poured for himself he lifted his glass to the light, then smiled at her. Rebecca sipped the wine; cool, heady and delicious it seemed very delicate yet instantly warmed the blood.

'To your friend Grey,' she said, lifting her glass. 'His wine is beautiful . . .' She glanced at the bottle, '. . . and very old, and I hope he won't mind our drinking it.'

'Grey is the most generous of men.' Cal drew out a chair for her. 'If he were here to see you he'd know why I chose that wine; he would have chosen it himself. It complements you, and it reminds me of the first time I saw you, here, in the wood. When you looked very young and . . .' He broke off, as Rebecca raised her face questioningly to his. Their eyes met for a second, and Rebecca felt the colour wing its way to her cheeks. Cal never completed his sentence, but turned away to the kitchen, returning with two huge earthenware dishes, one filled with rice delicately tinted and fragrant with saffron, the other with chicken freshly grilled, sprinkled with rosemary. Rebecca's eyes rounded; when she had tasted the chicken and the rice she laid down her knife and fork and regarded Cal accusingly. 'What lies you've been telling me! You cook well—very well . . .'

He smiled. 'Rice and chicken isn't exactly difficult . . .'

'Easy enough to mess up if you don't know what you're doing. And you obviously do . . .' She looked at him with narrowed eyes. 'I'm beginning to suspect you're like your friend Grey—one of those people who can turn their hands to anything . . .' She paused. 'You win prizes for your books. You handle a boat as well as Nico who's done it all his life. Now I find you can cook!' she paused. 'I shall test you. Let's see . . . Do you ski?'

'Uh huh.'

'Ride?'

'I'm afraid so.'

'Speak umpteen languages?'

'English, French, Italian, Greek. That's not umpteen.'

'It's bad enough. Disgustingly accomplished.' Rebecca looked at him gloomily. Cal sighed.

'I'm unmusical,' he offered. 'Tone deaf. Can't play a note. Is that any help?'

'I suppose it's something . . .' she said grudgingly, and Cal's lips lifted at the corner.

'I have masses of what Americans call personality defects,' he went on helpfully. 'Absolutely masses—whereas I'm sure you have none at all.'

'Such as?'

'Quick-tempered, impatient, intolerant . . .' He ticked them off on his fingers as he spoke. 'Unsociable . . .'

'I'd heard that before I met you,' Rebecca said, 'Your reputation ran ahead of you . . .'

Cal wrinkled his brow. 'Oh dear. I thought it might have done.'

Rebecca, taking pity on him, laughed. 'Oh, don't be silly,' she said. 'I didn't take much notice of the things I heard. And anyway, you're here to work, you must want to get on with your work in peace. You don't want a lot of interruptions . . . in fact . . .' she pulled a wry face at him, 'maybe I should go. Now.'

They were sitting opposite one another, so Rebecca could see his face quite clearly in the lamp-light. He did not smile in response to her teasing; instead she saw his face darken, and he reached across and clasped her wrist with a suddenness that startled her.

'You are not an interruption . . .' he said abruptly. 'You must know that already. I want you to know that. Never think it—ever. Will you promise me? No matter what happens? No matter how I . . .' He broke off and looked away. 'How I might behave . . .' he ended flatly.

Rebecca looked at him, startled by his sudden seriousness and by his vehemence, not understanding the abrupt change in his mood. He seemed to be trying to tell her something, perhaps even to be warning her, and the passion with which he did so alarmed and puzzled her. His grip on her wrist loosened. He looked away from her, then shrugged, and poured them some more wine. He laid his knife and fork together, though he had eaten very little she saw, and the relaxation he had shown earlier now seemed to have deserted him. Not liking to question him, and feeling suddenly shy once more, she finished her chicken, ate a little of the fresh fruit he offered her, and sipped her wine.

He asked her a great many questions then—about her father and mother, her sisters, the house she had grown up in, the school she had gone to, her work in London. Rebecca answered them all happily enough, for she could see that he preferred to question rather than be questioned, and he did so with skill and gentleness, drawing her out, so she recalled people and incidents she had not thought of for years; she spoke openly, evading his questions only when they touched on the agency and veered towards the subject of Conrad. Then she became purposefully vague; he noticed it, she thought, but said nothing. He made them some coffee, opened the second bottle of wine, and they sat side by side on the cushions before the hearth, just talking. Cal seemed to relax again. Gradually, slowly at first, then more fluently, he began to tell her a little about himself. His father had been English, he said, his mother American, but his father had died when Cal was only three, and then he had left England.

'Then I really went around from pillar to post,' he said, with a wry smile. 'My mother had very little money but she had a whole lot of relations. Mostly Bostonian maiden aunts who disapproved of her and who were delighted to take me off her hands so they could bring me up the right way. My mother's maiden name was Calvin—that's how I got saddled with my Christian name—and there were the Calvin aunts and the Cabot aunts, both equally grand and both equally disapproving of the others. However, they were united in their disapproval of my poor charming mother. She'd wanted to be an actress you see—and, well, as far as the Calvin-Cabots went, she might just as well have announced her intention of opening a brothel. Then she'd married my father, who'd been English, penniless, and to add insult to injury, a Roman Catholic, and who proved all their predictions of unreliability

by dying and leaving my mother a widow at twenty-six ...'
He smiled.

'So. I had a very odd childhood. My mother trying to get
jobs in summer stock and with second-rate touring
companies. Long holidays with elderly spinsters who started
off lecturing me and who pretty soon gave up and left me to
my own devices. Then, when I was about seven or eight, my
father's family suddenly weighed in on the act. They'd
discovered I wasn't being sent to a Catholic school, although
my mother had made all the usual promises about my
education when she married my father. So—at eight—with
prophecies of disaster from all the good free-thinking
Bostonian aunts, there I was, whisked off back to England, a
Catholic prep school followed by Ampleforth. Holidays with
English grandparents and, after they died, mostly with
schoolfriends. I hardly saw my mother again. She married for
the second time when I was about fifteen. I never even met my
stepfather. They were both killed in a car crash about six
months after the wedding ...'

He glanced away at the end of this speech, and Rebecca's
face softened. What a sad childhood, she thought. How odd
and how dislocated! If that little boy had grown up unsociable
and slow to trust it was hardly surprising. She leaned towards
him gently.

'So, are any of your family alive now? Your Bostonian
aunts? Did you have English cousins——'

'Hundreds of them, I suspect. It was that sort of family.
Endless ramifications.' Cal pulled a face. 'I never see any of
them. I lapsed, you see.'

'Lapsed?' Rebecca stared at him blankly, and he laughed.

'Left the church—the Catholic church. Well, not left it
exactly, but ceased to practice. They disapproved of that, very
much so. It caused strife and—well, in the end, it just seemed
simpler to stay out of their way.' He smiled bitterly.

'You mean ...' Rebecca hesitated. She had been brought
up within the Church of England, and her knowledge of
Catholics was mostly confined to hearsay about friends of her
mother's. 'You mean you lost your faith? At school? Later?'

'At Ampleforth?' He glanced at her dryly. 'Hardly. No—it
was later ...' He lowered his eyes, and she saw him hesitate,

quite expected that he would not go on, then he sighed and, not looking up continued in a low voice. 'When my mother remarried,' he said slowly, 'my stepfather had a number of children by his previous marriage. Three sons, I believe, though I never met them, and a daughter. After the car accident his daughter came over to England to live. My stepsister, Elaine.' He glanced up at Rebecca, whose skin had suddenly grown chill, and then away again. 'Elaine was older then I was, by—oh—ten or twelve years. She and I became very close. I—admired her—very much. It was largely due to her patience and encouragement that I began to write. Elaine became—in a sense—the family I never had. She was like a mother and a father to me, for many years she was one of my closest friends . . .' He paused.

'When she was thirty, thirty-one, something like that, it was my last year at Cambridge, she started having odd dizzy spells, half fainting, quite suddenly. She had multiple sclerosis, in fact, though it took them a long time to work out that that was what was wrong. They said that there was a possibility that she would be one of the luckier ones, that the disease might progress slowly, that she might have periods when she was virtually unaffected by it, though of course she must understand that no matter what treatment she received it would return—sooner or later; that there was no cure . . .'

He broke off and shrugged, his mouth now set in a straight and bitter line. 'As it happened it was sooner, not later. The disease advanced rapidly. She was paralysed—first partially, eventually almost totally, for the last eight years of her life. It finally took her two years ago. Some time before that I lost my faith. No, not even that . . .' He banged his hand down on the table beside him with a sudden anger that terrified Rebecca. 'No—I ought to be accurate. I didn't lose faith. I just looked at Elaine and at what was happening to her. And I looked around me at the world I lived in, at the things that happened, every day, to other people, perfectly innocent good people like my stepsister, who had never harmed anyone in their lives—children even—I looked at that and I thought that if there were a deity, and he were responsible for this, for all this, I didn't want to worship him, that was all. I didn't want to set foot in his church or offer him prayers or . . .' He broke

off abruptly. 'So, I didn't. I stopped. I stopped going to Mass.
I stopped going to confession. Elaine died . . .' He broke off
once more, with an abrupt dismissive gesture that belied the
pain in his eyes.

'I'm sorry,' he added quickly. 'I shouldn't have started on
all this. I can't think quite how I came to do so.' He turned
back to Rebecca for an instant. 'I haven't spoken of this
before. Not to anyone. Well, Grey knows, of course, but no
one else, and I shouldn't have inflicted it on you now. I'm
sorry . . .'

Rebecca leaned forward and took his hand. 'Don't be,' she
said simply. 'I'm glad you told me . . .'

There were a great many other things she wanted to say,
but she knew that if she tried to voice them she would put
them wrongly and they would sound trite and inadequate. So
she said nothing more, but simply pressed his hand and hoped
that he would sense what she meant. Perhaps he did; certainly
he did not recoil from her—and she had thought he might,
angry with himself for having revealed too much perhaps, this
man who guarded his privacy so strongly. They sat in silence
for a little while, her hand clasped in his, her head bent. At
last he leaned forward and pressed his lips gently against her
hair.

'It's very late,' he said. 'Much later than I realised—we
must have been talking for hours . . .' He paused. 'I must take
you home . . .'

Rebecca lifted her face to his, but before she could
answer she heard a slight sound outside—a footstep
perhaps, the snapping of a branch. Cal heard it too; she
saw him tense, start to rise. Almost at once there came
from outside a low whistle. Cal stood still: Rebecca,
startled, looking up, realised that he showed no surprise.
The next moment there was a tap at the door, it opened,
and Nico came in.

At first he did not see Rebecca, still sitting on the floor, her
figure half hidden from where he stood by the chaise longue
that was between them. He saw Cal, of course, and advanced
upon him quickly, his hand outstretched, launching at once
into a rapid flood of Greek, none of which Rebecca understood, though she thought she caught the word 'Circe' . . .

Something in Cal's expression must have alerted Nico to her presence, for suddenly the excited torrent of words stopped, he swung round, and—when he saw Rebecca—stared at her in embarrassed silence. Cal stepped forward smoothly; he held out his hand to Rebecca and helped her to her feet.

'We've been having dinner, Nico,' he said, 'and in fact I was just about to take Rebecca home—here . . .' He drew out a chair for Nico, and poured him a glass of wine, all with perfect composure. 'Sit down, have some wine. I'll be half an hour at the most. We can go off then, can't we? It won't be too late?' He turned to Rebecca then with a shrug and a charming smile. 'I'd completely forgotten,' he went on. 'Nico was taking me out fishing tonight. Conditions are perfect apparently—we should make a fine catch . . .' He took Rebecca's arm and began to steer her, gently but firmly, towards the door. Rebecca went, willingly enough. She said goodbye to Nico, and wished him good luck with the fishing, and then ducked out of the door, grateful to be in the dark again, and to have the shadows hide her burning cheeks. She blushed from embarrassment, but also from shame—shame for Cal, not herself. He had been lying, she was absolutely certain of that. He'd done it well, improvising quickly and easily, and Nico had taken his cue from him, but he had been lying, covering something up—every instinct in her body told her that.

Dully she climbed up into the Jeep beside him. It hurt, she realised, as the engine fired, and he pulled away down the steep track. To have felt so close to him, to have felt he had trusted her, and then to have him lie, flagrantly; it hurt.

He was driving too fast, she thought, his mouth a tight line, his expression impossible to read, but tension and anger visible in every line of his hard body. He was expecting her to ask questions, she thought, to quiz him about Nico. Well, she had no intention of risking that . . .

He braked sharply, she felt the rear of the Jeep slide, then he spun the wheel and they were back on the road to Gaios, driving fast. Rebecca glanced down nervously at her watch: why at this rate he'd get her to Gaios and be back with Nico in fifteen minutes, not thirty: if he didn't crash the Jeep and kill himself first, that was.

He hadn't spoken a word since they left the house, and that silence, the speed and violence with which he drove, brought a lump to Rebecca's throat; she felt tears prick behind her eyes and angrily blinked them back. She could control the tears, but not the disappointment and hurt she felt, the sense that now, for some reason she did not understand, everything was going wrong when, all day, everything had seemed so wonderfully, so gloriously, right.

He slammed on the brakes; the Jeep shuddered to a halt, and looking up, Rebecca saw that they were in the alley behind her flat, pulled up in the shadows close to the wall where they could not be overlooked. Cal switched off the engine, and in the sudden silence she saw his hands, pale and tense, gripping the wheel tightly. His head was bowed.

Quietly Rebecca picked up her bag, and reached for the door handle.

'Thank you, Cal,' she began, in a flat voice, 'Thank you for . . .'

'Damn it to hell . . .' With a swift violence he turned to her, and before she could move or speak, caught her tight in his arms, and pulled her roughly against his chest. For an instant she caught the scent of his skin, saw his eyes blaze darkly into hers, then he brought his mouth down on hers hard, and kissed her. He kissed her as angrily and as violently as he had driven that night through the dark, forcing her lips apart, one hand tightening around the base of her throat, the other tightening over her breast. The gentleness he had shown her earlier that day was all gone: he wanted her, and he wanted her to know it. She felt his body shudder against her as, blindly and instinctively, she reached for him, feeling some force in herself surge up and pulse through her with a violence that equalled his. He groaned against her mouth, then, as abruptly as he had caught her to him, he drew away from her, gripping her arms, forcing her to look up into his face.

He was asking her to trust him—she felt it keenly though he did not say the words, and she knew at once that she did trust him, completely, though she knew he had lied, though she was certain now that something was happening on the island, and he was somehow involved, and she had no notion of what it could be. She met his gaze, unspeaking, and after a moment what she felt seemed to communicate itself to him, for the tension went out of him, and his expression softened.

'Tomorrow,' he said. 'Can you come to me tomorrow? When you finish work? Come to the house? It doesn't matter if it's late—say you'll come . . .'

'I'll come.'

He smiled then, grimly, but he smiled. Then he was out of the Jeep, helping her down into the dark street beside him. She saw him hesitate.

'Your friend, Nicky—I get the feeling she's not very discreet . . .'

Rebecca smiled. Her confidence had come soaring back. She touched his arm lightly. 'Don't worry,' she said softly. 'I shan't say anything to Nicky. Not about today—or tomorrow . . .'

'If she asks?'

'I'll lie. If necessary.'

She looked up at him calmly. He gave her a strange look, a second of doubt, a moment of dry amusement, something like admiration. Then he bent and kissed her forehead.

'Well, well, well,' he said softly. 'I believe you would . . .' Then he turned away, and climbed back into the Jeep. The headlights came on, dazzling her for an instant. Then the engine fired. He said nothing more: no confirmation of their meeting the next day, no explanation, no farewell. The Jeep wheeled full circle. By the time Rebecca reached her door, looked up at the darkened windows of her flat, he was gone. She listened to the whine of the Jeep's engine as it mounted the hill behind the village, and then, when it had disappeared and all was silent once more, she took out her key and softly, quietly, let herself into the flat.

'God, but it's hot.' Michael Hamilton, leaning elegantly on the ship's rail beside her, drew out an immaculately laundered linen handkerchief and wiped his brow. Then he removed his crisp linen jacket, folded it neatly, and laid it down on the bench seat behind them. He looked at his watch.

'Not ten yet. I've never known it so hot here in April. Has it been like this long?'

Rebecca shrugged. She too was leaning on the rail of the ferry looking down into the water. She was hardly listening. She was calculating the time: another hour and they would be in Corfu. If Michael didn't delay too long there should be plenty of time to get all the things he said he wanted and still catch the four o'clock ferry back. If it wasn't delayed they'd be back in Gaios by seven at the latest; if she took the moped she could be with Cal as promised by seven-thirty, eight at the latest—it ought to be all right. She relaxed a little. She still cursed the fact that she'd gone into the office early and that she'd run into Michael, and she regretted being press-ganged into this trip—but still, he was her employer, she could hardly refuse . . .

'Hey—Rebecca, you're dreaming.' Michael smiled down at her, and she started. 'I said—has it been this hot for long? I couldn't believe it when I got in yesterday . . .'

'Sorry. I was miles away.' Rebecca looked up at him. 'And yes—I suppose it has been very hot—I hadn't thought about it really. I assumed it was always like this . . .'

Michael grinned. 'No way. In August, yes. But not at Easter. It's too hot, if you ask me. And close. Storm weather.'

'Storm weather?' Rebecca swung round to him anxiously. 'You mean you think there'll be a storm—today?' Her dismay was transparent, and Michael, misinterpreting it, smiled at her a little patronisingly. 'Worried it'll get rough? Don't be. If there is a storm it won't be today—I could be wrong, but I don't think so. Island weather you know—but when there are storms here they take a while to build . . .'

'So we ought to be able to get back to Paxos today as planned?'

'Oh, sure, sure. No problem.' Michael gave an airy wave. 'We can go straight to the market, as I said, I'll leave the buying to you, then I'll get the stuff sent down to the ferry. It was lucky I ran into you when I did, wasn't it? If I'd missed you I'd have had to do it all on my own, and buying food isn't my strong point. Wine now, I'm OK there, but food— hopeless.' He paused and looked down at her. 'You don't mind doing the food for the party? Nicky said you were such a terrific cook—and when I got in yesterday I suddenly got the idea. We did something similar a couple of years back, and it was a great success—we had a barbecue then, I remember, and all our villa people came. It was the high point of their holiday some of them said. So yesterday—there I was, mooching about the island on my own, feeling at a bit of a loss, no sign of you, no sign of Nicky—well, the wire should have reached you, but there you are, it didn't—so, there I was, at a bit of a loose end, and suddenly I thought, I know, we'll have a party. Celebrate Easter—take advantage of this super weather—put Rebecca to the test. Good idea, eh?'

'Terrific,' Rebecca answered mechanically. But Michael was in full flood, and seemed not to notice her lack of enthusiasm.

'Of course we don't need to get fish—Nico will take care of that for us. We'll give him a bit of notice—I thought we might hold it tomorrow. Friday—that'll be perfect. There's a great procession, Friday night, with candles, before the evening Mass at Gaios—did Nicky tell you about that? It's very picturesque, rather moving actually, even if you're an unbeliever like me. That will be OK, and it'll give us time to get everything organised, go round and invite all the villas and so on ...' He paused for breath. 'So, today, well, we should be able to get everything you need in Corfu town. Have you been to the market there? It's amazing. Stuff that never gets over to Paxos, alas. So, anything that takes your fancy, just order it, OK?'

With difficulty Rebecca wrenched her mind back to the problem in hand. She looked up at Michael. He looked bandbox fresh, in spite of the heat, bouncing with ideas and energy. Just looking at him made her feel exhausted.

'How many people will be coming, do you think?' she asked.

Michael shrugged. 'Eighty. Say ninety to be on the safe side. We've got about sixty people in the villas—some of them are children of course—and then our staff will be there, naturally Nico—he brought along some friends and they played bouzouki music for us last time. And Agape, Leandros—you know. Yes, about ninety, I'd say ...'

'And it's to be a dinner?'

'A dinner and a dance,' Michael said quickly. 'Start things

off as soon as it begins to get cooler. After the service—about nine-ish, something like that. Then there'll be time for music and dancing afterwards . . .'

'And you'd like me to prepare a traditional meal—a Greek meal?' Rebecca sighed. She could see this turning into a nightmare: dinner for ninety at one day's notice, in the open air, and no mention of any assistance from anyone.

'Oh hell, I don't know.' Michael looked vague. 'Can you cook Greek dishes? It would be nice I suppose . . .'

Rebecca gritted her teeth. 'I could try,' she said.

'Good girl.' Michael was already losing interest in the details. 'If there's any problems, let me know. And there's plenty of people who'll help out, I'm sure. Nico, for one—I gather you've made a bit of a hit with him. And Agape—Agape can cook I should think . . . We'll fix up a huge open air barbecue for you, the way we did last time. It'll be great, you wait and see. Last time Nico arranged all that. God, it was fantastic. You could have roasted an ox on it . . .'

Rebecca sighed and turned her face back to the sea. She made a private resolution that she'd go and see Nico first thing tomorrow. With his help she might just be able to organise all this in time, and, after all, Michael was right—it would be fun . . . Eating out under the stars, and then dancing . . . Would Cal come, she wondered?

'So . . .' Michael had lit a Gauloise and was leaning back on the rails contentedly, in the manner of a man who has just efficiently sorted out a great many problems with habitual ease. 'So . . .' He glanced down at her. 'You're liking it on Paxos? Settling in?'

'Yes. Very much.' This time Rebecca could answer him with genuine enthusiasm and warmth. 'I love it . . .'

'Ran into one of our groups yesterday—the Templars, is that the name? Staying up at Lakka?' He glanced at her sideways. 'They were full of compliments for you. Said you'd really gone out of your way to make their stay a happy one . . .'

Rebecca blushed. 'Oh—that's nice of them. I don't think I have done anything very special—but I'm glad they're enjoying themselves . . .'

'And Nicky. I had a brief talk to her last night when she got back from her boat trip . . .' There was a fractional pause, as if he hoped Rebecca might have been prompted to say where she had been the previous evening. When she said nothing, Michael continued. 'Yes, well, Nicky said she thought you were settling in. Enjoying the work. Making friends and so on . . .' Again there was a pause; Rebecca continued to gaze out to sea, and she felt him glance at her. 'Gather you even made a bit of a hit with Cal. Cal Ryder. And that's something none of our girls have been able to pull off before . . .' There was now open speculation in his glance, and Rebecca silently cursed Nicky and her indiscretion. She smiled up at him coolly.

'Mr Ryder? Oh, he seems very nice. I've run into him a few times. Just checking that the work up at the Villa Circe was on schedule and so on . . .'

'He's moving in at the end of the week, is that right?'

'Yes, Saturday,' Rebecca answered composedly.

Michael cleared his throat. 'Odd chap. Read any of his books have you?'

'One or two.'

'Like them?'

'I thought them very clever . . .'

'Anti-social sort of fellow. A bit distant I've always thought. Did you find that?'

'I didn't really think about it.'

'Where's he staying meantime? At that fellow Jameson's place—up on the west coast?'

'I believe so.'

'Bound to be. Only ever stays in one of two places. There or the Villa Circe. The two most inaccessible houses on the whole damn island. Typical.' Michael shrugged. Cal's taste for solitude appeared to irritate him. He lit another Gauloise. 'Of course he wanted to buy the Villa Circe, you know,' he went on, his manner suddenly confidential. 'Don't think he was too pleased when I nipped in ahead of him, and got it.'

'Really?' Rebecca looked up at him in surprise, and Michael, apparently flattered by her interest, smiled.

'Well, he used to rent it from the old farmer that owned it. Had done for years, I gather, before I started operating out here anyway. Then, one winter, the old boy died. Well, I was looking for houses to convert then, I was just starting up, hadn't a lot of capital, and that place was going cheap. So—I moved in pretty fast. Bought it from the old boy's widow, everything signed and sealed before Cal even heard of it. When he found out he tried to buy the place back from me. And, well, I didn't like his manner I suppose—he can be a bit haughty, you know, so, I dug my heels in. No deal. He wasn't too pleased. Doesn't like to be crossed, and isn't used to it, I'd say.' Michael paused. 'Well, he came round in the end. Agreed to rent it from me every year and that's what he's done, ever since. It's ironic, really. Wish I hadn't been so stubborn now. Wish I'd let him have the damn place. Frankly, I'd be glad to be shot of it . . .'

'Oh, but why?' Rebecca looked at him in surprise. 'It's such a beautiful house . . .'

'Oh, beautiful, yes. Sure. And nobody wants to rent it. Except Ryder. It's too remote. If the weather's bad it's very exposed. Every winter there's some damn storm damage—it's cost me a fortune repairing the damn place. And to cap it all last summer we had the Greek police crawling all over it— wasting my time, going through my records, interviewing me, interviewing the staff—it caused a lot of upset, I can tell you.'

Rebecca's eyes widened. She felt a little cold chill of fear run down her spine. 'The Greek police?' she said faintly. 'At the Villa Circe? Whatever did they want?'

'Don't ask me.' Michael stubbed out his cigarette irritably, and tossed the end into the sea. 'Some cock and bull story. Don't think there was a word of truth in it myself. Just some damn stupid rumour that had reached the mainland, and some hot-shot inspector from Athens thought he was on to a good thing—saw promotion ahead of him . . .' He paused, and seeing Rebecca's expression of incomprehension, shrugged. 'Smuggling,' he said tersely. 'I ask you. Damn stupid. But there you are. The Albanian coast is—what— fifteen miles from the north coast of Paxos? Twenty at the most. Albania's part of the Eastern bloc—more like Moscow than Moscow itself, so they tell me. So, apparently, there's a flourishing black market there in Western goods, and how do you get the goods into Albania? By boat. And where does the boat go from, according to Mr Hot Shot from Athens? Why,

Paxos. And where on Paxos? The Villa bloody Circe, that's where. It's got a landing stage—of sorts. It's the only likely house on the north coast. You can see the Albanian coast from there. As far as Mr Hot Shot was concerned that was it. Case proven. Damn stupid. I took him up there. I showed him the landing stage—what was left of it after the winter storms. Thought that would clinch the matter, that they'd all give up and go home. But no. They were here for weeks, crawling all over the place. God knows what they thought they'd find. I mean what the hell are you supposed to smuggle into an Iron Curtain country from a little tiny Greek island where no one has two drachmas to rub together? Illegal currency? Caches of blue jeans? I told them. Don't make me laugh, I said. You've been reading too many bad books at airport bookstalls. But it didn't do any good. Went through all my records. Who'd stayed there and when—well, that was simple enough. Only one main candidate. Our old friend Ryder. He turned up in the middle of the whole fiasco as it happened, and I must say I was rather surprised. I mean, I expected him to hit the roof. After all, he's pretty keen on being left alone to write his next best-seller, right? And now there's a Greek cop behind every bush. But he took it all in his stride, I'll say that for him. Took the Hot Shot out to dinner, patiently answered all their enquiries. I think it amused him rather, in his supercilious way, and in fact I was rather grateful to him, because it took the heat off poor old Nico. The Hot Shot had latched on to him, you see, because some fool had told him Nico had a caique and fished the waters to the north of the island, so they'd been pestering him and his family for weeks.' Michael smiled. 'So—Ryder was politeness itself, put himself entirely at their disposal, and eventually they saw sense and decamped. Thank God.' Michael sighed. 'I mean it was farcical really, but I was worried. The Greek police can be very tough, and if there had been any trouble, if rumours had got out—well, it would have killed my business stone dead. Overnight. Who wants to rent a villa in a trouble spot?'

'Of course. You must have been terribly worried...' Rebecca kept her eyes down. She hesitated. A horrible sick lurching feeling had started up in the pit of her stomach as Michael spoke, and a whole series of memories, little incidents, flashed into her mind and suddenly began to connect. Cal and Nico on the terrace at the Villa Circe; the way Cal had stopped her going into the house; the repairs to the landing stage; and—last night—Nico's late visit, his agitation and excitement, his shock when he had realised that Cal was not alone. She swallowed, and clenched her nails into the palms of her hand. She mustn't let her imagination run away with her—it was absurd. Cal Ryder, involved with Nico in smuggling black market goods into an Iron Curtain country from a tiny Greek island? Why, it was ridiculous. It made no sense . . . She cleared her throat.

'So,' she prompted lightly, 'was that the end of it? The police realised it was a wild goose chase? They gave up? They—they haven't been back?'

'Not to my knowledge . . .' Michael shrugged. He was gazing out across the water. In the distance, coming closer, was the outline of Corfu; they'd be there, Rebecca realised, in the next ten minutes. 'Maybe they're still keeping an eye on things. It's possible. I think it was just a storm in a tea-cup myself, but you can never be sure . . .'

'I hope so,' Rebecca said. Michael stretched, and grinned. His mind had already diverted to Corfu and their arrival, Rebecca could sense it. She swallowed. 'Of course, I suppose they might still be watching the place,' she said hesitantly. And suddenly remembered: the glint of light on binoculars—from the terrace of the Villa Circe. Yesterday.

A knot of fear suddenly tightened around her heart. Michael turned away from the rail with a smile.

'Might be,' he said casually. 'Not to worry though. Ryder said he'd keep an eye open for me. If there's any sign of trouble, he'll let me know. He promised . . .'

CHAPTER SIX

WHEN they docked at Corfu it was past eleven, the sun was high, and even Rebecca found the heat irksome. On Paxos there were always cooling breezes from the sea; here, in Corfu town, with streets jammed with Easter tourists, it was far more oppressive.

Michael insisted they have a drink first, which they did in a café overlooking the harbour. Then they were off, Michael's short plump figure darting ahead of her, and Rebecca almost running to keep up with him, as he negotiated the winding streets and alleyways that led to the market.

Nicky had warned Rebecca of Michael's energy and enthusiasm, which were unflagging, and on the few occasions when she had previously met him Rebecca had found both qualities engaging. But now she felt worried and on edge, the heat was giving her a headache, and Michael was driving her mad. The white suit he was wearing was a little too tight for him, and with his mop of dark hair and high colour, he was extremely conspicuous. Once in the market, Rebecca had expected him to leave her to get on with the shopping, but no—suddenly his interest in the 'feast' as he was now describing it, reawakened. He dashed ahead of Rebecca, passing from stall to stall like an excitable puppy, waving his arms, talking Greek with a pronounced English accent at the top of his voice.

Rebecca sighed, and trailed after him. On another occasion she would have loved this market, its stalls laid out under awnings, trestle tables piled high with purple figs and golden nectarines, with fresh oregano bound in bunches, the air heady with the scent of freshly ground cumin. But now, though she forced herself to concentrate, to calculate exactly what to buy and how much of it, another part of her mind was working away feverishly, trying to make sense of what Michael had told her. One part of her mind dismissed her own suspicions as laughable; another refused to let them go. She tried to piece together what Michael had said, and what she knew of Nico and Cal Ryder. It made no sense, it was absurd, and yet . . . She paused, weighing some fruit in her hand, and thinking. Nico was poor—she knew that. Most of the islanders on Paxos scratched a living, and although Nico made some money from his fishing and from his work for Michael, it must still be little enough. He had a large family— how many children? Eight, she remembered him telling her, with Dimitrios, who was about seventeen, the oldest. Could Nico have become involved in some black market trading? It was feasible, she could see that. And she could just imagine that Cal, his close friend, might find it amusing to be, in some way, involved with it. He was not exactly a careful or law-abiding man; he liked danger and excitement—that had been obvious the previous day in the boat. And the hot-shot inspector from Athens had been right on one count: if anything of that nature were happening, then the Villa Circe, with its panoramic view of the coastal waters between Paxos and Albania, was the perfect HQ.

She thought of the life Cal Ryder must live when he was not on the island, of which he had spoken briefly the previous evening—the life of a sophisticated and successful Western author, lecture tours, promotional tours for his books, rounds of smart parties. Yes, she could believe, just, that it might excite and amuse Cal to come to Paxos and break away from all that, to be involved in a mad buccaneering scheme that just happened to make his good friend Nico some money . . . After all, he wrote about crime, even if the crimes he dealt with in his books were of a rather different order. But his concern with plots, the meticulous dove-tailing of location and time and circumstance which made his books so clever and so intriguing—might not a man who loved creating plots enjoy actually being involved in one himself, enjoy working out with Nico the logistics of time and tide, of cargoes and their illicit transference?

The stall-holder was staring at her, she realised; Michael had, temporarily, disappeared, though she could hear his voice, exclaiming loudly in English, through the press and jostle of the crowds. Quickly she ordered some fruit, and turned away from the stall impatiently. She was being absurd, she decided again. It was too far-fetched. But still—she longed to be back on Paxos, and she longed to see Cal again. She would tell him what Michael had said, she resolved, that very evening. And she would tell him about that glint of light on binoculars from the Villa Circe . . .

She moved on from stall to stall, buying quantities of rice, kilos of the huge sweet Mediterranean tomatoes, tiny shallots, olive oil, the little black olives, so sour she had disliked them at first but which she had now come to love. To bite into those little olives was to taste Greece, Lawrence Durrell had once written, and she smiled to herself, remembering that, and beginning to relax a little. Whenever she thought of Greece, she realised, she would think of the island and she would think of Cal Ryder, of the first time she had met him, when he had stepped out, so suddenly, the tall, dark man in the olive grove . . . She stopped, missing Cal quite suddenly and with an intensity that took her by surprise. For a moment she forgot where she was: the clamour of the market ceased, she heard and saw nothing of the crowds around her, she thought only of Cal, and the memory of him was so intense, so sharp that it was for a moment as if her heart had stopped beating. She saw his face, with its dark watchful eyes; she heard his voice; she felt the touch of his hands and his lips, and she ached for him. Then the moment passed; she became possessed with impatience. Never had hours moved more slowly. She could not wait to be back on the ferry, to be with him again, to be held by him again, in the cool of the Greek evening.

Half an hour later she had completed her purchases. Her feet ached; she felt hot and exhausted. All she wanted now was to sit somewhere cool, in the shade, and wait for the ferry back. She peered across the eddying flow of people. Michael had disappeared again, and she couldn't leave without him . . . Tossing back her hair, which felt heavy and hot against her forehead and neck, she made for a patch of shade near the entrance to the market. She stood there, grateful to be a little cooler, her eyes running over the people in the square. Greeks—mothers and children; old women in headscarves and black dresses; in the corner, a little café; a priest in dark robes with a glass of ouzo and a tiny saucer of meze before him; an old man, fingering worry beads of amber; a little boy selling honeyed filo pastries from a tray around his neck; tourists, in bright butterfly-coloured clothes, laughing and gesturing to each other ... At the far side of the square one figure suddenly caught her eye and held it. An Englishman: he could only have been English, she thought, staring at him with amusement. Tall, grey haired, about sixty perhaps, carrying a cane and a rolled up newspaper, wearing, in spite of the heat, a pearl grey suit with a waistcoat, shirt and grey silk tie. He was very thin, with the faded good looks of an Edwardian matinée idol, and he was smoking a black Russian cigarette in a holder. He, too, was surveying the square; for a moment their glances intersected, and across the space that separated them, Rebecca caught the flash of forget-me-not blue eyes. Then the man turned, and strolled out of sight with an easy unhurried gait, as if he were wandering down Piccadilly on the way to luncheon at his club ... She watched him disappear into the narrow side streets, and as she did so the crowds beside her parted and Michael bobbed out of them, mopping his brow.

'There you are! Been looking for you everywhere! All fixed I hope? Yes? Everything under control? Jolly good—anything I can do? No? Fine ...' He took her by the arm. 'Drinkies? Yes?'

'Yes,' Rebecca said, with relief. 'If I don't sit down soon, I'll fall down ...'

Michael laughed jovially. He seemed in high good humour. He began to steer her through the crowd. 'No problem. Piece of luck. Oddest thing. Just bumped into an old friend of mine. Well, used to be a friend, knew him at school, haven't seen him for years. Something in the embassy in Athens now. On holiday with his wife, staying with some Greek high-up who has a villa here. Invited us both for drinks. Big place up near the Casino. We'll take a taxi. Come on. Bear up. Mad dogs and Englishmen and all that. Through here ...' He ducked out of the market into a narrow street, and began waving his arms over his head.

'Taxi! Taxi! Ah—here we are ...'

Before Rebecca could speak she had been bundled into the back of a huge old-fashioned saloon that had screeched to a halt in front of them. Its windscreen was decorated with pictures of saints and plastic flowers. Michael heaved himself in next to her and gave lengthy directions in loud Greek. The driver grinned; there was a flash of gold teeth.

'Yes. Yes,' he said. 'No problem. I know this place. Get you there, sir, pronto, super-quick . . .'

The car screeched off, narrowly avoiding a group of pedestrians. Rebecca leaned back on the seat and sighed.

'We will still be in time for the ferry won't we, Michael?' she said weakly.

Michael patted her knee. 'No problem. No problem. Quick champers then back to the harbour. Masses of time. Don't worry. Much better than fighting for a table in some damn tourist trap. You'll like my friend. Terrific chap. Sweet wife. She's called Jonquil. Odd name. Suits her.'

'What's your friend called?'

Michael leaned back on the seat. He looked every one of his forty years, Rebecca thought, with amusement. He also looked like a schoolboy who'd just been given a day's holiday. He smiled seraphically.

'Carstairs,' he said. 'Can't for the life of me think what his first name is, but it doesn't matter. Always called him Clickey—don't know why—seemed to suit him. Helluva spin bowler, I remember that. Clickey Carstairs. You'll like him, Rebecca . . .'

As it happened Rebecca didn't terribly like Clickey Carstairs. Not that it mattered either way, but when she was introduced to him and to Jonquil, his wife, she took an instant dislike to him. About Michael's age, he was slender and small; his cool silk-clad wife towered over him. Everything about him was smooth: he had a smooth, pinkish English complexion, and thin fair hair impeccably smoothed down. He had pale blue eyes that instantly wavered away from you, he looked as if he never needed to shave, and his handshake was languid and limp.

'How lovely,' he said vaguely, when they were introduced, and instantly turning away, 'Michael, have you met Costas? You haven't, have you? Costas, this is Michael Hamilton, yes, an old friend of mine. Owns rather a large slice of Paxos now—you know, villas and all that. Michael this is Costas

Andropoulos, Ministry of the Interior. Bit like our Home Office, am I right, Costas? Surprised you two haven't met before actually. Champagne, Michael? Or G and T? No, I'll stick to Perrier . . .'

They were gone, without a backward glance. Rebecca looked at Jonquil Carstairs and Jonquil Carstairs looked somewhere over Rebecca's left shoulder.

'So hot,' she murmured. 'And you're working with Michael on Paxos. How super for you. I hear it's the most divine little place. Quite unspoiled. We might . . . Costas has this yacht, you see, and really Corfu is impossibly crowded, don't you think? So we thought we might visit it, on the yacht. Over Easter you know . . .'

'Visit it?' Rebecca had failed to follow this, which had been spoken in low tones accompanied by many vague gestures.

'Why, Paxos.' Jonquil's eyes widened. 'Isn't there an Easter procession or something? So lovely . . .' Her eyes focused on what was clearly a familiar face and she gave a little sigh. 'You must be dying for a drink. I'll send the waiter over. Excuse me a moment . . .'

With a drift of silk she, too, was gone, and Rebecca felt only relief. The party was being held on the terrace of a spectacular and opulent villa. Behind them the walls of the house glittered white in the sunlight; below them the terraces led down to a shaded garden, bounded by a low wall, which overlooked the roofs of Corfu town and the bay beyond. All around her guests jostled and milled; men in shiny black suits and dark glasses gestured and talked. Most of the other guests seemed to be Greek; a couple of the men cast glances in her direction, but Rebecca had no wish to talk to them, or to be landed with Jonquil Carstairs again. So quickly she made her way to a waiter, claimed a glass of Perrier, and took it down to the lower terrace and the shade of the trees. No one else seemed inclined to follow her, and she heaved a sigh of relief. There was a fountain there, cool water tumbling from a succession of stone scallops into a pool green with the foliage of lilies. Rebecca stooped and let the water run over her wrist, then, thankful for the shade and the quiet, went to sit on the low wall shaded by the tall black spires of the cypress. She sat there, her back to the guests on the terrace above her, and looked out over the waters of the Ionian. She thought of Cal; she sipped the long glass of iced water, and rubbed the little beads of condensation on the glass against her forehead. For the first time that day all her speculations ceased and her anxieties fell away. The garden was still; the scent of the cypress was dusky and sweet.

She must have sat there some time, gazing out at the water, at the boats which, tiny at this distance, moved to and fro from the harbour. Her mind was still far away when suddenly, hearing nothing, but suddenly becoming conscious that she was watched, she looked up with a start. Just behind her was a man, a man of about sixty, in a pearl grey suit. He was tall, and she had to shade her eyes against the sun to look up into his face. When she did so, she saw that he had bright blue eyes, and that he was regarding her with amusement. She had the feeling that he might have been there, glass in hand, watching her, for some time. When she turned, he lifted his glass in a companionable salute, and then put the empty glass in his pocket, took a step forward, and smiled at her.

'Hello,' he said, as if they were old friends.

Rebecca looked at him uncertainly. There was something in his face that she liked at once, but the step forward had been partly a lurch. She suspected he might be a little drunk.

'I saw you in the market place earlier,' he announced. He had a beautiful voice, and a dated voice, affected to modern ears, though without affectation. A pre-war English upper-class voice; if he were drunk the voice did not betray that fact.

'You are Rebecca, and you work for that plump man in the white suit who doesn't get on with me, alas, at all. Except I don't know quite why I should say "alas", since I don't get on with him either. And that plump man is now rather the worse for drink—I know the symptoms—which is not in the least surprising, because that awful little creep Carstairs has been pouring champagne down his throat ever since he arrived. He's now being rather voluble, not to stay indiscreet, and so I thought I'd come and tell you. That man is a menace. He needs a minder, and while you are far too charming to be a conventional minder, there is no one else to hand. So I came to tell you. Michael needs rescuing, and I for one would be awfully glad if you'd do it . . .'

He smiled at Rebecca at the end of this odd speech, and Rebecca stared at him. She had no idea who he was, and he seemed to see no need to explain; she felt simultaneously taken aback—wrong-footed—and also amused. She hesitated, glancing up to the terrace above them. As she did so, Michael hove into view, conspicuous among the dark-suited Greeks. He was sandwiched between Clickey Carstairs and their host; as Rebecca turned, he grabbed another glass from a passing waiter, and spilled part of its contents down his shirt-front. She stood up quickly.

'Oh dear—I think you're right. Thank you for the warning. I'll try and get him away. We ought to leave anyway—we have to catch the ferry.'

'Ah yes.' The clear blue eyes met hers, and she hesitated, unnerved suddenly; the stranger's regard was amused, and slightly knowing. As if, she thought, he knew why she was so anxious to catch that ferry, and was perfectly aware that it had nothing to do with Michael. As she hesitated, the man touched her arm lightly. 'Don't hurry. I didn't mean you to do that. Five more minutes won't make much difference, I think, and you'll catch the ferry easily.' He paused. She saw his eyes scan the group on the terrace, then move lazily away.

'Lovely house, don't you think? And with a fascinating history. Built for a White Russian princess with a taste for gambling. She could walk from her garden to the Casino, and they say that sometimes, when she'd had a winning streak, she used to collect her winnings, and stand here, on the edge of the terrace, and just toss them over the parapet. Thousands of drachma notes, just fluttering down on to the houses below. Chic, don't you think? Though I doubt if it's true...' He glanced down at her, and when Rebecca didn't answer, he smiled. 'Ah—a puritan. You don't approve? You're probably quite right. I was always too fond of *gestures*. Especially *extravagant* gestures. There was a time in Zagreb once—but no, I mustn't digress.' Rebecca looked up sharply, but if he noted her reaction he gave no sign of it. His eyes were scanning the figures on the terrace once more, and he sighed.

'Do you know,' he went on imperturbably, as if this were a quite normal conversation, 'that if you go to parties in Washington D.C., and you find yourself talking to a rather taciturn man and you ask him what he does—do you know that if he says "Import-Export" you can be quite certain he works for the CIA?' He laughed. 'I simply couldn't believe it at first. It seemed so silly. They're all using the same phrase. And then later, I discovered that the British could be just as silly. I'm sure you're aware that all our embassies abroad have Intelligence Officers—we never call them that of course, we call them something else. In my experience we usually give them a cultural tag. Oh, sometimes they vary it. They run out of inspiration. They just call them Third Secretary. But often it's cultural. Because, of course, being English we disapprove of culture anyway, and certainly see no need to represent its interests properly in our embassies abroad. So—the long and short of it *is* . . .' Here he paused dramatically. 'Whenever I meet an embassy man and he says he's the cultural attaché, I think to myself—"Ah ha!" I think.' He paused again. 'That man Carstairs says he's the cultural attaché.' Another pause. 'Personally, I shouldn't think he'd know the difference between a sonnet and a quartet. What would you say?'

Rebecca looked at him blankly. She was beginning to think that if he wasn't intoxicated he must be mad. 'I don't quite understand,' she said slowly. 'Are you trying to tell me that man Carstairs is in Intelligence? Why should I care?'

'Because from the moment Michael arrived Mr Carstairs has been plying him with questions about Calvin Ryder, that's why.' The blue eyes met hers once more, their expression lazily benign and yet sharp. Rebecca paled. 'Apparently Jonquil—*can* she be called Jonquil? Really an absurdly unfortunate name for a woman that shape—apparently Jonquil has a passion for detective fiction in general, and for the crime novels of Cal Ryder in particular. She seemed awfully hard put to remember their titles, *I* thought but that might be uncharitable of me . . .'

'Please.' Rebecca interrupted him. 'Why are you telling me this? I don't understand at all, and . . .'

'Oh, really? I thought you might.' He looked at her sharply and then shrugged. 'Never mind then. Just take it from me, you would be doing me a favour, and Cal, if you could persuade dear loquacious Michael to leave. To stop talking about writers and their odd taste for isolated villas with a good view of the Albanian coast, and their liking for night fishing expeditions—just get him to leave, could you do that?' His gaze had grown colder, and harder as he spoke. 'You're a woman, after all. Can't you say you have a headache, or something? Can't you . . .'

Colour winged its way into Rebecca's cheeks. She still didn't understand, but the drift of his words was enough. If Michael's drunken indiscretions were some kind of threat to Cal, then she would shut Michael up and get him away somehow—if she had to faint on the floor at his feet she'd do it. She started towards the terrace, and then swung round.

The tall thin man was watching her closely.

'Who—who *are* you?' she stammered.

He smiled, in a way she did not entirely like, and gave her an odd half-bow from the waist. 'Forgive me. I quite forgot. I thought you must realise. You have been to my house. I'm Grey Jameson . . .'

There was a moment's silence. Rebecca, torn between her desire to get to Michael, and her disbelief at what she had just heard, hesitated. 'You're Grey Jameson? But . . . I thought you were away. In England or . . .' She stammered to a halt. She met his eyes, and composing herself, growing calmer, she said carefully: 'How did you know I'd been to your house?'

'Cal told me.'

'He can't have done!' The words were out before she could stop them. 'I don't understand! It's not possible . . . last night . . . You mean you spoke on the telephone?'

Jameson smiled. 'Certainly not.'

'Then how . . .' Her voice trailed away.

He shrugged. 'You were on Paxos yesterday evening; you are in Corfu this afternoon. Why shouldn't the same be true of me?'

'Because you weren't on the ferry this morning! There is only one and you weren't on it, I'd have noticed you if you were, and . . .' She broke off. Her distress was so sudden and so acute that it was difficult to control. All she knew was that she wished, wished passionately, that Cal should not have discussed her with this man.

He stepped forward, his expression a little gentler than it had been before. 'My dear.' He took her arm and turned her gently but firmly back towards the terrace. 'Let me give you a piece of advice, will you? Don't ask questions, and don't get involved. Just go up on the terrace and get Michael Hamilton out of here. And when you get back to Paxos—stay out of Cal's way.' He hesitated. 'It's unfortunate that you met, and it's unfortunate that Cal can be weak when it comes to a beautiful young girl. So—stay away from him, before you get hurt. That's what he'd prefer—I happen to know . . .'

'How do you know?' Rebecca heard her own voice rise, and felt sudden pain knife through her.

'Because he told me so,' Grey Jameson said quietly.

There was a little silence. Their eyes met. Rebecca's mouth set in an obstinate line; she tilted her chin. 'Then he can tell me himself,' she said fiercely. 'I don't think Cal's the kind of man who'd use you as an emissary. Goodbye, Mr Jameson . . .'

Then she turned, quickly, so he should not see the expression on her face, and ran up the steps to the terrace.

They caught the ferry with ease; it was then late leaving. Michael found himself a seat inside the saloon, propped himself up between a hiker's kitbag and an old Greek peasant woman with a cage full of chickens, and promptly went to sleep. He stayed asleep for the entire journey, and Rebecca, standing up on deck staring out across the darkening water, had no inclination to wake him.

By the time they reached Paxos it was well past seven, and the light was fading fast. The little square by the harbour buzzed with activity. All the seats outside the cafés seemed to be full; a group of young girls were decorating the outside of the little white church with palm leaves and spring flowers; waiters from the tavernas were carefully stringing coloured lanterns between the oleander trees.

'Getting everything ready for the procession tomorrow evening,' Michael said, joining Rebecca on deck. He looked sheepish, and very pale.

'I say, Rebecca . . .' He plucked at her sleeve as they went down the gangplank. 'I'm most awfully sorry. Made a complete ass of myself. Can't thank you enough for getting me away. Can't think what happened to me—must have been the heat, I suppose, and damn Clickey kept filling up my glass when I wasn't looking . . .'

'It doesn't matter, Michael, honestly. Forget it. Are you feeling all right now?'

'To be perfectly candid, no. I feel bloody awful. Kind of Zulu drumming going on in my head. I think I'll just go back to the flat and lie down . . .'

'I'll see you home.' Rebecca sighed and took his arm. 'It's no trouble—I pass your house anyway . . .'

'Haven't got a good head for alcohol, never had. 'Spect Clickey remembers. Don't drink much usually. Thought champagne would be all right . . .'

Michael kept up his rather peevish litany as far as the door of his house. It was clear he was feeling extremely sorry for himself; he announced that he would feel a lot better if he had some really strong black coffee. Rebecca hesitated; she was already late, and anxious to get away, but she could sense it wasn't going to be easy to get rid of Michael. So, briskly, she marched him indoors, settled him in a chair, and quickly made some coffee so strong that the spoon nearly stood upright in it.

'There,' she said, laying the tray down beside him, 'coffee. And now Michael I have to go. I'll see you in the morning . . .'

Before he could protest, or start asking questions, or think of something else he might need, Rebecca was outside. Her own flat was only a few streets away. She paused for a second, feeling the dark air balmy, scented with salt, hearing the sounds from the square—laughter and voices, someone had begun to play a guitar. Then she started to run lightly back to the flat: she would shower and change, she thought, it wouldn't take more than five minutes, then take the moped and be off . . . She glanced down at her watch: not so late, nearly eight. She would be with Cal by eight-thirty . . .

As she paused by her front door, fumbling with her keys, a shadow detached itself from a near-by wall. Light footsteps. Seeing movement from the corner of her eye, startled, Rebecca looked up. A little Greek boy was standing in front of her: about nine years old, bare-footed, in a torn T-shirt and cut-offs. Under a jet black fringe of hair; his eyes glittered in the fading light as he looked up at her.

'*Kyrie*, Kyrie Farrell?'

'*Ne . . .*'

He pressed a scrap of paper into her hand. Then he turned and scampered off.

'*Perimenas parakalo . . .*' Rebecca called after him. 'Wait—oh please wait . . .'

But the boy was gone. She peered into the shadows after him, then slowly unfolded the piece of paper in her hand. She could just read it, and the message was brief.

'Not tonight. I'm sorry. I will come for you when I can. Cal.'

Rebecca stared down at the piece of paper. After the suspense of the past day, the endless ferry journey back from Corfu, when she could think of nothing but the fact that each minute that passed brought her closer to Cal—after that, her disappointment was the more acute. She looked back once more over her shoulder, ran to the end of the alleyway, but there was no sign of the little boy. She couldn't be certain, but she thought it had been one of Nico's younger sons . . . Desolately she turned back, and let herself into the flat, which was in darkness—clearly Nicky had already gone out. She held the piece of paper tight in her hand, unhappiness and also anxiety welling up inside her. She had wanted to see him so much—and she needed to see him, she thought, disappointment kindling anger. She needed to tell him they had been watched from the Villa Circe. She needed to ask him about Michael's story, about meeting Carstairs, about the extraordinary interview with Grey Jameson . . .

In her room she switched on the light, and sank down on the narrow bed. She was tired, she knew that, but it was a nervous kind of tiredness that charged her with a dreadful restless energy. She stood up again, paced back and forth, opened the note once more and read it again. It was terse, to say the least, and that hurt her. No explanation, hardly an apology. Why not tonight? What was happening tonight that meant he could not see her?

She stopped still, staring blankly across the room. Was something happening tonight, something that had been planned for another night, something that had, for some reason, been changed? She paused in her pacing; the room felt stiflingly hot. She crossed to the window and threw it open, looking down at the empty street, at the dark water lapping against the stones. She stiffened, suddenly alert, then she crossed the room, turned off the light, went back to the window and peered out into the gathering dark.

Yes, she had been right. There was a yacht coming in—a large white ocean-going yacht. Even as she watched, it edged stern-on to the quay: she heard voices, in Greek; a man, dressed in white, leapt on to the quay with a mooring rope.

Pressing herself against the curtains, Rebecca watched, puzzled and alert. Large yachts did visit Paxos—many of them in the summer, according to Nicky, although there had been very few this early in the year. But they moored in the main part of the harbour usually, near the central square, not here. There could be no reason to moor at this, the shallower end of the quay, unless you wanted your arrival to be unobtrusive . . . She stared; the yacht was large and expensive; above its wheel-room its roof bristled with navigational radar equipment. As she watched, the man in white tethered the mooring rope. He called out something, in Greek, and two other men appeared on the aft-deck. Rebecca leaned forward in disbelief, straining her eyes. Then the two men looked up, looked along the quay; what light there was caught their faces, and she recognised them at once. Carstairs, and their host at the party that morning—what was his name? Costas, that was right, Costas Andropoulos. And Michael's words came back to her: *some Greek high-up, from Athens* . . .

She hesitated, her senses quickening. Carstairs' wife had mentioned something about a yacht, something about their coming to Paxos for the Easter celebrations—but that wasn't until tomorrow. Why, to be here now they must have left Corfu soon after she and Michael had caught the ferry . . .

She stared out into the darkness. Andropoulos said something to Carstairs, and the Englishman nodded. They turned and disappeared through a door that must lead below decks.

For a moment Rebecca sat absolutely still, her pulses racing, her mind accelerating. Everything Michael had said, and everything Grey Jameson had hinted, clashed and jumbled themselves in her mind. She stood up, her hand tightening around Cal's note.

She knew only one thing, and she felt it acutely. This arrival was not accidental. It connected in some way with Cal, with Nico, with whatever it was that was going on on this peaceful island. And Cal was in danger: suddenly she felt certain of it. He would not know, could not know, that these people were here. He would not know—unless she told him.

She knew then what she must do. Decisiveness came to her, flowing through her veins like adrenalin. Quickly she moved away from the window. She did not put on the light, but felt for her clothes in the darkness. The black dress—where was it? Hands trembling, she found it, and pulled it on. She slipped her feet into light sandals, and fumbled in the drawer beside her bed for her torch. There; she had it. She slipped torch and note into her pocket, and crept back to the window. Silence. The yacht was in darkness; there was no sign of movement.

Quickly she crept to the door, closed it softly behind her, and fled silently down the stairs, out the side door, and into the little courtyard. Yes, there were the mopeds. As quietly as she could she opened the gate into the alleyway, and pushed the bike out: not a sign of anyone. Music drifted on the night air; the street was deserted.

She made herself push the bike a little way through the back streets of the village, until she was well away from the harbour, then, her pulses hammering in her head, she kicked the starter handle. The engine fired; its noise seemed terrifyingly loud. In a second she was astride it, urging it up the hill and out of Gaios, praying that for once, in the cool of the evening, it wouldn't balk at the hill.

Her prayers seemed to be answered; the machine chugged, and slowed, but it made it. With a sense of relief, of intoxicating relief, she crested the rise, and looked back. Below her lay the roofs of Gaios; lights. Ahead of her lay the dark. She switched on the headlamp and accelerated away. The wind caught her hair and rushed over her body. It was downhill now, almost all the way to the olive grove and the turning to Grey Jameson's house. Cal, she thought, Cal. The road stretched before her, dark, unlit, uninhabited. She urged the machine down it, as fast as she dared. The wind rushed in her face. Looking up, she saw that the stars were blotted out by cloud, that the moon, scarcely visible, was in the first thin sickle of its cycle. Cal.

He felt closer to her every second. She had not a second's doubt that she would find him. The wind moved the trees and rushed against her skin, and she felt that on the wind, through the dark, he called to her.

She left the bike half-way up the track that led to Grey Jameson's house, when it became obvious she could take it no further. Better anyway to approach the place quietly, she thought to herself, as she dragged it off the path and concealed it as best she could behind some olive trees.

Then she set off on foot, moving silently in her sandals, her breath catching in her throat as the track grew more rutted, the incline steeper. She reached the place where, that first day, Cal had stopped her, and paused, tense, beneath a tree, peering ahead. Her eyes were used to the dark now, and she knew she was very near to the house, but she could see no lights, could hear nothing. She hesitated, and then went on, moving more slowly now, feeling for some reason that she should be cautious, should not loudly announce her arrival.

The clearing—she had reached it. She stopped again. She could see the house now, it loomed up to her right through the olives. Shuttered, dark; there was no sign of lights. Carefully, quietly, she moved forward. The Jeep was there, parked in the usual place, and she felt a sudden surge of relief: he must be here then, he must.

It was terribly quiet; the silence raised prickles on the back of her neck. Just the shifting of branches, and in the distance, the suck of the sea beneath the cliffs. Carefully she inched her way towards the house. Once a branch snapped under her foot, and the sound seemed immensely loud, like a pistol shot. She froze, but nothing happened, and she moved forward again. She reached the house.

It was in total darkness, the outer shutters closed, with no chink of light showing through them. Carefully, running her fingers over the panels of the door, she tapped once, twice, very lightly. Nothing happened. No stir. No answer. She tapped again, and then very carefully, stealthily, tried the handle. It turned, but the door did not budge. Frightened now, her anxiety mounting irrationally, she pressed her shoulder against it. It didn't move an inch.

She stepped back, trembling, disappointment flooding through her veins. That he should not be here, that this journey through the dark had been in vain—this had simply not occurred to her. He must be there—he must! She stood there, feeling suddenly cold in the chill of the night air, her mind working feverishly. The Jeep was here, but the house was locked. If Cal wasn't here then there was only one other place he could be—the Villa Circe. The realisation made her feel sick and exhausted. It was so stupid of her: why had she not thought of that before? Why hadn't she planned, worked things out, instead of just rushing off into the dark like an idiot . . .?

She set her mouth. Well, now there was nothing else for it. If Cal were at the Villa Circe, then she would have to go there. She'd just have to go back down the track again, get the bike, and . . .

She stiffened, every nerve in her body suddenly alert. She had heard something, she was sure of it. Just faintly, a muffled sound, but *something*. She stood absolutely still, straining her ears, fear tightening her throat, and making beads of sweat start out on her brow.

There it was again, a voice, she thought, though she couldn't be certain, and she couldn't tell from where it came. It seemed to be below her, but that was impossible. She trembled. Now she could hear nothing, just the distant crash of surf on the rocks. She swallowed, her throat dry and taut.

'Cal?' Her own voice, hardly more than a whisper, startled her. There was no answer.

Above her the branches of the olives lifted on a gust of wind. They shifted, a ghostly grey against the darkness of the sky. Very carefully, her limbs feeling tight and stiff with nerves, she began to pick her path away from the house. One step. Another. She let her breath out on a sigh. She must have been mistaken; her nerves were playing tricks with her, that was all. She mustn't waste any more time. She had to get back to the bike, and then . . .

She knew, a split second before it happened, that there was someone behind her. She heard nothing, but her senses registered danger. Alarm clanged in her mind, tensed the pores of her skin: she started to swing round, opened her mouth to cry out, and the hand grabbed her out of the dark. It came from behind, wrenching her off balance, a man's hand, clamping itself violently and painfully over her mouth and nose, so the cry never came and she could hardly breathe. She was pulled off her feet, up and back, slamming against something hard and damp that smelled of sweat and the sea. There was more than one of them: her senses, reeling, registered that. She saw nothing but swirling dark, an arm, the branches over her head.

Then someone had her arm, her right arm, and they were twisting it up behind her back, violently, grunting with the effort, and the pain was terrible in its suddenness, like a blinding light. She wanted to cry out, through the pain, through the flesh that was pressed so suffocatingly tight over her face, and she heard someone say something, an exclamation—not English, not Greek—in a language she had never heard, rough and guttural. Then there were footsteps running, a voice she knew, Cal's voice . . .

She struggled then, through the pain and the shock; she found just enough strength to kick back, to squirm aside. For a second, one glorious second, the hand over her mouth slipped, and air gushed back into her throat and lungs, half choking her. She opened her eyes through the white light of the pain, and she saw him, just for an instant: Cal. He was clothed in black, from head to foot, and the blackness gleamed wetly in the thin light. His hair was wet, plastered against his head, water ran over his face in rivulets. His hand was reaching up, up towards her throat, and he was saying something, something she didn't understand, his voice harsh and low, and his eyes—they glittered blackly at her with a terrifying rage. She saw him, and saw his anger, for a second, lit by pain as if illumined by lightning. Then something hit her, hard, on the side of her head, and she knew she was falling, falling, into the dark.

CHAPTER SEVEN

SHE came round and it was dark—terribly dark, so black she thought for a moment that her eyes were blindfolded, or that she had lost her sight. She gave a little whimper of fear, and then, as consciousness seeped back, became aware of other things. It was bitterly cold; something had been thrown over her, some kind of cover, she could feel its weight, but it gave little protection: coldness stiffened every limb in her body. When she tried to move, and found she could not, she realised why she felt so stiff. Her hands and her ankles were tied, and the bonds were tight, they cut into her skin, and with even the smallest movement they seemed to tighten further. Her hands and her feet felt like ice; and she was lying on something cold, cold and dreadfully hard, with bumps and indentations that bit into the skin of her back . . .

She moved, then lay still. Fear rose in her in a great swooping wave; she tried to cry out, and found her throat dry and constricted with fear, so that barely a sound came out. The fear took her and engulfed her; she felt herself begin to shake. And then, slowly but surely, it began to pass, to ebb, and her mind started working again. Carefully, using all her concentration, she closed her eyes, and then opened them again. She was not blindfolded, and she could see—but she could see nothing. Wherever she was it was totally dark, and totally silent.

And yet not silent. Very carefully she stopped struggling, and lay perfectly still and listened. She tried to channel all her senses into just this one; she strained her ears, and then she could hear it, quite clearly, as she would have heard it before if fear had not blotted it out. The sea; the sound of the sea. The noise was oddly distorted, slightly echoing, but it was there, a swirling, sucking sound, the occasional slap of water against rock . . . Rock. She was lying on rock—cold hard rock that pressed against every bone in her spine. Spreading her fingers as far as the bonds allowed she touched the ground below her and felt its smooth coldness: rock.

The fear came back then. Feeling rock beneath her she immediately imagined it must be just above her head also; her senses pulsed. She could sense it, pressing down on her, just above her face. Oh God, where had they put her—and where had they gone? Had she been left here to die, in some horrible cramped place? Was the sea coming closer, was that it? Was she being left here to drown?

She heard her own breath come in pants, felt her limbs tense and the bonds tighten; she could taste salt in the air, salt against her lips. For a moment the fear eddied out of control again, spiralling up within her, and then, slowly but surely, she got it under control once more. Think; she must think, not let her imagination run away and play tricks on her.

Very carefully, moving no more than an inch at a time, she began to ease herself upwards, until she was half kneeling, half crouching. Blindly, she felt the dark behind her back, and felt nothing, only space. Cautiously, she lifted her head, and encountered nothing. She sighed, then made herself breathe deeply and slowly. She was not in a constricted space; there was plenty of air, she could feel its currents cold against her face now. And the sea was not that close; wherever she was it was quite dry. If only there were just a glimmer of light . . .

She froze then. She could hear something else, above and beyond the sound of the sea . . . There, she heard it again. Movement, the sound of footsteps, voices, a crash, then an exclamation . . . She listened intently; the sounds ceased.

And then she remembered the torch. It was in her right-hand pocket; if she could just ease her bound hands downwards, slip it out on to the rock beside her . . . Very carefully, grimacing as the ropes cut into her skin, she eased her arms to her side. Her fingers were stiff and awkward, and she could not turn her hands; she bit her teeth against her lip, concentrating every ounce of strength into her effort. There, she had it, it was out of the pocket. Now—if she could just . . . She felt the smooth plastic casing under her fingertips; she inched it up into the palm of her hand, feeling for the switch. She almost had it, if she could just . . . Her hand slipped. With a moan of despair she heard the torch roll over the rock, then a crash, startlingly loud, as if it had fallen a little way and the casing had cracked. She gave a little moan, and let herself slide down again against the rock. Whatever had been covering her had fallen off when she moved. Now it lay half under her, and gratefully, she sank back against it. She closed her eyes; she could have slept; she wasn't sure.

Time passed; she had no idea how long; she lay there in an odd dreamlike state of semi-consciousness, in which images mixed and married and swam back and forth in her mind, like fish, like seaweed, drifting back and forth, now connecting, now disconnecting, half perceived, half glimpsed. Then, quite suddenly, she knew she was not alone.

She tensed, every nerve in her body alert. She strained her eyes but could see nothing, just blackness, unrelieved. A sound, very soft, bare feet over rock, moving cautiously; someone there with her in the dark, someone trying to control their breathing as she tried to control hers. A slithering sound . . .

She lay absolutely still, forcing herself not to move. Someone or something was beside her; she could sense their presence in the air. She felt the sweat break out on her brow; she opened her mouth to cry out, and a hand came down over it. The hand was damp, but with an animal alertness she knew it was his hand, Cal's hand, and for an instant of blind terror all the images of his books surged in her mind. Then the hand moved. She felt the fingers slip gently over her skin like silk; she shut her eyes quickly; they touched her lids. He sighed. Then his hand moved again, over her face, to the side of her head. They touched her there, and she felt an instant's pain; then they laced themselves in her hair. He gave a groan—a ragged sound, harsh and pained. Then, she felt his body, close to hers, his arms, sliding around her, lifting her. He lifted her easily, in one swift movement, as if she were weightless, and pressed her against him, moving quickly now, feverishly, with a terrifying impatience. She felt his chest hard against her breasts, felt the texture of what he was wearing—smooth, cool, damp, not cloth, her mind thought confusedly, something else, then she remembered him as she had last seen him and realised, of course, a wet-suit, that was it, and—oh, God he strained her body against him, so tightly she could hardly breathe. Hideous fears and imaginings coursed through her mind: he meant to kill her, or rape her. That was why he had come back, that was the reason for that vicious anger she had seen in his eyes before they'd hit her . . .

Fear made her body go limp. She sagged against him, she felt his heart hammer against her face. He was breathing fast; his hands pressed against her face and lifted her back, he was saying her name now, over and over again. 'Rebecca, oh Rebecca . . .' His mouth was against her ear, after the cold of the rock his body felt terribly hot, and she wanted to cry out, scream, but she couldn't, no sound would come . . . And then his mouth came down on hers.

She started to fight him then, with a suddenness and strength that came from fear of him and fear of the dark. Quite instinctively, having no time to think, she wrenched her head back, and threw herself sideways, squirming out of his grasp. The suddenness of her movement clearly took him by surprise, because for a moment he lost his grip on her. She fell back, the hard rock slamming against her spine, knocking the breath out of her body, and then she tried to roll away from him, over the rock out of his grasp, kicking out blindly with her feet as she did so. He gave a cry of surprise, a grunt of pain, for a moment she was free, slipping across the rock, and then he had her again. She felt his arms reach for her, hard hands catch her shoulders and stop her slide, then his weight was on her, he was astride her body, and he was pinning her to the rock. He started to say something, she felt his hand move up to her throat, and she wrenched herself desperately once more, hearing her dress rend and tear, but not caring.

'Rebecca . . .' He was trying to hold her, pushing her down. She struggled wildly, feeling his strong thighs press against her, his weight bearing her back. He was panting now; her own breath was a series of wild hysterical gasps. She writhed under him, arching her body back, and she knew he was saying something, but she wasn't going to listen, she didn't trust him . . .

She felt his hand brush her lips, and in an excess of fear she tried to bite him. She felt her lips graze his skin. He gave a sharp exclamation, and then she realised that whatever had been happening, he had not been using his full strength, but tussling with her merely, as if she were a child. Now she heard him swear; he caught hold of her by the upper arms, his grip vice-like, so she could not move, and he shook her once, very hard, so the breath was knocked out of her body. Then he pushed her down and back, letting his full weight come down on her, so for an instant she felt every line of his hard body pressed against hers. He was straddling her now, she was trapped between the power of his thighs. Dimly, through her terror, she heard him saying her name, but she would not listen to him, would not stay still. That was what he wanted, she thought confusedly, he wanted her to stop struggling, and then . . .

He was reaching his hands up to her face. Violently, using all the strength she possessed, she wrenched her head away, tried to bring her leg up between his thighs. He gave a muffled exclamation—'Keep still, damn it—Rebecca . . .' And then fiercely, desperately, as still she struggled and tried to cry out he put first his hand, and then very deliberately, his mouth, over hers. At the touch of his lips, the thrust of his tongue, she felt her whole body go rigid under him. He too tensed, there was a moment of hesitation; she thought with an irrational rush of triumph that he was going to relent. Then he groaned against her mouth, and his kiss deepened.

He kissed her then with an extremity of passion, holding her by the hair, ravaging her mouth. The grip of his thighs tightened, and she felt his body harden and then thrust cruelly against her. With his other hand he felt for her body, pulling at the torn dress, wrenching it aside, cupping her breast to the suck of his mouth. She cried out then, a long low moan of fear, but fear of herself as much as of him, for she felt her body begin to betray her. Something had ignited between them, a flame of excitement that coursed up through the nerves of her body, and made her slacken and relax against him. She fought it down, but she knew it was conquering her; she wanted him; he made her want him, even now, even like this, even in the dark.

She could not touch him—could neither fend him off nor answer the mounting fierceness of his caresses. She could not deny the moist sweetness which flooded her veins, the pure animal instinct that made her arch her back, that made the full nipples harden and point under his tongue. She trembled, feeling him shudder against her, knowing he was not in control now any more than she was, feeling his hands roam her body with a quickening ardour and urgency. Summoning every ounce of her willpower she forced herself to do the one thing of which she was, just, still capable. She went limp in his arms, let her body lie slack against his straining, let him part her lips, but forced herself to give no response to the quest of his mouth and tongue. It was passive resistance, but it was resistance none the less; she felt him sense it, and she felt it anger him. He lifted himself; she knew, through the darkness, that he was looking down into her face. For a moment he stopped, he did not move, did not kiss or touch her, and she felt the hectic languor almost betray her again. She wanted to cry out, to lift her body up to him again, but she did not.

Then, very deliberately, coldly, she thought, he moved his hands down over her body. He parted the material of her dress, touched the full curves, the swelling veins, of her breasts, and she bit back the moan that almost escaped her lips, and lay still. He moved his hands on down, his fingers cool, hard, questing, and exactly skilled. He knew where to touch her, and how, knew precisely, and did so, running his hands in a firm parabola, over her belly and down to her thighs. He pushed her dress up, stroked, very lightly, the moist soft skin of her inner thighs. Then he removed his hand; she heard him fumble at something, and then the rip of a zip fastener. Then, with a swift angry gesture, he caught her and lifted her, and she realised he had opened the wetsuit jacket, that he was pressing her bared breasts against the hard muscles and damp hair of his chest. She groaned then, she could not prevent herself, and she heard him give a low exclamation of triumph.

'No lies . . .' He caught her face and forced it up to him in the dark. Dimly, for a second, she glimpsed the glitter of his eyes. His fingers tightened their grip on her hair, and he rocked her back and forth against him, speaking so his mouth was almost against her lips and her whole body cried out to clasp at him.

'Don't try and lie to me. You can't. Your body can't. I know. I knew from the first moment we met, and so did you.

You want me, even now, even like this . . .' His voice caught in his throat. 'Rebecca . . . Tell me. Just tell me that . . .'

His grip had become more gentle. When she didn't answer him, he swore, harshly, his hold tightening once more. He bent his head to her throat, pressing his lips against the pulse that beat wildly under her skin. He arched her back with one quick easy movement, so her breasts were lifted to him, then he lowered his mouth to them with a low groan, sucking their hard tips, then moving again, at once, lips parted, to claim her mouth. She gave in then; it was too strong, and she couldn't fight it any longer. With all the passion that had built in her, she kissed him back, and the release was blinding. She felt his joy and excitement instant in his response; his arms tightened around her protectively; he held her in a long embrace. Then, very deliberately, still not speaking, he felt behind her and slowly undid the bonds that held her hands. He caught them between his, and chafed them, and she felt the blood course painfully back.

Then he knelt; she felt metal glance against her legs; a tug, and the ropes around her ankles fell away. Very gently, with a patient tenderness, he stroked her feet, her ankles, her legs, and then, when he judged—and he judged exactly—that the pain of their loosing was ebbing, he drew her upwards, so they knelt, facing each other. In the darkness, calmer now, both trembled. He took one of her hands, her freed hand, and very gently laid it against the bare skin of his chest, over his heart. Then, slowly and deliberately, and she felt his gaze as he did so, he drew her hand down, and further down, over the taut muscles of his stomach until they rested over the hard thrust of his flesh. She gave a little incoherent cry and felt him quicken and move against her there. He clasped her tight, an odd desperation in his embrace; she felt her own body quicken in answer, and then gradually grow still.

'You know me . . .' he said, his voice low, with a contained passion. 'You know me. And now—we most stop this madness. Stop it at once, before we both lose control . . .'

Rebecca cried, a little. With exhaustion, with confusion, because some things were over and a great many more were beginning, because something had happened to her, that night, in the dark, and she knew that no matter what else happened she would never be the same again, but that these events, this man, would colour the rest of her life, like wine in water.

She told him why she had come, and what had happened to her that day; the meeting with Grey Jameson, the party at Corfu, the arrival of the yacht, her fear that the Villa Circe had been watched. Once she began to speak, in answer to his first gentle question, she found she could not stop. She just went on, not even thinking of all the questions that thronged somewhere at the back of her mind. And Cal listened, patiently, alertly, holding her gently in the curve of his arms. When she had finished, he sighed deeply, and she swung round to him.

'Where *are* we? I was so frightened. It's so dark. I could hear the sea . . .'

She had reached up to touch his face, and she felt him smile.

'You wanted to come here,' he said gently. 'Can't you guess? The cave of Aphrodite . . .'

She drew in her breath sharply. 'Aphrodite's cave? But that's not possible! I don't understand . . . Someone hit me. Not you—someone else, and then I don't remember anything . . . But I was at Jameson's house—up on the cliff. How could we be in the cave? Why is it so dark . . .'

He laughed softly. 'It's not just one cave—it's a network of caves. This is one of the inner ones. Quite dry. Well above waterline and quite safe. No one wanted to hurt you, or kill you. If they had done, they'd have been quite capable of it. It would have been very quick and very silent. But the men who caught you—the one who hit you. They're good men. They don't kill young girls—even when they come blundering in out of the dark at the worst possible moment . . .' He paused, and touched the side of her head gently. 'They had to make sure you didn't cry out. I'm sorry if they hurt you. I had a moment's terrible fear—outside the house. They got to you before I did. For an instant, I feared . . .'

'You looked angry. Terribly angry. I was afraid of you . . .'

Again the soft laugh. 'Not angry with you.'

'But how . . .' She turned to him impulsively. 'Cal—explain.

please. I don't understand anything. How I got here—those men—who they are—anything.'

There was a little silence, and he took her hands. When he began to speak he did so slowly and carefully, no emotion in his voice. 'We brought you down here from the house,' he said. 'Not by sea. The caves all interconnect, this part of the island is riddled with them, they must be thousands of years old. There's a passageway; it leads out of the upper caves and it ends in the cellar under Grey's house. He discovered it years ago. I imagine it must have been quite useful to whoever first built the house, whenever that was. When Grey found it, it was partly blocked. It hadn't been used for a very long time. He and I, and Nico, unblocked it.'

'But *why*?'

'For a hiding place at first,' he answered simply. 'I would imagine it had served that purpose in the past. When these islands were part of the Venetian empire; in the last war, when the Germans occupied them, almost certainly.'

'Then Nico is smuggling goods into Albania?' She stared at him with rounded eyes, and he laughed gently.

'Not goods. People. And not into Albania. Out of it. Now do you understand?' There was a silence. Rebecca looked at him uncertainly, and then, in the darkness, felt for his hand. After a pause, Cal went on, speaking slowly and carefully.

'Do you know anything about Albania? Very few people do. It's virtually a closed country; there are very few Western visitors. It was annexed to the Eastern bloc after the last war; with Bulgaria it's become one of the most Russianised states . . .' He paused. 'If you want a run-down of its politics you must ask Grey, not me. He spent time there before the war; when he was in the diplomatic service he was posted to Yugoslavia and Bulgaria—its two nearest neighbours besides Greece; he speaks Serbo-Croat. He's visited Tirana—that's the capital—and he still has friends there, though of course he wouldn't be allowed into the country now. Grey can tell you the politics; all I can tell you is about my friends . . .'

'Friends?' Rebecca turned to him. 'You mean Nico?'

'Nico, primarily. But others also.' He sighed. 'You see, the Albanians are a mixed-race people. The boundaries of that part of Europe have been in constant flux for centuries, and so now there are people living there who are, if you like, Albanian. There are also Turks, Rumanians, and Greeks. Whatever race you are originally it's not possible to leave. Greeks, Turks, Rumanians—they are all now Albanians, and they have to remain there. The regime is strict; it doesn't happily grant exit-visas to those who happen to be unsympathetic to its political aims.' He paused.

'It looks so beautiful, doesn't it? I've often thought that, when I've been up at the Villa Circe, looking across the sea. That beautiful purple stain on the horizon; that mysterious country.' He stopped and spread his hands. 'I try not to think of it from a political point of view. I don't know enough of the rights and the wrongs. All I know is that there are people over there who do not find Albania beautiful, who want to leave, and aren't allowed to do so.' He shrugged. 'If you like, that's how it began.'

'You agreed to help Nico get them out, is that it?'

'That's it.' He sighed. 'We first tried about five years ago. One family. Greek. Fishermen caught the wrong side of the curtain that came down at the end of the last war. They were cousins of Nico's. He intended to bring them out anyway. Grey and I agreed to help him. Grey was more use than I could ever be. I was just another pair of hands really, additional manpower, and I was renting the Villa Circe, which helped. But Grey did the important work, because he has the contacts. The family couldn't stay here, you see. They went to the Greek mainland. It was Grey who got them there, who took care of their papers and so on.' He hesitated. 'That first time, I had doubts. It would have meant trouble for Nico, serious trouble, if we'd been caught. There was a certain amount of danger—not much, not the first time, but some. But Nico was my friend. He asked my help. I could not refuse. And—well, we were successful.'

'And—since then?'

'Not many.' Cal sighed. 'Each year, a few. Always Greeks. Once a family, with young children. Over the last five years it's twenty-five, maybe thirty people. Most of the time I don't even know their names. Grey keeps in touch with them. I feel . . .' He hesitated. 'I feel that whatever else I've done or failed to do, that was worthwhile.'

There was a little silence. In the darkness, Rebecca moved closer to him.

'Your stepsister . . .' She hesitated. 'Elaine. Did she know you were doing this?'

'Yes. She knew.' Cal's voice was flat. 'After she died, well, I went on with it partly for her sake. I would have done so anyway, but Elaine understood, you see. Not the politics. Not that. But—she knew what it felt like to be a prisoner. She was a prisoner of her illness. She understood Greece, and the Greeks. And she knew what it felt like—to want to be free.'

Rebecca pressed his hand. 'And now,' she prompted gently. 'What now?'

'Now——' she felt him shrug angrily. 'Now it is difficult. Michael told you about the police, last year? The smuggling story? Well, that was a cover-up on their part—the line they spun him, that's all. He bought it, of course, which suited their purposes. They knew quite well what was going on. I think . . .' He paused. 'It's difficult to say. I think the authorities in Athens would have turned a blind eye if they could have done. They didn't want to make waves. It was a small-scale operation, they knew that much, even if they didn't know the details, and the people being brought out, well, there were very few of them, they were of Greek origin, they weren't politically involved in Albania, they were just Greeks who wanted to get back to Greece. But, of course, if the Albanian government had started to make a fuss, to pressure them—and Grey thinks that's what happened— then, for form's sake, they would have to take a stand. Greece and Albania share a long border. They wouldn't have wanted this to blow up into a major diplomatic incident—particularly since it involved two Europeans, Grey, and myself. There could have been quite a fuss. Still could be. I should think that's why your friend Carstairs has turned up now.' He paused.

'You see, this is the last trip. We'd agreed on that, Nico and Grey and I. And the men we've brought out tonight are rather different. There are eight of them. All young. All of Greek descent. All active opponents to the Albanian regime. Each of them facing, at best, a life sentence if they remained in Albania. Their leader is Nico's nephew.' He paused. 'If we can get them off Paxos, and away to new lives on the mainland, everything should be OK. There'll be a big fuss behind closed doors, and some residue of ill-will between the Greek and Albanian governments. Then it will die down. But if we can't—and this time the Greek government will make a discreet but concerted effort to stop us—then the eight men will be handed back.' He paused grimly.

'I think, I hope, that we are still a few jumps ahead of them. We moved the operation forward. We shifted everything from the Villa Circe to here. Instead of using boats, we decided to use inflatables. They were stored at the Villa Circe, they were there the day you first came up there—do you remember? When I couldn't let you go into the house ... Then, tonight we brought the men in on inflatables, the way you and I did it the other day, at high tide, into the bay, and then into the caves. The transfer from their boat was very quick. We got them in here in darkness, and very fast. No boat can get into the cave now, that's why we used the inflatables. No one could follow us, if we had been seen, and only a few islanders know about the link between the caves and Grey's house. Those who do would never talk. Your turning-up caused momentary consternation, but apart from that, so far, so good. We'll take them off tomorrow night, during the Easter procession and the celebrations ...'

He broke off, and there was a sudden heavy silence. Rebecca felt a cold and horrible premonition; it came to her on his words, chilling her skin. She swallowed.

'We?' she said quietly.

'Grey and I.' He paused. 'And Nico. But Nico will be coming back.'

He shifted slightly beside her, and she sensed his hesitation, knew, on some shaft of intuition, why he had explained all this to her, so patiently and at such length. Instinctively she drew back from him a little.

'You're not coming back to Paxos?'

'No.' He spoke with finality, but even so she grasped at straws.

'But you will come back? Eventually? When everything has quietened down?'

'No.'

'But you must! Surely—the island means so much to you,

and . . .' She broke off. *And I shall be here*, she wanted to add, and knew she could not. He sighed, and in the darkness he reached for her hand.

'Rebecca. Try to understand. I shan't come back, and I can't come back. This is over. This episode in my life will be over. If I come back, if Grey comes back—don't you see? They know we're involved, they don't know how exactly, but they know we're involved. If Grey or I return here things will never get back to normal. There are police on the island now. They've been here ever since last summer. They watch us. They watch Nico. If we come back, sooner or later Nico will try to start up the operation again. I know he will. And sooner or later, he'll get caught. If we leave, he'll accept it. He'll know it's the end. And eventually—well, the authorities will know it's over, too. They'll pack up, and they'll go. They'll leave Nico and his family and the island in peace. No trouble. No incidents. The way it always used to be . . .' He broke off, and she could hear the strain in his voice.

'I've thought about this and thought about it. I've argued it back and forth, with Grey. With Nico. And we've decided. We must leave. I've accepted it now.' He paused. 'That is—I had accepted it. And then you came. That made it harder.'

Rebecca felt her blood grow slow and chill; a little knot of pain settled around her heart, and caught in her throat.

'Why?' she heard herself say in a small voice.

'You know why.' He turned to her impulsively, lifted his hands in the dark, and cradled her face up to his. 'Because I want you . . .' He hesitated. 'Very much. More than I can say . . .'

'Then let me come with you,' she cried impulsively. 'Please, Cal. Let me . . .'

'No. It's too dangerous.'

'I don't care. It doesn't matter . . .' Her voice rose. 'If you won't do that, then let me come to you later, somewhere else, wherever you like. I'll meet you. Join you. Please. We could . . .'

'No.'

'Why not? Oh, why not?' She turned to him pleadingly, not caring any more that he should hear the pain she felt, all pride gone.

'It wouldn't work.' He moved away from her roughly. 'Rebecca, you're too young, you'd get hurt. I'd hurt you and I don't want that. You're sweet and impetuous, and you don't realise what you're saying and no . . .' He lifted his hand and placed it lightly over her lips as she tried to interrupt him. 'No. I'm not going to argue about it. That's it. I've decided, and I know I'm right. Just believe me, understand. There are reasons . . . factors . . . that make it impossible.'

The finality in his voice cut her to the quick. She sat for a moment very still, her mind working with a curious vivid speed, a flow, like dreaming. A thousand incoherent memories and thoughts flashed into her head, then she felt herself steady, her mind still, and she knew that what she felt, and thought, was of great simplicity. She loved him, she thought, and for a moment the power of the emotion, welling up in her in silence in the dark, was so intense that she thought he must hear her feelings as clearly as if she had given them voice. She loved him; beyond that she could not see or think.

Carefully, as he sat silent beside her, she reached out her hand to him.

'All right,' she said, with a meekness she did not feel. 'All right. But may I ask you something . . . Two things?'

She thought he smiled. There was a pause, and then he said, a little sadly, 'Of course. What are they?'

'If you take the men off the island tomorrow night—during the celebrations—if you need distractions while that is going on, will you let me help you? I think I could.'

'You might.' He hesitated. 'I had thought of that too. If there was no danger—yes, there might be a way, something you could do . . .' He paused, and she felt his gaze. 'And the second thing?'

'What time is it?'

'Late. One in the morning . . .'

'When must you leave here?'

'In two—three hours' time. When it starts to get light. The men are sleeping now. They will stay in the caves. But at dawn I have to meet Nico.' She had reached her hand up to his face, and felt him frown. 'The second thing?' he prompted.

'Stay with me here,' she said softly, touching his lips with her fingers. 'Oh won't you? Stay with me until then. Until dawn. Until you have to go . . .'

She felt him draw back, just a little. A sigh escaped his lips. Very gently she took his hand, and guided it to her breast. At the touch of her flesh she felt him start, and she summoned all her willpower, all her resolve, all the certainty she felt, and pushed it out to him through the dark.

'Stay,' she said softly and insistently. 'Just this once. Just this night. You're leaving tomorrow. Please. I promise never to ask you for anything else. Cal. Give me this night. These hours. This dark. Please, Cal . . .'

She reached up and kissed him gravely and chastely on the mouth. She felt his resistance, then sensed his slow surrender. His lips quickened against hers. She heard her heart beat very loud, and pressed his hand against its hammering. He sighed.

'Cal . . .' she said once more, and with a great winging sense of peace, she drew him down beside her.

They stood under the trees, under the olives where, that first day, he had stopped her. The first light of the morning was slanting through the trees; the horizon was cloudy, pinkish; the birds had begun to sing. Cal took her in his arms, and looked down at her. His eyes shone darkly, and his face was troubled. Rebecca met his eyes; she felt that the joy she felt must light her face, and hoped it did, hoped he saw it. He held her gently:

'Last night . . .' He hesitated, awkwardly. 'I knew you weren't badly hurt. I came back to you as soon as I could. I knew they'd tied you, and—Oh Rebecca.' He broke off, then smiled at her sadly. 'I know what you thought. But I came to release you, not to hurt you . . .'

'I know that. Now I know that. I was frightened. That's all. It doesn't matter now . . .' She pressed her hand against his lips.

'But it does.' He frowned. 'Rebecca, you should have told me. If I'd known I wouldn't have . . .'

'I know,' she said simply. 'That's why I didn't tell you. I wanted you to be the first. I'm glad you were.' She drew away from him quickly. 'I'll go now . . .'

He hesitated, then clasped her to him strongly, held her for a moment, burying his face in her hair. Then he drew back, and although she could see anxiety and consternation in his eyes, she could see also that his resolution had come back.

'I must go to Nico.'

'I know . . .' She stepped back.

'But I'll meet you as planned.'

'Until then.'

'You'll be safe?'

'Quite safe.' She turned. 'Goodbye, Cal.'

He didn't answer her. Their eyes met, just for a moment, then, abruptly, he turned and disappeared through the trees.

Rebecca stood still for a moment. She was wearing an old sweater of Cal's over her torn dress, and she held it close around her for a moment. She looked back to the cliff meadow, with its secret cave beneath it, and to the lightening sky, and then up to the silver grey branches of the olives. Her heart lifted. Somewhere, she knew, sadness lay in wait for her. But not yet, she thought, she would not let it come to her yet.

She began to run down the path, slowly at first, and then faster, feeling a wild happiness, feeling part of the new day, the dawn and the birds' singing. Not yet, she thought, as she found the bike and lifted it. Tomorrow, when Cal had gone, perhaps, but not yet.

She climbed on to the bike. Before day she would be in Gaios.

CHAPTER EIGHT

WHEN she reached the flat she saw Nicky's window was still shuttered. She paused outside the house, looking along the quay. The Andropoulos yacht was still there, but there was no sign of life on it; the curtains of its cabin windows were still drawn. Quietly she let herself into the flat, and crept into the bathroom. She showered, and washed her hair. She bundled up the torn black dress, and hid it at the back of her cupboard. Then she dressed carefully—one of her prettiest frocks, pale blue cotton with cap sleeves edged with lace. It showed off her tan, and her slender figure, and today, dealing with Michael and with Carstairs, as she and Cal had planned, she wanted to look her best.

When she was dressed, she made herself some coffee, padding out to the tiny kitchen in bare feet. She was grateful for the cool of the tiled floor under her feet; even so early it was already hot, and there was a haze over the water—that meant it would get hotter still.

She took the strong black coffee back into her bedroom, and curled herself up on the window seat. Then, slowly, meditatively, she began to comb out her long dark hair. From here she could watch the yacht, and she could think.

She bent her head; the comb slipped through her hair; she thought of the night, and the cave, and of Cal, and the sweetness of the memory pierced her to the quick; she felt her body pulse as if he touched her still. She was glad of what she had done; her spirit rejoiced at it, and she knew it had been right. If Cal was to leave, if, after tonight, she was not to see him again, and he had spoken of his leaving with such finality that she accepted it—if he was to leave, then she was doubly glad. This memory would remain with her always; she hoped it would remain with him, too. Their union had seemed to her to be inevitable, and of a curious magic, part of the island, the fulfilment of some spell it wove. She smiled to herself, hugging the memory to her: she thought of Aphrodite, the most

127

dangerous of the gods, born on the sea foam, the giver and the destroyer, and she felt a cool fatalism take possession of her. She had had the goddess' gift; she would not think ahead to the reckoning—not yet at least, not yet.

She thought of Cal, who was not fatalistic, who, for all his love of Greece and the Greeks, would, she thought, never achieve that strange equilibrium they could show, in both triumph and disaster. No, Cal was all struggle, all effort. She sensed fight in him, that he fought against circumstance, against injustice, against human nature, even against himself, rebelling, combatting, those things he saw around him which he believed should change. She could imagine, she thought, the vain struggle he must have put up against his stepsister's worsening illness, and the anguish it must have cost him when the efforts failed. Usually, in such circumstances, people gave in; they comforted themselves with clichés: 'It's for the best,' 'One has to think of it as release.' She could never imagine Cal saying such things: Cal's reaction to adversity would be anger, a proud rage: and she admired that in him, pitying meanwhile the hurt it caused him. Last night she had felt that, in passion and in tenderness, their lovemaking had brought him some solace—she hoped that it was so.

On the yacht outside two crewmen had begun to swab decks; the night-fishing boats were returning to the quay, their catches glittering and writhing silver in their holds. From Nicky's room, she heard sounds of stirring. She stood up. It was time to put the first part of Cal's plan into action.

She breakfasted with Nicky, and then, as arranged, met Nico in the market square. They sat in the café, discussing plans for the party that night, and for Michael's 'feast', as if, just then, they had no other worry in the world. Two of Nico's younger sons joined them—one the little boy who had brought Rebecca the message the previous night—and they undertook to cycle off round the island, and pass on the invitation to all the guests staying at the villas. Then Nico, drawing back her chair for her, said he would take her down to the beach where the barbecue was planned—it was just the other side of the village.

The beach was deserted—a beautiful place where Rebecca

had often gone swimming. Wide, long and sheltered, fringed with olive groves, it was the perfect place for a party, and carefully Rebecca went over the plans. The fires for the barbecues would be here; friends of Nico's would arrange the delivery of all the food to be cooked, the chairs and tables, the lanterns; a group of musicians would play there; Nico had already arranged that Agape and his wife would take care of the second course—they were baking already, he said, there would be *paklava* and *kataifi*, and Agape would make her speciality, her famous *ghalaktoboureko*—a very fine crisp pastry with pine nuts and egg custard and a special syrup— she was famous for it. The salads, with feta cheese and olives, Rebecca would find all these were prepared by the evening; all she would have to do would be to supervise the cooking of the main dishes, the fish, the young lamb, the chickens, the fresh okra, and aubergines, the kebabs and the rice. There would be plenty of helpers, one of his daughters and his niece would be bringing all their friends; he thought there would be red mullet, caught that morning, and perhaps some lobsters.

'Nico—there will be nothing left for me to do . . .' Rebecca smiled at him, and glanced at him sideways.

'You will be occupied enough, I think.' He had been staring out to sea, a slight frown knitting his brows. Now he turned to her, and she saw that his face was serious. She nodded quickly, knowing he did not refer to the food or the party, and with a quick gesture he turned to her, caught her hands, and pressed them between his.

'*Efaristo*, Rebecca, *efaristo* . . .' he said. He hesitated. 'After—you are staying on the island, *ne*?'

'Yes. I shall be staying,' Rebecca answered quietly.

She saw a moment's puzzlement in his dark eyes, but he was naturally courteous, and he asked no further questions, but merely nodded.

'You shall have friends here,' he said simply. 'Always.'

Rebecca pressed his hand in return, touched by the warmth with which he spoke.

'We Greeks . . .' he paused. 'It is sacred for us, the debt of gratitude, you know? If ever I, or my family, or my friends . . . If we can ever be of help to you, you have only to ask. You will remember that, *kyrie* . . .'

'I shall remember. Thank you, Nico.'

He released her hand, and they turned back to the path. Nico glanced back at the sea, and then up at the sky. Again Rebecca saw he frowned.

'There will be a storm,' he said, as they began the climb back to the village. 'I can smell it in the air, and see it in the water.' He paused, lifting his hands in that odd fatalistic gesture Rebecca had come to know so well.

'Not tonight. I hope not tonight,' he added.

Rebecca left Nico in the market square, and then made her way to the offices. When Michael was on the island he liked to have a meeting with his staff each morning, to check on their movements for the day, and to make sure that all the work that needed to be done, and any last minute emergencies, would be taken care of. The meeting—just herself, Michael and Nicky that day—was due to begin at ten, and when Rebecca opened the office door, she knew she was in luck. Michael and Nicky had been deep in conversation; when she opened the door, they both started guiltily, and Nicky blushed bright scarlet. Rebecca greeted them casually enough, and went to make coffee, smiling to herself. Clearly, just as she had intended, the things she had told Nicky at breakfast had been repeated to Michael without delay.

When she rejoined them she sat down in a chair, and yawned ostentatiously. Michael and Nicky exchanged glances, and Michael suppressed a grin.

'Been out on the tiles, Rebecca? I thought you were going home when you left me last night?'

'No, no,' Rebecca said airily. 'I was going out . . . I was a bit late. I'm fine though. I've seen Nico, we've been down to the beach—everything's in hand.'

'Good. Good.' Michael gave a knowing smirk. 'Now, if we can just run over the details. Timing, who's coming exactly, that sort of thing . . .'

They went over the details exhaustively. Then they went over the guest-list. The honeymoon couple on Anti-Paxos were coming over; the Templars were coming, and the Templar children except the baby; some of the more recent arrivals . . .

'The Sullivans,' Nicky put in, and Michael grinned.

'Well, I didn't think they'd stay away, not if you're going to be there, Nicky. Now. Who else?' He consulted his clipboard lists, and then looked up suddenly at Rebecca.

'Cal? Cal Ryder? What about him?'

He made Rebecca jump, and she had no difficulty in blushing. 'Oh yes . . .' she said tentatively. 'I . . . I think so. He said he would come.'

'Oh? You've seen him then?' Michael's gaze became more intent, and again Rebecca repressed a smile. Since she had, that morning, given Nicky a highly coloured and innaccurate account of a 'dinner-date' with Cal Ryder which had ostensibly taken place the previous night, and since she was quite certain Nicky had wasted no time in passing on this piece of gossip to Michael, he knew perfectly well that she had. She glanced at him demurely, however, and lowered her eyes.

'Oh—yes. I ran in to him. I mentioned it. He seemed—quite keen to come.'

'I can imagine,' Michael said dryly, and Nicky giggled.

Rebecca, deciding the moment had come, gave what she thought was a pretty passable imitation of shy embarrassment. 'In fact . . .' she went on. 'I meant to ask you, Michael, and now we're on the subject, Cal—Mr Ryder that is—he did ask if I could meet him, up at the Villa Circe at lunchtime, today. He's moving in to the villa tomorrow, as you know, and there's quite a lot of—er—last minute arrangements to make. And, as everything's in hand for tonight, I thought you wouldn't mind, that . . .'

She let her voice trail away.

'Lunchtime?' Michael raised an eyebrow. 'Well, yes, of course, Rebecca.' He paused, and gave a dry cough. 'Yes. If Cal—Mr Ryder that is—Nicky, please, there's no reason to laugh—If Cal wants some help settling in, then of course you must give it. You won't be away too long, though, will you?'

'Oh *no*,' Rebecca breathed. She clasped her hands together and raised shining eyes to Michael. '*Thank* you . . .'

Nicky made a gurgling noise. 'The *beds*,' she said. 'I mean—you won't forget to check the *beds*, will you, Rebecca? After all, the place gets very damp, and it hasn't been aired for months, and lying on damp beds can make you terribly *stiff...*'

'Yes, yes, well, that's enough of that, I think,' Michael said quickly. 'Now, before we get on with the rest of the work—are there any other problems?'

There were not, and the meeting ended soon after. Rebecca spent the rest of the morning preparing for the dinner that night, and then, about twelve, made her way back to the square where she had parked her moped. Her heart lifted when she saw that, across the square, seated at one of the café tables with Michael and Nicky were Clickey Carstairs and his wife, and the Greek official, Costas Andropoulos. Apart from Costas, who sat sprawled on his small chair, his eyes moving lazily over the square, no one noticed her arrival; the other four were deep in conversation. Purposefully Rebecca made her way to their table.

'No, please,' she said, as the men started to rise to their feet. 'I'm not staying. I just wanted to check with Michael.' She paused; they were all looking at her expectantly. 'Is it all right if I go up to the Villa Circe now, Michael? I shouldn't be too long...'

She was rewarded; neither Carstairs nor Costas said anything, but she caught the minutest of glances pass between them. Costas' brown eyes lifted to her face with new interest.

'Rebecca's helping Cal Ryder move into the villa,' Michael said, just as she had hoped he would.

Carstairs gave her a wide smile. 'Oh, really?' he drawled. 'He's staying on then? Good. Jonquil's longing to meet him, and I don't know, I thought he might be leaving—something you said yesterday, Michael. Must have got hold of the wrong end of the stick...'

He raised his eyes speculatively to Rebecca, and she gave him a sunny smile. 'Oh *no*,' she said with emphasis. 'Cal's going to be here for *months*. He's just been waiting for the Villa Circe to have some repairs done ... It looks marvellous now. The roof's fixed, and the damp—and the landing stage is like new now ...'

It was enough. The hint registered with both men; she saw a slight tensing in their limbs, another quick shared glance. She held out her hand. 'Goodbye—Mr Carstairs. Mrs Carstairs.

Mr Andropoulos. So nice to run into you again. And thank you for the lovely party yesterday . . .' She began to turn away, then turned back, as if the thought had just struck her. 'But you'll be here tonight, I hope? You'll be coming to our party? You must—we're laying on a feast, and there'll be music, and Mr Ryder will be there . . .'

'Oh, certainly, certainly.' Carstairs gave her a small cold smile. 'We wouldn't dream of missing it, would we, Jonquil?' Jonquil, who had in fact hardly been listening to this conversation, and certainly exhibited little interest in meeting Cal Ryder, gave a little jump. She smiled a practised diplomatic wife's smile.

'Oh *yes*,' she murmured breathily. 'Delightful. We're *so* looking forward to it . . .'

Rebecca lifted her hand in a quick wave, and turned away with a smile. Glancing back, as she reached the far side of the square, she saw that Costas was watching her departure thoughtfully. The others had already bent their heads again in conversation. Good: Rebecca hoped profoundly that Nicky and Michael were regaling them with gossip. If they believed she and Cal Ryder were close, were romantically involved, so much the better. Then, she knew, they would watch her, thinking that through her they could watch Cal. They would be wrong, of course—after tonight, very wrong. But it served her purposes.

Half an hour later, she met Cal at the Villa Circe. He took her hand, and led her out on to the terrace, so their figures were outlined against the sky. At the bottom of the track that led up to the villa a Greek whom Rebecca had never seen before on the island, was laboriously loading stone from the roadside on to a cart. Out to sea, about half a mile off, a fishing boat rested, apparently at anchor. Cal took her in his arms, and kissed her. It was a long embrace. When he drew back a little, Rebecca laughed softly.

'You fraud,' she said, against his ear. 'Whose benefit was that for? The labourer's or the fisherman?'

'Both.' Cal met her eyes; his sparkled with a glint of mischief. 'For mine also, however . . .'

Rebecca frowned, as if in disbelief, and he kissed her again, even more thoroughly, as if to remove all doubt that he spoke the truth. When he had finished, and she had recovered her composure, she told him of her successes that morning, and he smiled grimly.

'Good. Excellent. So—they think we're having a wild affair, that I'm staying on the island for a while at least, and that I'll be using the landing stage here to bring the men in—you didn't get any hint, any suggestion, that they knew they were here already?'

'Nothing.' Rebecca shook her head emphatically. 'They picked up on the landing-stage repairs, just as you wanted. They'll be watching this villa, I'm certain of it—well, they already are, by the look of it.'

'Oh, I think so. But we want to keep it that way. That's excellent.' Cal's tanned fingers began softly to massage the skin at the base of her neck.

'And they think we'll be together tonight—at the party?'

'I think so. I told them we would be. They'll watch us just the same, I suppose, but they'll expect us to be together.' She paused. 'Just as you wanted,' she finished, fighting down the ache that she knew crept into her voice.

But Cal heard it; his arms tightened around her, and he cradled her against him. He kissed her forehead, gently, and tenderly, but he said nothing more. Rebecca swallowed.

'Anyway,' she went on, her voice gaining strength again. 'As of now, the excuse is that I'm helping you move in. But none of them believed that. Actually, this is a romantic tryst . . .'

'Good.' Cal smiled. 'Then perhaps we should give them their money's worth. Shall we go inside?'

He drew her gently by the hand through the shadowed doorway, and into the cool interior of the villa. Rebecca trembled a little, and his hand tightened around hers. He led her into the main bedroom that faced out to sea, and then, crossing to the window, closed the shutters. He turned back to her.

'I think we'll disappoint them this much, don't you?' he said dryly. 'Subterfuge is all very well. But I don't intend to have my lovemaking witnessed through a telescopic lens . . .'

He looked at her, across the shadowed room, and at his

words Rebecca felt a sweet weakness take possession of all her limbs. His face grew serious, and he crossed back to her, tilting her face up to him, and looking down into it, his eyes dark, and a little sad. 'How long do we have?'

'An hour . . . not more than an hour . . .' Rebecca said. Her throat was very dry, and her voice faltered.

He drew her to him with great gentleness, and slipping his hands beneath the cotton of her frock, eased it down from her shoulders, so her throat, and her breasts were suddenly laid bare. A sigh shook him; he caught her against him roughly, and Rebecca gasped as she felt the hardness of his body, the warmth of his skin against her. Instantly her body responded to him. *This might be the last time*: the thought spun into her mind, heightening the eroticism of the moment with a new and painful urgency. She clung to him, knowing her body had yearned for the release of his touch and his thrust, every moment since she left him. That he felt the same want and the same need, she had not a second's doubt: she could feel it arc through his body, this longing, as it arced through hers; their bodies spoke with more eloquence than any words.

Fiercely he drew her to the bed; their fingers fumbled with impatience at their clothes. When they were naked, he caught her against the length of his body with a low cry. She reached for him, feeling his flesh leap at her touch, and he entered her almost at once, slipping into her body, taking her down, straight down to a place where darkness moved and swelled like the sea.

He came quickly, shuddering against her, his body outpacing hers, but Rebecca was content. She lay, tranquil in his arms, desire for him eddying through her veins, lapping her, pulsing up through her like a gentle tide. And then, almost at once, she felt him stir once more. He bent his mouth to her breasts; he lifted her body up to him; their limbs entwined, relaxed, moved, and entwined once more. Slowly this time, gently at first, then with a mounting fierceness, he made love to her anew. He could make her respond; he knew it. She saw his eyes darken with the triumph of possession as her head fell back against the pillow, her throat arched to him, and her body opened, opened to him.

'Oh my darling,' he said once, and the sound of his voice,

the other things he said, his passion and his dispassion, his urgency and his control, all this quickened her flesh. She felt the pale globes of her breasts harden under the rough suck of his mouth, she felt herself moist, felt their skin touch like silk with their sweat as he moved on her. She felt heat build and build intolerably, fiercely, in the dark caves of her body, felt him move, withdraw almost, so she cried out, then thrust more fiercely.

'Now,' he cried, his lips against hers, and out of the dark, light pulsed through her blood, and she came with him to the hammer of his heart.

After, bewildered, shaken, she cried a little, and he held her until their breathing stilled. They slept, and Rebecca dreamed, but even in sleep their bodies stirred against one another, as if they must touch, must make love again, as if nothing could satiate this demon each had awakened in the other's flesh. Later they showered, and there, again, under the stream of water, as it gushed over their heads and throats, desire made them catch suddenly at each other with quick impatient hands, and he took her, standing up, under the rush of the water, their climax then not tender at all as before, but angry, fierce, quickened by the knowledge that they must part.

Out on the terrace he pressed his hand between her thighs, and kissed her mouth. Below them the Greek labourer straightened up, as if resting a moment from his labours, and, out at sea, there was a tiny flash of light on glass, there and then gone. Cal drew back, and Rebecca, looking up at his face, at the strong planes of his cheeks, the dark shadow of his eyes thought, just for a second, *He cannot go. Not now. He cannot* . . . Then she saw his mouth tighten, and she knew that already he was remembering the men in the cave, the expedition that night, and that with a man's greater ease his mind was already moving away from the pull of their lovemaking, back to his main preoccupation, back to practicalities.

It was not so for her, but she did not resent the facility in him. She lowered her eyes, hoping he could not read her mind, and started to turn away.

She saw her own shadow move and waver over the paving;

he held back, then, suddenly went after her. At the top of the steps he gripped her tight again.

'Remember, Rebecca,' he said, with a sudden fierceness. 'We can do that, at least. I shall. Remember . . .'

She didn't answer him; she could not, then, have trusted herself to speak. She half nodded, turned quickly away, and as she reached the bottom of the steps he lifted his hand. The gesture was a little false—for the benefit of the man below, no doubt. 'Until tonight,' he called, a little too loudly. 'We'll meet by the church? Yes? Before the procession?'

'Yes,' she called back, waving also. 'I'll see you then . . .' For a moment she saw him, tall, dark and still, outlined against the light. Then she set off. When, at the bottom of the track, she greeted the workman, she glanced back. The terrace was already empty.

'You're not getting into this too deep, are you, Rebecca?' Nicky linked her arm through her friend's, and glanced at her curiously. They were setting off to the procession; they paused on the quay; it was not the first of Nicky's questions that evening.

Rebecca shrugged. 'I don't know what you mean . . .'

Nicky came to a halt, and turned Rebecca round so she faced her. Her plump features wore, Rebecca saw, an expression of genuine worry and concern.

'Yes, you do,' she said firmly. 'You know quite well. Oh, come off it, Becky, I'm not an innocent, even if you are. You look . . .' she hesitated. 'Well, if you want to know, you look like a woman in love—and one who's been making love too, come to that. Sort of, I don't know, flushed, and glowing at the same time, and a bit languorous as well, as if half the time you were thinking about him, and whatever it is you two have been up to together . . .' She broke off abruptly, her teasing tone failing her. 'You know what I mean,' she said, more gruffly. 'You look beautiful; these last few days you've really come alive. Everyone can see it—even old Michael. It's highly alluring, you know, as if you're giving off some extraordinary charge. And now you've bought a new dress, and you're actually wearing some make-up for once, which I've never seen you do, and . . . Oh, Becky . . .' She caught something in

Rebecca's eyes even as she spoke, and her own face suddenly crumpled with an odd, almost comic dismay. 'Look,' she said. 'Tell me to mind my own business if you like—but watch yourself, will you do that? I'm fond of you, you know, and it was me got you out here, and I'd hate you to be hurt . . .'

'Why should I be hurt?' Rebecca looked at her closely. Nicky lowered her eyes in embarrassment, and then shrugged.

'You know,' she said. 'Cal Ryder. I mean—it's all so sudden, and . . . oh, God.' She pressed Rebecca's arm. 'He's bad news, Becky. Believe me. Listen to me, before it's too late.'

'Maybe it's too late already.' Rebecca tilted her chin, and met her eyes challengingly. 'And why is he bad news?'

'He just is. You remember the stories I told you? He's ruthless, Becky. Be sensible—it's OK for him, maybe he suddenly feels like a holiday romance, who knows? But what's going to happen at the end of the season? He'll go back to London, or Paris, or New York. And you'll be left nursing a broken heart. Or worse . . .'

'Nonsense.' Rebecca felt her lip tremble, and she turned away. 'Cal isn't like that . . .'

'Isn't he?' Nicky paused. There was a little silence. Nicky shifted her feet miserably, and looked down at them, and Rebecca, strained by pretence, and by genuine concern, fought down the anxiety. She would not prompt her; she would not listen. It wasn't true. If Cal was leaving, and leaving much sooner than Nicky realised, it didn't mean he didn't care for her, she told herself passionately. In his way, he did, she believed it. What had happened was special to him, as it was to her, and if she didn't understand why they must part, she could accept it, none the less. It didn't mean Cal felt nothing, that he was just using her . . . She swallowed, and in a low voice Nicky went on.

'You see—that girl Rosalie,' she said, her voice miserable now, so Rebecca had no doubt that she would, for once, much rather not tell this story, 'the one who worked out here, the one who was nuts about him—you remember? Well, I didn't tell you all the story . . .' She hesitated, and Rebecca felt a sick surge start up below her heart. 'The thing is—well, Rosalie doesn't give up easily. She got nowhere here, true enough.

But, in London, it was about two years ago ... Oh, I don't know the details, but she went to some conference Cal was speaking at, and afterwards she went up to him, and re-introduced herself as it were, and—well, the long and the short of it was they ended up going out to dinner, and then they went back to her flat. Maybe Rosalie came on strong, I don't know, she was quite capable of it, and she was very pretty in a chocolate-boxy kind of way. Anyway, according to her, they went to bed together. She said that, before they did, he warned her, said he didn't intend to get involved, the usual sort of thing, she didn't believe it, being her. So, they spent the night together—and he was incredible she said, *it* was incredible, and then——' She paused, and Rebecca stared stonily straight in front of her.

'And then, well, he dropped her. And how. Quite viciously. Wouldn't contact her, hung up on her when she tried to ring him, and finally told her in no uncertain terms that she was a one-night stand and as far as he was concerned, she could go to hell ...' Nicky broke off and shrugged. 'There you are. End of story. I don't pass judgment, I don't exactly blame him. He was honest at least. But—this is the point—according to Rosalie she wasn't the first or the last that he'd treated like that. Later on, she heard stories. How he'd use someone— take up with them for a night, a week, a month, never much longer, and then drop them just the way he dropped her. She wasn't altogether a fool, though she could be daft about men. She said he only had room for one love in his life, and that was his work. Period. So—if you can accept that, if you don't mind that, fine, go ahead, forget I spoke. But I know you, Rebecca, I've known you since school, and you can't fool me. I always thought that sooner or later you'd fall, and when you did it would be heavier than anyone. You're not the type to brush things off, say, oh well, that was just an affair, on to the next one. You're not like that. Are you, Becky?'

There was a little silence. Rebecca felt a bleak despair enter her heart and settle there.

'Oh, I don't know,' she said at last, making her voice light to hide the pain in it. 'I can always learn I suppose. Thank you, Nicky. I know you meant well. But let's not talk about him any more, OK? Please ...' She took her friend's arm, and began to pull her towards the square where, already, the lanterns were lit and people were gathering. 'Please,' she said again, as Nicky held back. 'I don't want to think about it. I don't want to worry. Not tonight. Tonight it's a festival ... Come on, Nicky ...'

Nicky hesitated, then shrugged and allowed herself to be drawn along the quay. They passed the Andropoulos yacht, which was blazing with lights, though there was no sign of its occupants, and finally reached the square. Nicky's face wore a sulky, slightly sullen expression, and she said nothing as they walked; Rebecca knew she resented the fact that her advice was not being taken, as she thought, and Rebecca registered her displeasure, but said nothing. She couldn't explain to Nicky, not now, and she had, somehow, to control the pain and the anxiety which she could feel spiralling inside her. She set her mouth tight, and deliberately wrenched her thoughts away: she had to trust her own instincts, she thought passionately; she trusted Cal, she accepted what he had told her, and if she stopped trusting him now, because of a piece of old gossip, what did that make her?

When they reached the square it looked so lovely, so magical, that it helped to ease her spirits. The light was paling to pearl grey: the square itself, and all the small boats that bobbed against the quay, were decorated with hundreds of paper lanterns. They hung from the masts of the sailing boats, they hung in necklaces between the oleander trees, glowing like jewels, ruby red, emerald, sapphire, and topaz. All the tables outside the cafés were lit with candles, and crowded. Between them the waiters hurried with golden bottles of restina, with glasses of clear ouzo, saucers of lemon, and black olives. The air was rich with the scent of flowers and the dark smell of Turkish coffee. The entrance to the tiny white church had become a bower of flowers, wild orchis, gathered from the hills of the island, intertwined with green ferns and dried palm leaves. Everywhere there were children, in a state of high excitement, running after one another, weaving in and out of the crowds that were gathering, calling to one another ...

Rebecca looked around her with pleasure, and felt her heart lift a little. She recognised many faces: the Templars, the Sullivan cousins, the honeymoon couple, sitting slightly apart from the others, their arms around each other. On the far side of the square, she saw, growing more alert, that Michael had assembled a large table: Carstairs was there, looking like a parody of an Englishman abroad, in a white suit, worn with an incongruous panama hat, which even as she watched, he removed, so that he could mop his brow with a large white handkerchief. Next to him, resplendent in turquoise silk, her hair bound up in a turquoise turban, her majestic bosom sporting three rows of pearls, was Jonquil. Next to her was Costas Andropoulos, wearing a dark suit.

As Rebecca glanced in his direction she saw him turn and say a few words to a man who stood just behind their table. The man bent forward to listen, nodded, then melted away into the shadows. Costas leaned back in his seat; lazily his eyes roved over the square and the press of people. Rebecca shrank back a little behind the Sullivans, who had come across to greet Nicky, and looked at the crowd with closer attention. Many islanders she recognised, and of course families staying in the villas. Nico was there, with Leandros and their wives, Yianni, who ran the best taverna on the island . . . But there were also, she realised, a number of faces she did not recognise: men, Greeks, unobtrusively dressed, but somehow slightly alien, outsiders, she felt it instinctively. She began to count the strangers, four, six, a group in the corner, talking together, there must have been a dozen at least, perhaps more. She felt certain they were police of some sort, and that it was Costas Andropoulos who was responsible for them. None approached him, but all, like him, kept their eyes on the crowd. They moved, they mingled, but they never relaxed for an instant.

She tensed, only half attending to the Sullivans and to Nicky and then she heard the music, and the singing. It was still a little in the distance, but others in the crowd heard it too, and a general cry went up. Nicky touched her arm.

'Look——' She pointed in the direction of the olive groves above the village. 'The procession is coming . . .'

Rebecca looked. At first she saw very little, just flickering light behind the soft grey shapes of the olive trees. It appeared and disappeared, as on the night air the sound of women's voices and the pluck of strings drifted at first clearly then less distinctly. Then, as they came out of the grove, she saw them: at the head of the procession the black robes and tall headdress of the priest; above him, fluttering in the air, a gorgeous banner of gold and silks enbroidered with an effigy of the patron saint of the island; behind it others, banners of saints and banners of angels, lit by the light of torches, swaying on their poles, advancing down the hillside. Behind the priest came a group of men, their heads and necks bared, and behind them the young girls of the island, dressed in white, garlanded with flowers, each holding in front of her a flickering taper, their voices raised in the lilt of a Greek hymn. Behind them came the musicians, some of them children, some of them men: the hymn they played was not sad nor sonorous, but gay and triumphant, an affirmation of Easter. Over the sound of the strings, she could hear the rattle of tambourines, the shake of silver bells, the insistent beat of little drums.

She caught her breath at the loveliness of it; the crowd stirred, all over the square people began to stand up, for a moment even the children stilled. And then, across a space in the crowd which opened like a path, magically, she saw Cal. He was wearing black; a stranger might have taken him, momentarily, for a Greek, an islander, until they noted his height, and the easy negligence of his dress, which was European. He saw Rebecca in the same instant, and halted; he lifted one hand in the slightest of signs, and in a second, hardly conscious of moving, she sped across the square to his side. He caught her, and held her against him for a second. Rebecca shut her eyes. Her senses reeled with the scent of lilies, the rustle of palm leaves, the chime of bells. Then she opened her eyes and looked up at him; the dark eyes met hers, he pressed her arm in secret greeting, a lover's touch in a crowd, eloquent only to her. He smiled, and bent his head, seeing the question in her eyes.

'All well,' he said softly. 'Stay with me, Rebecca. Stay by my side . . .' He paused. 'Until I give you the signal . . .'

'The signal?' She looked up at him, hesitating.

'When I kiss you,' he said. 'When I kiss you like this,' and drew her to him.

CHAPTER NINE

FOR almost an hour the procession had wound around the streets of the village, at its head the banner of the saint, at its tail an ever-growing crowd: islanders, children, visitors. Now, at last, it had entered the little church, which was crammed with people to the doors, and beyond.

Rebecca and Cal, who had joined the procession just behind the musicians, and just ahead, Rebecca had noted, of two of the men, the strangers she had noticed earlier, were now in the main body of the church. Before them were three or four rows of simple rush-seated chairs, most of them occupied by island women, all wearing black, all with their heads scarved, all bent over their rosaries. Behind them was a more mixed congregation, many islanders, but also visitors, children who were constantly hushed, Michael's party, and, flanking the doors, several of the dark-clothed men, who stood, arms folded, heads half-bowed, eyes watchful.

But after a few minutes of the service, Rebecca forgot them all. She saw only the priest, gold vestments now worn over his black robes, as he moved back and forth, back and forth, before the cloth of the altar. The Greek Orthodox service was totally unfamiliar to her, and she had been unprepared for its beauty and its majesty. The air was heavy with incense, much of the service was sung, intoned by the priest in deep bass tones, the responses from the congregation higher and lighter. The music lifted her heart, and moved her close to tears, the more so because she wanted herself to respond, but knew none of the words, though their sense reached out to her. She bowed her head, knelt, stood, and then offered up a silent, awkward Anglican prayer, remembered from the colder and austerer churches of her childhood. Beside her Cal was very still. She imagined he must have been to such a service before on the island, she thought he might know the responses but he kept silent. His face, averted from hers, was tense, and closed.

Rebecca realised suddenly that this might be the first time

143

he had been in a church since the death of his stepsister, and her heart went out to him in sympathy. Instinctively she felt, had felt ever since he had told her that story, that Cal had proudly cut himself off from something he sought, which had been, before, a source of solace and strength to him, and which, the more he sought to deny, the greater its power over him. She bowed her head once more, and the church was suddenly still. The music stopped; the singing ceased, the candles guttered, and for an instant, so powerful had been the preceding invocation, the peace in the church was palpable. No one moved, even the children were silent. The priest stood, two palms lifted.

Then, slowly, there was rustling and movement. In front of them, observing island precedence, a very old woman was rising painfully and slowly to her feet. On either side the hands of younger women reached out to lift and aid her; with slow halting steps she passed along the narrow aisle, came to the step below the altar dais, stopped, and then knelt. She was followed by others; old women, young girls, then a young boy, then a group of men. All knelt, and Rebecca, seeing suddenly the chalice and the wafers, realised they had reached the moment of communion.

The space was limited. Each communicant took the wine, and the bread, and then crossed themselves, and then drew back, and another knelt and took their place. It was very quiet, and very calm; Rebecca watched, and felt the calm flow through her like a stream of water. Then, beside her, Cal stood up. He did not look at her, or touch her; he moved to the aisle, followed the others, knelt as they did, did as they did. He returned to his seat beside her, and for one quick moment, covered his face with his hands. They were shaking. Then gradually they stilled, he lowered them, and lifted his head.

For a moment Rebecca felt confusion: her mind groped after the little she knew about his religion, half-absorbed facts, things she had read, or heard spoken, all jumbled together, uncertain and messy. She felt a sudden lurch of alarm; surely for Cal to take communion he should first have gone to confession, and he must not have taken food or drink, and ... then, as suddenly as the anxiety had begun, it fell away, to be replaced with a great sense of joy. Apart from the niceties of dogma, this must mean that somehow, perhaps just now, tonight, in this tiny church, Cal had refound his faith. And in that she rejoiced, for she had seen something of the anguish which losing it had caused him.

The ceremony was over. Softly, as the last of the communicants rose, the singing began once more. Then the doors at the back of the church were flung open, the singing grew louder: the priest leading, the congregation began to file out. Cal took her arm, lightly, led her down the aisle and out into the close perfumed air of the square.

After the still of the church the noise and the movement were confusing. It was as if, the service over, all the emotions summoned up by it now spilled over, were translated, at once, with a wonderful Greek ease, into gaiety and celebration. As the last of the congregation came out, a band in the square struck up. The priest, Rebecca saw, now sat at a favoured table outside the café: a waiter was bringing him coffee and sweet cakes; one of the children was sidling up to him to feel the stuff of his robes. The lanterns bobbed amid the trees, the crowds milled back and forth, all the lights of the houses and the cafés shone bright against the darkness. There was a burst of laughter from one of the tables; someone was trying to dance. Rebecca stood still for an instant, drinking it in, the lights and the music, the dark sky above, all the stars obscured by cloud, the shifting black of the sea beyond the quay. On a fierce impulse, she turned to Cal, and touched his arm.

'I'm glad,' she said. 'Oh Cal—I'm so glad . . .'

He turned to her, half amused, the corners of his mouth lifting, 'Glad of what?'

'Everything,' Rebecca said, thinking he must know the chief source of her happiness.

He pressed his hand lightly over hers. 'I am too,' he said quietly.

When Rebecca and Cal reached the beach where the picnic feast was to be held, they were ahead of the crowd, though not of Michael, who was there already, rushing up and down the ranks of charcoal grills, inspecting a pot and a baking tray here, and great bowls of salad there, the chickens that sizzled on their spits, the lamb that was roasting.

'Thank goodness you're here,' he said impatiently, when he set eyes on Rebecca. 'I thought that service was never going to end. Oh, hello, Cal, glad you could make it. Now, Rebecca, tell me, it all looks OK, but is everything under control? There's a lot of people coming you know . . .' He looked at his watch agitatedly. 'It's gone eight already, I told people to start coming at half past, we ought to start serving the food at nine at the latest. That lamb doesn't look nearly cooked to me, and I can't see any plates, and—oh God, did you remember to ask Nico about the muscians?'

Rebecca smiled at Cal, and sighed. 'Michael,' she said patiently, 'everything's in hand, there's no need to worry. The lamb's nearly done, the chickens will be perfect in another half hour. The musicians will be here any moment, and all the plates and things are over there, under the tree, on the trestles . . .'

Michael gave a sheepish smile. 'And I can keep quiet and mind my own business and let the pro get on with it, you mean? OK. I'll let you take over, and I'll get out of your hair. Fancy a drink, Cal?' He took Cal's arm and began to draw him towards another trestle table, resplendent with bottles and glasses. 'How are you? Everything OK up at the Villa Circe? Yes, I only got in the day before yesterday—haven't laid eyes on you. Where have you been hiding yourself?'

With good grace Cal let himself be drawn aside, and Rebecca slipped away. She quickly and deftly completed the last preparations for the food, checked that everything that was needed was there and ready in place, and then joined Agape and a group of younger women, led by Nico's daughter, Ariadne, who were supervising the cooking of the chickens.

She pressed Agape's arm. 'Thank you,' she said. 'You've taken care of everything. There's nothing left for me to do . . .' She caught the flash of gold teeth as Agape smiled up at her. The younger girls giggled, and nudged one another. Rebecca saw them glance in Cal's direction, and then back at her, and caught a flood of whispered Greek. She sighed. Was it possible to keep anything secret on such an island? She thought the younger women would not know, but did Agape know, she wondered, what would be happening that night, on the other side of the island?

The men, making their way stealthily through the network of caves to the sea? The shallow, fast, inflatables that were prepared, and that would carry them, on the flood of the tide, over the lethal rocks, through the swell of water between arch and cliff, and then, fast, out to sea, to the lee of Anti-Paxos, where Grey Jameson, and another boat, the boat which would take them to the Greek mainland, awaited them? The plan—which Cal had only outlined to her, giving no details and no times, though she knew the tide would be in flood not long after midnight—the plan seemed to Rebecca fraught with danger, filled with a thousand details that could easily go wrong. Did Agape know of it too? Did she fear for Nico, as Rebecca feared for Cal? Did she think, as Rebecca did, that the device of attracting all attention to the Villa Circe, in the wrong part of the island, might fail? That rocks might catch the smooth rubber hulls of the inflatables? That, out to sea, patiently patrolling and watching, there might be ships that would be alerted by the noise of engines, by the presence of Grey's boat, however stealthily it had been brought in?

The questions sped through her mind as she looked down into Agape's lined face, and met the gaze of her faded but sharp brown eyes. For a moment fear, fear for Cal, gripped her; her hand tightened on Agape's arm, and something in the old woman's eyes seemed to register her feelings. Agape's face grew serious; she pressed Rebecca's arm; she glanced up at the sky. Rebecca followed her gaze, saw the heavy cloud, felt anew the heavy warmth of the air, and thought of what Nico had said about a storm. She looked back at Agape, dismay in her face, and Agape gave a magnificent shrug, as if with one defiant gesture she could dismiss it all, just with her human will: the chances of the undertaking, the danger of the sea, the threat of the elements, any ingenuity of Costas Andropoulos and his officers. Then she laughed, a full, throaty, wonderful, cracked laugh, and made that odd gesture which Rebecca had come to know so well: the hand lifted, palm upward: *leave it to the gods* . . .

Rebecca left her then, obscurely comforted, though whether

by Agape's cheerful fatalism, or by some well of superstitious instinct of her own, or, even, by what had passed that evening, she could not tell. Cal came to her side, quiet, attentive, never far away as she busied herself with the food; guests began to arrive, in twos and threes first, then in larger numbers. Soon, under the lanterns, the beach was full. The musicians arrived, and struck up: gay, driving village music that drowned out the sound of the sea, and drove away like demons the last of Rebecca's fears.

Gradually, as people began to queue up for food and for wine, the crowds began to resolve themselves into groups: but no matter how they shifted and moved, Rebecca saw that Carstairs and Andropoulos were never far away. Neither man was drinking; they both helped themselves liberally to food, and talked animatedly enough to those who joined them but, somehow, apparently without effort, they were never far away. Cal, Rebecca saw, neither ate nor drank; whenever she was close to him, she could sense the tension in his body. So attuned was she to him that she felt it acutely, yet no one else would have known, she thought, marvelling at his composure as, easily, charmingly, he helped others to food and wine, joined in their conversation.

She turned away, for a moment, to check the serving of the last helpings of rice and salad, and then, turning back, felt Cal's arm come around her shoulders.

'Miss Farrell—Rebecca, isn't it?' Carstairs was suddenly right next to them, smiling broadly.

'I simply must congratulate you on the food—absolutely delicious—what a feat! Can't be easy, preparing all this, out in the open and so on—and it's marvellous. Really terrific. Don't know when I last put away so much . . .' He paused, and smiled benignly upon Cal. 'I'm sorry, butting in. You must think me jolly rude. We haven't met, I think? I'm Carstairs, Hugo Carstairs—our embassy in Athens. Just over here on a quick Easter trip. Lovely island—like paradise, isn't it?'

Cal agreed gravely that it was, indeed, just like paradise, and Rebecca dutifully introduced them. Carstairs then took a slightly theatrical step backwards.

'No! You're Ryder? Gosh, my wife's absolutely dying to

meet you—great fan of yours. Now—where's she got to? Jonquil? Jonquil?' He peered around him as if expecting Jonquil to materialise from the bushes, and when she did not, turned back with a sigh.

'Just like a woman! With you one moment, disappeared the next. Where can she have got to, I wonder? She'll be furious if she misses you, absolutely furious . . .'

'No cause for alarm,' Cal said smoothly. 'The party is just beginning. Michael's parties tend not to get into their stride until midnight—and there'll be dancing soon. Perhaps your wife would honour me with a dance, later?'

'Oh, yes, certainly . . .' Carstairs looked momentarily disconcerted. 'Waltzing on the sands, what? Like the *Owl and the Pussycat*, Edward Lear, you know? How does it go? *Then hand in hand on the something sands, they danced to the light of the moon* . . . Very jolly.'

'Very,' Cal agreed solemnly. He glanced up at the sky. 'Except there is no moon tonight, of course. A shame that . . .' He looked at Rebecca and smiled. 'It's the only missing element in a perfectly romantic evening . . .'

Carstairs blinked. He looked from Cal to Rebecca and back to Cal. Rebecca, on cue, obligingly snuggled closer to Cal, who smiled charmingly at the discomfited Carstairs.

'I'm so glad you like the island,' Cal went on smoothly. 'It's very quiet and very beautiful. I've been coming here for years—are you staying long?'

Carstairs shuffled his feet. 'Not sure exactly,' he said. 'Depends rather. Not long I shouldn't think.'

'Well, perhaps, if you stay a few days, you and your wife would like to join me for lunch one day? I'm renting a rather marvellous villa—a bit remote, but the most magnificent view. We could arrange some fishing for you, if you were interested, couldn't we, Rebecca? You'd like that, I think. Are you interested—in fishing?'

There was the minutest of pauses, before the word 'fishing'. Rebecca caught it, and marvelled at Cal's insolence; Carstairs caught it too, and stared up at Cal, screwing up his eyes, clearly uncertain whether the words carried a hidden meaning, or were just a casual invitation.

'Oh yes. Er—yes,' he managed finally, as Cal smiled down

at him. 'Fine idea. Terrific. Jolly nice of you. I must mention it to Costas—Costas Andropoulos, we're here on his yacht—run into him, perhaps, have you?'

Now it was Cal's turn to scan the bushes around them as if one of them might conceal Andropoulos's portly person. He turned back to Carstairs with a smile of polite blankness. 'I don't think so,' he said. 'No, I don't think I've had that pleasure. He's here with you tonight?'

'Somewhere . . .' Carstairs craned his neck and scanned the crowds. 'Ah yes. Over there. Talking to Jonquil, my wife. I'd better join them—I'll tell them we've met. Jolly nice to run into you finally, heard so much and all that . . .'

He began to back away nervously and Cal called after him, his voice drawling.

'Do ask your wife to save me that dance—won't you?'

'Dance? Oh yes, yes . . . Certainly . . .'

Carstairs disappeared through the throng and Rebecca let out her breath in a long sigh of relief.

'That was wicked,' she breathed. 'And dangerous. He's not as stupid as he looks.'

Cal shrugged. 'He's the least of my worries. He's just HMG's minder, that's all. So, if anything happens, and a diplomatic row blows up, they've got someone here to quieten things down as much as possible. Try and keep my name and Grey's name out of it, that's why he's here, so the whole thing becomes an incident between Greece and Albania, no British involvement. It's not him that worries me, it's the Greek that brought him here . . .' He turned away with a tired gesture and Rebecca turned with him. For the moment they were alone, no one was in ear-shot, and she plucked at his sleeve.

'But Grey,' she said in a low voice. 'What about him? Won't they be watching him, too?'

'I think not.' Cal gave her a dry smile. 'It's a great advantage to have an established reputation as an alcoholic. As far as Carstairs and Andropoulos are concerned, Grey's on another of his benders. It began some while before he crashed Andropoulos's party on Corfu—the one where you met him—and it came to a fairly spectacular climax shortly after you left. A table got smashed and a lot of glasses broken, I believe. Grey doesn't do things by halves. He was carted off to a hospital on Corfu that he's been to before, and as far as they're concerned, he's still there, fighting off the DTs.' He smiled. 'It's another of the reasons that they're fairly relaxed. They think something might happen, it's true. But from their point of view it's likelier to happen when Grey's sobered up. In fact he was never drunk in the first place, and he's most certainly not languishing in a hospital bed. But we have some assistance there, and I'm pretty sure they don't know that. No—everything is going according to plan. Relax, Rebecca. Don't worry.' He pressed her arm. 'Listen, the music is starting again. We should dance. You know what to do, don't you?'

Rebecca nodded silently. 'What time is it?' she said.

'Eleven,' Cal said shortly, and Rebecca thought—*about an hour to go. And then I shall never see him again.*

She bent her head, biting her lip, and Cal drew her into his arms. 'Listen,' he said fiercely, his lips just by her ear. 'Listen, Rebecca. I wish it wasn't like this. I wish it with all my heart. I want you to believe that. Will you believe it?'

'Yes,' Rebecca said, and hoped it was true. She believed it now. She just hoped she'd go on believing it. After.

By the time the dancing began it was clear that Michael's copious supplies of wine and of Greek brandy, were beginning to take effect. The noise of conversation and laughter was becoming louder and increasingly uninhibited. First a few, and then more and more people were swept up into the dancing. To and fro the couples swirled over the sands. One of the Sullivan cousins attempted an energetic jive to bouziki music with Nicky, was defeated by the beat, and fell in a heap on the sands. The honeymoon couple withdrew to the privacy of the olives, where they could be glimpsed, locked in one another's arms. Jonquil Carstairs and her husband took up an extraordinary and stately foxtrot; some of the island men joined arms, and, shoulder to shoulder, began a glorious, wild, leaping Greek dance, punctuated with much shouting and thigh slapping.

In Cal's arms Rebecca was spun to and fro, close to the sea, back towards the trees, over to the musicians, where Costas Andropoulos stood alone, watching the dancing couples, and then back to the other side of the sands. Even old Agape was

dancing, with her husband; the island girls, shyly at first, and
then with increasing gaiety and delight, began another of
the village dances—linking arms, advancing and retreating,
advancing and retreating, to the ranks of their sweethearts
among the island men. It was a beautiful dance—very
decorous, very formal, for the island women, Rebecca knew,
were strictly watched over by their families, and guarded
until the day of their marriage. The magic of their dance,
and the lilting swooping music that accompanied it, drew
others to their ranks. Slowly, shyly at first, then gaining
confidence, some of the visitors to the island, Cal and
Rebecca included, took up the laughing gestures and the
invitations to join them, and took their places in the two
ranks.

Cal was opposite her. The men advanced; the women
retreated. Then the men drew back, and with formal swaying
steps the women advanced upon them. It was a mimicry of
courtship, a dance of love, and as she advanced and withdrew,
with Cal's tall, graceful figure now drawing closer, now
further away, Rebecca thought: Let me remember. Let me
remember him like this . . .

Then, as the dance drew to its stately conclusion, as if at a
signal, the musicians started up a new tune. People found
their partners again; couples began once more to circle, to
leap, upon the sands. Rebecca glanced to where the band
played, and frowned: a minute ago Nico had been among the
musicians. Now he was gone; his eldest son Demetrios had
taken his place. She stiffened, looked down at her watch. It
was a quarter to twelve.

One of the Sullivan cousins appeared, out of breath, at her
side, and demanded a dance; Cal, bowing gracefully, handed
her over. As she spun away, she glimpsed him again, leading
the majestic figure of Jonquil Carstairs on to the sands. The
Sullivan cousin danced like a dervish; what he lacked in skill
he made up for in speed. Gasping, made dizzy by his spins,
Rebecca saw olives, dancers, sea, olives, spin before her gaze
like pieces in a kaleidoscope. She glimpsed Nico—at least she
thought it was he, dancing with another island woman. She
saw Ariadne, his daughter, together with a friend, go up to
Costas Andropoulos, and laughing, brooking no denial,

tossing back their beautiful dark hair, draw him, too, into the throng.

Everyone was dancing—old Agape had Carstairs by the hand, and was drawing him over the sands with the energy and grace of a much younger woman. All the strangers, the dark quiet men who, all evening, had stood at the edges of the circle, they too were dancing, and they were getting caught up in it, she could sense it, in the mad gay vortex of the music, in the abandon of the dance.

She spun and saw that Jonquil was now dancing with her husband again, a quickstep now, not a foxtrot. She spun again, clutching on to the Sullivan boy to avoid losing her balance, and she saw Cal dancing with Nicky, more slowly than the others, Nicky saying something to him, she saw, above the tumult of the dance. Then she was spun again, the music quickened, and everyone began to change partners, spinning from one person to another so for a moment she was with Nico, a few steps, another spin and it was Michael who held her, then another islander she did not know, then one of the dark strange men, then Chris Templar, who laughed aloud as he gripped her.

'Isn't this marvellous?' he cried. 'Such fun! I'm being danced off my feet and I love it . . .'

And then, quite suddenly she was with Cal again; his hard arms held her close against his chest, so tightly she was almost suffocated, and before she knew what had happened, he had drawn her to one side of the circle, apart from the dancers, with their leaps and their whoops. And the music was changing, it was slowing, and the beat was becoming more insistent, and Cal had drawn her over to the trees, to a place she knew, a place Nico had pointed out to her, and her heart slowed, and her blood went cold, and she thought: *Now; it's now.* They were under one of the lanterns, clearly visible to any one of the dancers, should they look up at them, and Rebecca thought that some of them did, and might have halted, if their island partners had not urged them on.

And then Cal's arms came round her. Looking up into his face she saw it cold, and hard; purposeful, but also she thought angry, and that she did not understand. He turned her, like a puppet, like a doll, so her back was to the dancers.

He held her against his hard body, and ran his hand down her spine, until it lay across her flank, and he caressed her gently, with a gesture that anyone watching from the dance-floor must have seen. He did not speak; not one word; that was the hardest part. His eyes burned into hers for a second, a minute, an eternity, and then he bent his head and kissed her full on the mouth.

Rebecca wanted to cry out: it seemed so cruel that the last piece of duplicity should be a kiss. Her mind thronged with a million things she wanted to say to him, and ached with the knowledge that now, above all, she must say none of them.

He kissed her, and went on kissing her. Gradually, she realised that as he kissed her, he drew her out of the light and towards the shadow. She knew then, they had planned, he had instructed her, what she had to do.

And so, then, dutifully, she did it. She pushed him away, suddenly, as if he had just said or done something which went too far, and she half-wanted to stop him. Cal drew back, then moved to her again. He bent his lips to her hair, and to anyone watching it must have seemed so obvious: a man, pleading with a woman: the oldest scenario in the world. *Let me; No; Please; No; I beg you, I love you, please; Well, maybe, maybe . . .*

Except actually he said nothing, and she said nothing; it was a mime, no more. He apparently pleaded, she apparently resisted. He grew more importunate; his arms came around her again, he caressed her again; she weakened; she raised her hands to his face and apparently questioned him; he reassured her; he began to pull her away, away from the eyes of others, into the dark, into a place where, in private, they could continue their lovemaking.

One last apparent hesitation; one last apparently persuasive kiss which was like gall on Rebecca's lips. Then, and she let herself be led, he drew her out of the light and into the dark. They were in the trees; her heart was beating a trip-hammer refrain in her head; his breath was coming fast. Unaccustomed to the sudden dark she reached for him, felt him grasp her hands, draw her deeper and deeper into the olive grove, so she stumbled, though his feet were sure. Deeper; the music was muted now; then he stopped.

They stood apart, not touching, the pretence over. They were in a little dell, a grassy place, a ring of flowers and herbs beneath the bent trunks of the olives. Cal reached for her two hands, lifted them, and raised them to his lips. She thought he said her name; she had to bite her lips not to cry his. And then he was gone.

He moved like a wild creature, or a tracker, making no sound. One moment, in the dim light, she could see him; the next he had gone. She stood alone, staring at the greyish trunks of the trees, and then underfoot, to her right, she heard the crackle of a branch. She turned, and the young islander she had been expecting was at her side. Even in this light she could see he had been well chosen; tall for a Greek, he was near to Cal's height. He had the same build, the same darkness of hair, and he was wearing almost the same clothes. He hesitated; this Greek boy. His name was Alexis, she knew that much; and she knew that he was another member of Nico's huge island family, a cousin, she thought Cal had said. He was too young, no more than eighteen to Cal's thirty-two. Close up there would have been no confusion between the two men, but the likeness was enough for their purposes.

He gave Rebecca an odd, formal, half-bow. He shook her hand. 'We must be quick, I think,' he said softly. 'They will follow to check, that much is certain. You will permit me?'

He took off his jacket and laid it carefully on the ground. As if in a dream Rebecca watched him. From the beach below them she heard the music alter pace once more, and the boy Alexis lifted a hand to her.

'Please. That is the signal. Their dancing partners will let them go now, they know what to do. Please, Miss Farrell, please. We must hurry . . .'

With a quick movement he lay down on his back on the gound, the jacket under his shoulders. He held up his arms to her. Rebecca looked at him, and then, her mind starting to work again, knelt down beside him. Politely and stiffly, he put his arms around her.

'You have no need to worry,' he said, with a smile, a flash of white teeth, then an expression of great seriousness. 'I have sisters. Many of them. And this is an honour for me, to help

Mr Ryder. We will do nothing wrong. I am full of respect. But I must hold you . . .'

Awkwardly he drew her into his arms. And Rebecca lay the way Cal had instructed her to lie, across Alexis, the upper half of her body resting on his chest, her hair, loose, falling down in a thick curtain over his face. The boy Alexis gave a nervous sigh of relief.

'I thank you,' he said politely. 'It is very useful, your hair, I think. And now, if you will permit me, I will put my arms so, and my hands, so—that is all right? It will look all right? You are quite comfortable?'

He looked up at her with an expression of such serious solicitude that Rebecca felt an hysterical wish to laugh. She fought it down, and lay still.

'And now—we listen. I shall hear them, do not worry, and when they are close, if you will permit me, I must be kissing you, but only a little bit. And you will say his name. And they will watch for a bit, and they will be deceived. I even wear English shoes—Mr Ryder thought of that, a good touch, don't you think?'

They lay absolutely still. Rebecca could feel the tension in the young man's body, knew he strained his ears to hear the first footfall. And she realised that she too was afraid; she could feel the panic, the sort of edged nervousness that you felt as a child when you first played hide-and-seek in the dark, and you could sense, as you crouched somewhere, not daring to breathe, that the searcher was stealthily, quietly, coming closer. She bit her lip: they had to get this right; it had to be convincing. For Cal's sake; for Nico's sake; for the sake of the eight men who must, even now, be making their way down through the caves to the sea.

Alexis's hand tightened on her arm; he nodded slightly. Rebecca had heard nothing above the distant beat of the music and the sigh of the sea. Then a branch cracked underfoot; through the veil of her hair she saw a torch-light among the trees which almost at once went out.

'Now . . .' Alexis's mouth was against her ear, even so the word was hardly audible. He began to stroke her back, very gently, and not very expertly, rather like a man stroking a dog, some mad dissociated part of her mind noted, and hoped it would appear enough. Footsteps, hardly audible, a branch moving; there was more than one of them, and then, every nerve in her back electric with tension, as if her skin could see her instincts were so alive, Rebecca knew someone had stopped and someone was watching them. She gave a deep sigh.

'Cal,' she said. 'Darling Cal . . .'

Alexis's arms tightened around her; she moved a little, as if in response, and lowered her face chastely to his as if they kissed. There was quiet; her eyes were open; Alexis's eyes were open; again, through the veil of hair she caught the quickest beam of light and then it was gone. Alexis clearly dared say nothing; his English was good, but heavily accented. Instead, he too sighed, and moved his body just a little, and began with one hand to stroke, and then to hold, her hair. Rebecca lifted her head very slightly, just an inch or so, as if a kiss had been broken off.

'Darling Cal,' she murmured. 'Dear Cal—I love you so much. Oh, yes . . .'

A long sigh; her own voice saying to this boy, to the watchers, to the air, the things she had longed to say to Cal. It sounded soft and husky. She felt curiously glad that it had been said, even if Cal himself should never hear it.

She lowered her head once more, and Alexis kissed her very gently on the lips, and then on the cheek, and then—he was very young after all—on the lips again. Rebecca, beginning to suspect that he might be slightly less capable of restraining himself than he had boasted, sisters or no sisters, began to tense, and moved away from him slightly. She stroked his arm; touched his hair; a branch moved—God she thought, would they never go away? The same thought clearly struck Alexis at the same time, because, with a suddenness and an expertise that took her by surprise, he moved his hand firmly down over her bottom to her thigh, and slipped it under her dress. True, once his hand was hidden, he did nothing more, but Rebecca began to panic. They must have seen enough, surely, these men? All they needed, Cal had gambled, was to be sure he had not slipped away, that he was here, with her, happily engaged in lovemaking for some while. Greeks were not voyeurs; once they had made sure of that, they would withdraw to a respectful distance. And, yes . . . he was right. They were going, she could sense it; the softest of footfalls, further away the crack of an olive branch underfoot. It was working; it was working . . .

Alexis sensed their departure too, she knew it, but they had their instructions and neither of them dared move, or speak, for some while. Alexis's face, she saw, opening her eyes again, wore a look of fixed concentration that she did not attribute entirely to the fact that he too, was listening intently. Eventually, he gave an odd groan.

'This is very difficult for me, Miss Farrell,' he said politely into her ear. 'Much more difficult than I had thought. You will forgive me. I am only a man and you are very beautiful. I think that they have gone, but meanwhile, if you will not object, I shall just count to myself quietly . . .'

'Count?' In spite of herself Rebecca felt a smile come to her lips. Alexis regarded her very seriously.

'But yes. I have been assured. That is the best way. It is just that I have not had a lot of practice . . .'

He shut his eyes then, and presumably counted, for the exercise eventually seemed to work. Then he said against her ear: 'My eyes are good in the dark. We must move a little. I think they have gone, but I want to be sure. Now . . .'

And he sat upright as he spoke, lifting Rebecca with him, keeping her cradled against his chest, keeping his face apparently buried in her hair. They sat like that, crouched together like children, and for the first time that evening, Rebecca felt a breath of wind against her skin. It lifted her hair, she saw the branches of the olives lift and sway. Alexis tensed; he looked at his watch.

'Five more minutes, Miss Farrell,' he whispered. 'And then we can go. There is a storm coming, I think . . .'

They lay back again on the grass, quietly, for five minutes as he said. Rebecca listened to the distant music, to the sea, and tried to calculate. How far would they be by now? Just embarking in the inflatables, or already setting out to sea? Cal, she thought, and for an instant summoned up all her strength, all her resolve, into one great effort of will. *Oh let him be safe. Let them be safe* . . . She felt the first drops of rain on her skin, just as Alexis, with a quick movement, drew her to her feet.

'Come. Quickly,' he said in a low voice. 'It is beginning, the storm. It will help us, I think . . .'

She heard the hesitation in his voice; saw the new anxiety in his eyes. She could complete the rest of the sentence, she thought: the storm might help them, but would it help Cal, and Nico, and the men who were with them? She knew it would not.

With a quick movement, Alexis bent, picked up the jacket, and drew her through the trees. Even as they hurried, their footsteps suddenly terribly loud, Rebecca heard cries of dismay from the beach below. The music faltered, and suddenly it was as if the heavens opened, and rain began to fall. It fell drenchingly, with astonishing force, so her thin dress was soaked in an instant, and her hair plastered to her face. Alexis began to run, pulling her after him, and below them, behind them, there was a shout. They plunged on through the trees, up a steep rutted incline, and there, just as the trees thinned, and Rebecca realised they had reached the road, Alexis drew her to him.

'Quick,' he said. 'Like this—it helps, the rain, you see?'

He put an arm around her shoulders, drew his jacket over their two heads, as if to shelter them from the rain, and then urged her forward again at a run. As he did so there was a terrible, rending, cracking sound, and for an instant the streaming earth, the bent olives, the black road ahead, and Cal's Jeep, which was parked there, were lit with jagged blue light. Rebecca cried out instinctively, and Alexis urged her grimly on. Behind the Jeep, a little way down the road, at a discreet distance, another car was parked. Beside it, outlined for a second by the lightning, stood two men, obviously as astonished by the suddenness of the storm as they were.

Alexis had the Jeep's keys ready in his hand; the doors had been left unlocked. Ducking, running, still sheltering under the jacket, they ran to the Jeep's side, and Alexis fumbled with the handle. Rebecca glanced behind at the two men, just visible in the darkness: they seemed rooted to the spot.

'Hurry, darling,' she called loudly. 'I'm getting soaked . . .'

The door was open. Alexis ducked in and pulled her after him. The door slammed, the headlights were on, the engine had fired, the wipers were streaming with rain.

They were off; neither of them spoke, though Rebecca saw Alexis watched grimly in the driving mirror as he accelerated down the road.

'Are they following us?'

'Not yet. But they will do. It is no matter. Mr Ryder assumed that they would. And now it is all the more logical, do you see? We go to the Villa Circe because of the rain, because we want to kiss under a roof—what could be more natural? And we shall stay there some while, and they will see you leave in the morning, and smile to themselves. They will think Mr Ryder stays in bed late that morning, because he has not slept so very much the night before. With luck it will be hours before they find they have been duped . . .'

'I hope you're right . . .' Rebecca strained her eyes anxiously ahead of them. Alexis was driving very fast; the Jeep careered over the rutted road; its tyres screeched on the bends. Rain lashed the windscreen; the trees, caught in the headlights, bent against the onslaught of the wind and the rain. There was another crash of thunder, a jagged vicious fork of lightning; for a second the road ahead of them was electric blue, then dark again. They had passed the turning to the Templars' house, to Lakka; they were passing the turning to Grey Jameson's house. Rebecca turned her head as they flashed past, but the track leading up to the house was dark and deserted—no cars, no sign of men.

'Oh, Alexis,' she said. 'Will they be all right? Do you think they will be all right?'

Alexis's mouth set grimly. 'We shall know tomorrow.' He shrugged. 'Meanwhile—there is nothing we can do, you and I.' He gave Rebecca a dry sideways glance, looking suddenly much tougher, and much older than he had done earlier.

'You could say a prayer,' he added. 'I have said some prayers, earlier this evening. But you could say some more, why not? To an old Greek god, maybe—you could try that. Poseidon, for instance . . .'

When they reached the track that led up to the Villa Circe, it was almost obliterated by rain—it looked like a waterfall. But Alexis merely swore, apologised for swearing, slipped the gears of the Jeep, and let it inch and crawl its way up. They made it, somehow, and Rebecca thought how visible they must be. The headlights snaking up the track could be seen from miles; occasionally, if there were any watchers, the Jeep must have been vividly outlined against the scrub by the lightning. When they reached the terrace, Alexis helped her out, pulled the jacket over their heads, raced for the doors, and pushed her inside. All the shutters were closed; now he locked the door, and switched on the lights. Quickly he checked each of the rooms, then, coming back to where Rebecca stood, tense, soaked with rain, shivering by the fireplace, he smiled.

'You should take a shower,' he said kindly. 'Maybe borrow some of Mr Ryder's clothes. I will light a fire. Then we shall eat a little—it is always good to eat when one is nervous. Please. Do this. Mr Ryder would not want you to hold a cold . . .'

Rebecca smiled at him. 'Catch,' she corrected gently. 'Catch a cold. Your English is very good, Alexis. You can even swear in it . . .'

Alexis looked abashed. 'I am learning it now for five years,' he said. 'At first, on my own, from a book. At college now, in Athens. Then, when I am perfect in it I shall start a travel agency, and become a millionaire. I have it all worked out . . .' He paused. 'You really think I speak it well?'

'Very well,' Rebecca said gently.

She left him then, and went into Cal's bedroom. As quickly as she could she pulled off the wet dress, and showered, feeling the warm water course over her body, and trying to shut her mind to all the memories that surged up, here, and in Cal's room.

In the bedroom there was a simple wooden chest of drawers; opening it she found all Cal's clothes laid out neatly. She looked at them—the jumpers, the shirts—and ran her hand sadly and lovingly over them. His clothes were here; his shaving things were in the bathroom, there were books by his bedside, some loose change and pens on the table. It was carefully done: nothing to suggest that Cal had left, that he intended never to come back . . .

She sighed, trying to turn her eyes away from the bed, to shut out the images that sped into her mind. She selected a pair of old jeans, a shirt and a sweater. The jeans had to be laced round her waist with a belt, and rolled up at the bottoms; the shirt was as voluminous as a nightshirt, and about as alluring, though that didn't matter now, she thought, and the sweater hung about her slender body in folds. She completed the whole ensemble with a pair of socks many times too large, and then slipped out of the room and shut the door firmly behind her.

Alexis straightened up proudly from the fire: the logs there had been lit, and now blazed cheerfully. Her wet dress had been carefully draped over a wooden chair in front of it; on the table were bread and cheese and steaming mugs of coffee. Alexis looked pleased with himself, and so anxious that she should approve his efforts that Rebecca forced herself to eat and drink a little, though she had no appetite.

While she toyed with her food, Alexis talked. He was excited by the night's exploits, proud of what he thought was the successful part he and Rebecca had played in them, and he had the natural resilience of the very young. His worries about the storm, about the safety of the others, were soon distanced by talk. He told Rebecca his life-story, and that of several members of his family. And Rebecca, who knew she would not sleep, was content to listen. He told her of his admiration for Nico—his second cousin by marriage, and at length began to speak of Cal, whom he had first met, he said, when he was a very little boy. It was Cal, it seemed, who had encouraged him to learn English, who had helped him with the exercises, and it was Cal who had given his parents the money to send him to college in Athens.

'Cal did that?' Rebecca looked up at him.

Alexis nodded. Mr Ryder had said that he owed Alexis's parents a debt of gratitude—for some trifling things the family had done for him, Alexis added proudly—and so he had asked if he might be permitted to repay them in some way, in this way if they were willing. And, Alexis said, they had been, with a little persuasion from him. He hesitated. Mr Ryder understood the Greeks, he added. There was a word—*philotimia*—it was not easy to translate, but *honour* came close to it. It was very important to Greeks, and Mr Ryder possessed it.

He hesitated. Had Miss Farrell known that Mr Ryder had had a sister, who had been very sick, who was dead now?

Rebecca nodded. 'Yes, I knew that,' she said. 'He told me about her. His stepsister, Elaine . . .'

Alexis's face grew sad. He had known Miss Elaine, he said, first before she was ill, and then after. A long illness. It had been terrible.

'And very terrible for Mr Ryder, I think,' he said at last, and his eyes met Rebecca's frankly across the table. 'He suffered for his sister. He looked after her himself. He fought to make her well again—she was his family, I think . . .' He hesitated. He lowered his eyes.

'You have known Mr Ryder long, Miss Farrell?'

The question took Rebecca by surprise; she shook her head. 'No. Not very long.'

'But you love him?' The question came straight out, and Rebecca felt the blood rush to her face. Alexis smiled. 'No matter. I am impertinent. I know so already, from tonight— from what you said tonight. So, tell me, Miss Farrell, you will be married, I think? Soon, I hope? On the island, maybe? It would be a good thing: Mr Ryder should have a wife, and children . . .'

'No—no . . .' Rebecca said quickly. 'No, please, Alexis, you're quite wrong. It's . . . it's not like that . . .' she finished lamely. Alexis looked perplexed; his dark brows drew together in a frown. He appeared to think she was being unneccessarily coy; then, seeing her obvious embarrassment, he collected himself.

'I am sorry,' he said stiffly. 'I should not have asked. But I thought . . . my mother thought, when Mr Ryder spoke of you, when he came to our house to ask me to do this thing tonight . . .' He broke off. 'My mother will be disappointed,' he said forlornly. 'She said to me after that she was expecting a wedding, that when Mr Ryder spoke of you he looked alive again, that he was happy once more—and he has been unhappy for a long while . . . But still.' He cut himself off quickly, seeing Rebecca's expression. 'My mother is getting old. She is a romantic. She wants me married. She wants everyone married. Also of course . . .' He hesitated, 'Well, she is Greek. She has lived on this little island all her life. She doesn't know about ... about the English,' he floundered slightly. 'She doesn't understand that it is possible, sometimes, to love, but not to marry ...' He cleared his throat gallantly. 'I understand, of course, but then I have been to Athens ...'

'Ah well.' Rebecca said gently, 'You would understand ...' She looked away, so Alexis should not see the expression in her eyes, and he sighed.

'All the same though,' he said. 'It is a pity ...'

There was a little silence, and then Alexis stood up. He had clearly decided that this matter, deep and impenetrable, even to one who had been to Athens, should be discussed no longer. He gave a large yawn. He asked Rebecca where she would like to sleep, and when she said she would stay up a little longer, asked if she would forgive him, but he was very tired ... He settled himself in a chair before the fire, closed his eyes, and—as far as Rebecca could tell—went to sleep almost at once, apparently without a worry in the world. When his breathing became deep and regular, she fetched a rug, and covered his knees, and put out the light. Then she sat quietly in the dark, listening to the sound of his breathing, and to the wind outside, which was slowly, hour by hour, lessening.

She watched as the first rays of thin light crept through the shutters. She listened as the birds began to sing. Finally, at about six, she took her dress from the chair, folded it, unlocked the door, and slipped out of the house.

The light was breathtakingly clear; it danced on the sweet, newly washed earth, on the still blue of the water below. The air smelled of an English spring-time; after the days of intense heat it was new-washed, cool and balmy against her skin.

She would stay in Cal's clothes, she thought. He wouldn't mind that, at least.

She walked slowly down the steps from the terrace, found the little shelter where Cal had promised her bike would be left waiting for her, found the bike itself. Attached to the handlebars was a little bunch of fresh ferns—she had not been expecting that. It was his parting gift, maybe.

She looked out over the landscape. Down below, at the bottom of the track, the Greek was standing by his cart, just as he had been the day before. Glimpsing Rebecca's figure, he at once bent to the ground, and began to lift stones.

She climbed on to her bike, and started the little engine. And then, with regret sharp in her heart, cutting into her like a knife, she began the journey back to Gaios.

CHAPTER TEN

SOMETIMES, in her mind, she composed letters to him, though she never put anything on paper. They were not even letters really, just fragments, scraps, sentences and phrases—things she had wanted to say, and had not said; things she saw, which she wished she had seen and shared with him. As the days passed, one and then another, so slowly, time creeping at a dull sluggish pace, those words were her greatest consolation. Letting them flow in her mind, groping to express things that she knew never would be expressed—this brought Cal closer, for a while. That and her memories; for a while they shored her up and helped to ward off the other moments, the more frequent moments, when the pain and the grief she felt were so acute they were like knives in her flesh.

She went about her work; she did as Nicky asked her to do, or Michael. She felt their quiet solicitude, their reticence, their English refusal to intrude, their sympathy which neither of them could quite bring themselves to express. But she was not at ease with their evasion; she was happier with the Greeks she knew on the island, with Agape, with Leandros, with Nico, whose left arm had been badly broken, but who dismissed his difficulties fiercely. In the face of unhappiness the Greeks were forthright; they accepted it as proper, as something to be honoured and endured, not hidden away. So, to Nico, who in any case knew the truth, Rebecca could speak of Cal sometimes; to Nicky and to Michael, who did not, she said nothing.

One night, it was a Thursday, and so must have been only six days after the night of the storm, though it felt to Rebecca more like six months, Nico asked her to come to dinner at his house. The invitation was casually given, but Rebecca knew its real purpose: at last Nico would give her a full account of everything that had happened, she thought, accepting gladly. So far, observing caution, and having his arm tended, which had necessitated a journey to the hospital in Corfu, Nico had been able to see her only briefly, and had told her very little. She had been content with that: in a way, the details were not important, but now, looking forward to the evening, Rebecca felt her heart lift, felt happier than she had done for days. He would speak of Cal; just to hear his name would ease the depression that clung to her—and the exploits of that night, yes, she realised, she did want to know exactly how it was that—after coming so close to disaster—all had been successfully resolved, and Cal and the men with him had got away safely.

All day she looked forward to the evening; the hours seemed to drag even more than usual. The weather was warm once more, but without the oppressive closeness that had marked the days before the storm. She was busy, but the Easter rush was over; at the end of this week a large number of the villa parties would be leaving. The next few months would be quieter, Michael said. There were some specialist groups coming to the island, some coming for a sailing course, others to go walking, and to study wild flowers, but the rush would be off until, gradually, it began to build once more towards the busiest months of July and August.

'How do you feel about it, Rebecca?' Michael said. He had asked her to join him for lunch in the square, and now sat opposite her, sipping a glass of ouzo.

'Feel about what?' Rebecca concentrated her attention, which had been wandering.

'Well, about staying on and so on . . .' Michael looked a little flustered and embarrassed. 'I mean, the thing is—when you first agreed to come out here, it was a pretty loose arrangement on both sides, no stop-date and all that. But . . .' He paused and looked at his hands. 'Well, I'd like you to stay on. Very much. You've been a terrific help to me, in fact, I can't think now how we managed without you!' He smiled. 'You get on with things, the visitors like you, you work well with Nicky . . .' He paused, raising his eyes to her face. 'What I'm trying to say is—I've talked this over with Nicky, and she's very keen—I'd like to make a few changes, and they involve you.'

'Changes?' Rebecca looked at him uncertainly.

'Developments, put it like that.' Michael paused, and lit a

cigarette. He drew on it deeply; Rebecca thought that he was looking pleased with himself—obviously he had one of his plans, and his only concern was how she would fit into it.

'The thing is—I've done very well here on Paxos, but I think I've taken it about as far as I can go. Any more visitors and the place will become spoiled. So, for some time now, I've been looking for another way of developing the business, and I think I've found it. There's a couple of other islands, also in the Ionian, both of them pretty much the way Paxos was when I first came here. And I'd like to start up my operation there—extend it. Run things just as we've done here, do it gradually, and so on. But the thing is it'll take a lot of my time. If I'm going to go ahead, and I have to decide soon, then I have to be sure I can leave things here in safe hands.' He paused. 'Your hands and Nicky's, to be exact.'

Rebecca stared at him. 'You mean we'd be in charge on Paxos—completely?'

'Exactly.' Michael smiled. 'What I'm proposing is this: a kind of partnership, you and Nicky would become my partners. I'd still pay you both a salary of course, a rather higher one than you're getting now, but you'd also be in on a profit-sharing basis. You two would run the Paxos side of things, and I'd take over all the business of the two new islands—finding the villas, getting them fixed up, bringing in the first visitors and so on.' He paused.

'That's the part of the work I like best, really, and it's the part I do best. You two don't really need me here, I've realised that. The machinery is all set up, you could run it perfectly, even improve it . . .' He paused. 'There's disadvantages as well as advantages from your point of view, I won't pretend there isn't. You'd both have to stay out here, for instance, for most of the year, and it may be idyllic now but it can be pretty tough and lonely in the winter months. You could have a six-week break, that was what I discussed with Nicky, to go back to England, but it would obviously have to be during the winter when things are quiet. Apart from that you'd be here. And you'd be in charge. If things started to go wrong, if we were losing money—not that I see that happening, but anything is possible—well, it would affect you both. And it'll be damned hard work—there's no getting away from that. So—how do you feel?'

Rebecca hesitated; she looked down at the table in front of her. 'I—I don't know, Michael,' she said at last, conscious that he was watching her closely. 'I'd have to think it over. Talk to Nicky about it. I mean—it's a very generous suggestion, and I'm very grateful—but, if you could give me a day or so . . .'

'Sure, sure . . .' Michael waved his hand expansively. Then his face grew more serious. 'The thing is . . .' he began, a little uncertainly, 'well, I don't want to butt in or anything, but, oh hell—I just want you to know, Rebecca, that I'm damn sorry about what happened. With Ryder.' He coloured as he spoke, and went on, the words coming out in a rush. 'I mean, I'd quite understand if, after all that, you felt you wanted to cut loose from here at the end of the season and never come back. Obviously, well, it's only natural, your attitude to the island must have been affected—but, Rebecca, I'd like to think you wouldn't make a hasty decision because of that and say "no". You've a lot of friends here . . .' He paused; ne was now scarlet with embarrassment. 'People who know your worth, even if Ryder didn't. People who admire you, and like you, and who would welcome your staying. Nico, of course, but others, too, myself included, and . . .'

He broke off, and Rebecca saw to her surprise that he was not simply embarrassed but also angry. He suddenly banged the table, so his empty glass jumped half an inch. 'And I may add, that if ever I run into Ryder, in London or whatever, I shall give him a piece of my mind. Tell him what I think of him and no mistake. I'd never have thought it of him, you know. I mean, I knew he could be difficult and so on, but deliberately to take up with you and then . . .' He broke off, seeing Rebecca's expression, and his face softened. He reached across the table and patted her hand. 'There! I've upset you, and I didn't mean to do that. But it does make me angry. Still—the thing is, Rebecca . . .' he hesitated. 'You're young, and you're very lovely, and you've got your whole life ahead of you. I can see you've been hurt, even if you'd rather I couldn't see it. But, it won't last, believe me. One day you'll wake up and you'll wonder what all the fuss was about.

You'll forget him. Honestly. You won't believe me now, but it does happen . . .'

'Does it?' Rebecca felt the sharp prick of tears behind her eyes, and turned her face away. It was Michael's awkward kindness that had done that, she thought, angrily. She had done well enough up to now; she wasn't going to weaken and burst into tears now, like an idiot. Not until she was alone in her room anyway.

'Of course it does, of course.' Michael hesitated and cleared his throat. 'The thing is—I have to ask, Rebecca, because it affects you and it affects all the plans we've been discussing— Is he coming back?'

Rebecca stared fixedly at the ground. 'No,' she said. 'He's not.'

'Yes, well, I'd heard as much . . .' Michael sighed. 'I don't understand the half of it. He ups and leaves, out of the blue. That damn pansy friend of his does the same thing—he's putting that ramshackle old farm of his on the market you know—the one on the west coast. Apparently wondered if I might be interested in it—damn cheek! And Ryder simply leaves me a cheque to settle the rental on the Villa Circe for the summer, lets me know that anything he'd left there can be disposed of, and announces he won't be renting that villa or any other on Paxos in the foreseeable future. Odd. Damned odd.

'I mean it was so unexpected. The night of the party he seemed fine—all set to be here for months—and then, what happens? A message a couple of days later. By which time he's gone. Melted into the air. No one saw him leave. Said goodbye to no one. Well, I suppose he must have said goodbye to you . . . Oh! I'm sorry, putting my big foot in it yet again.' He paused to draw breath, and eased himself in his chair a little awkwardly. 'I mean—it's as if he was running away—and I'd have said he was the type who'd never do that. And running away at a time when if he had any sense, if he had eyes in his head, he had the best reason of all for staying . . .' He looked pointedly at Rebecca as he said this, and when she did not answer, there was a silence. Eventually Michael looked at his watch. He drained the last dregs of ouzo from his glass. He stood up.

'Well,' he said, more formally. 'No point in crying over spilt milk. Will you think about what I've suggested, Rebecca? I hope you'll say "yes"—I mean, in a way, it's perhaps easier isn't it, making the decision, if we all know Ryder's gone for good? Then he doesn't complicate the issue, which is all the better. Nicky was rather afraid he might.'

'Oh no.' Rebecca lifted her face to his. 'He doesn't complicate the issue. He doesn't affect it at all.'

'Good. Good.' Michael appeared quite convinced by the calmness of her tone, and relieved that the whole conversation was over. 'Well, I'll be off then. I'll see you later. You talk it all over with Nicky—yes?'

Rebecca nodded and raised her hand in a brief salute as Michael hastened away. She smiled dryly to herself: how funny some Englishmen were, with their horror of all emotion, their intense awkwardness in speaking of it. She had begun to suspect of late, and Nicky had hinted as much, that Michael's embarrassed concern for her was not entirely that of an employer for an employee, but that something deeper and more personal was involved. She hoped she was wrong, though something in the way in which he had looked at her, and had made his suggestions about the partnership, had made her fear that she had been right. In which case, of course, she would have to refuse his offer. She didn't want Michael to fall in love with her, or think he had done so— Michael the comfortable bachelor! She didn't want him to be hurt—and if there were any danger of that she would have to say 'no'. And on the whole, she thought, she wanted to say 'yes'. Because, just now, she wanted to go on with her work, which she liked and knew she did well, and because she had come to love the island, this place of magic and beauty, where every curve of the coast or the road reminded her of Cal.

She could go back to London. She felt confident in herself now: she was sure she could find work, pick up the threads again, either cooking there as she had done before, or finding another job similar to this one. She would not go back to Conrad's agency although her mother had written to say that Conrad had visited her, and pleaded for Rebecca's address, and—not given it—had asked her mother to tell her that he apologised for everything ('Whatever *that* means,' her mother had written) and that everyone at the agency wanted her back, to name her terms . . .

No, certainly not there. And the thought of London did not attract. No, here, if it was possible. She felt, obscurely, that it was in this place she had found herself, and here, for some time at least, she should stay.

She stood up, abruptly. There was no point in dreaming; she had work to do, and she had already dreamed here too long. She had to go and say goodbye to the Sullivans, and to the Templars, both of whom would be leaving that evening, and make sure that all their arrangements were in order. There were the villas for the wildflower study group to be checked . . . She stretched, and set off, glad that her thoughts and concentration had to be channelled into something practical.

She collected her moped from the flat, and was just wheeling it along the quay, when around the corner came three figures: Costas Andropoulos, wearing dark glasses and an expression of extreme bad temper; Carstairs, and Jonquil, who, today, was eye-blinding in a cruise-suit of violent flowered pattern. Rebecca almost ran into them; there was then no way of avoiding them, and in any case all three had come to a halt. Andropoulos scowled at her, Carstairs hesitated and then gave her an uneasy smile, and Jonquil gave her a slightly blank stare.

'Oh, hello,' she said, in response to Rebecca's mumbled greeting, and clearly not remembering her name. 'How are you? Isn't it the most lovely day? We're just leaving—it should be wonderful out at sea today don't you think? So calm. Just like a lake . . .'

'Oh, you're going?' Rebecca managed to keep the triumph out of her voice: if they were going, they must be giving up. Good.

'Yes, yes.' Carstairs began fussily to urge his wife forward. 'We've stayed rather longer than we meant. It's back to Athens and paperwork I'm afraid . . .'

'And we missed Mr Roper!' Jonquil, refusing to be urged, stood her ground.

'Ryder, darling, Ryder . . .'

'Or course, *Ryder*! Didn't I say that? I meant to . . . Yes, and now we've missed him, and he was *so* charming the night of that lovely party. He wanted us to go fishing with him, didn't he, Hugo? And now we shan't be able to . . .'

Hugo made an odd irritable noise and gave his wife a most undiplomatic nudge in the ribs.

'No, we shall not.' This time it was Andropoulos who spoke, his voice smooth, making Rebecca jump. As the others moved to one side he held his ground so Rebecca could not pass. He looked down at her, the light flashing against the glasses, and his face unsmiling. 'But then Mr Ryder has already left the island, has he not, Miss Farrell? Rather a sudden change of plans, I gather. You, in particular must be disappointed.'

'Me?' Rebecca met his gaze boldly. She tilted her chin. 'Why me in particular?'

'Oh, no matter. Obviously I mistake. I thought you were such close—friends.' He paused. 'I watched you together at the party, you remember, the night of the storm. When you—danced—together so charmingly . . .'

The words hung in the air for a moment, and Rebecca had not a second's doubt what he meant, and that he knew the part she had played in all this. He smiled coldly, and she thought: he's furious—what will this mean for him, demotion?

'Oh I see!' She smiled back at him sunnily. 'Well, you're right of course. We were friends, and I shall miss Mr Ryder, but then friendship laughs at absence, doesn't it, Mr Andropoulos? Isn't there a saying—friendship knows no boundaries?'

'Or borders,' he said. 'Yes, I think you're right, Miss Farrell.' He paused meaningfully, as if to make sure she had picked up on the reference to 'borders'. Then he smiled once more. 'Still, it is a pity. Mr Ryder will not be returning to Paxos, I gather?'

'No.' Rebecca regarded him steadily.

'And I regret but I am unlikely to be returning myself. Such a shame. But pressures of work—'

'Of course,' Rebecca said solemnly.

'I wonder . . .' He paused; glanced along the quay to Hugo Carstairs and Jonquil, who were boarding the yacht, and then turned back to her.

'If you should see Mr Ryder again, would you give him a brief message from me?'

'I told you—' Rebecca cut in. 'I shall not be seeing him . . .'

'None the less.' He interrupted her. 'If you should happen to run into him—at some later date. Remind him of me, will you? And say—"A Greek *first*." He will understand. We had a most interesting conversation, he and I, the night of the party. "A Greek *first*," you'll remember, Miss Farrell?' He held out his hand, and shook hers. 'Goodbye, Miss Farrell. *Entaxi* . . .'

And with that he was gone. Rebecca turned and watched his portly figure stroll along the quay, and climb aboard his yacht. He did not look back. A few minutes later one of the crewmen cast off, and Rebecca stood and watched the yacht ease away from the quay. She watched it until it was well clear, and had manoeuvred into the channel; she watched it until it began to head out to sea, a frown of puzzlement on her brows. She had no idea what he meant, and no likelihood of delivering his message, and the thing that puzzled her most of all was that it had been delivered with a dry amusement, as if he knew something that she did not know, and he found that advantage funny.

All afternoon she was kept busy, however, so that soon all thoughts of Costas Andropoulos, and all attempts to decode his meaning, were forgotten. She joined Nicky to say goodbye to the Sullivans, who departed with many promises to write and to return the next year, and left her in Gaios, looking depressed and on edge—which Rebecca attributed to the Sullivans' departure. They would talk about Michael's proposal tomorrow, they agreed, though Nicky, rather short-temperedly seemed to think it needed little discussion. 'Oh, yes or no, Rebecca,' she said grumpily. 'I mean there's not that much to discuss, is there really? It's a super offer. We'd be mad to refuse—anyway, I haven't time to talk about it now . . .' She broke off, her face taking on the closed expression which Rebecca had come to know well over the past few days, and which she had assumed was due to embarrassment on Nicky's part, a wish, for once, not to pry.

'I mean—you're not going to be influenced by all this

business about Cal, are you?' she burst out finally. 'Michael thought you might be—but I can't see it. He's gone and he's apparently not coming back—I warned you. The best thing for everyone would be to get on and forget him ...'

'I intend to try. I told Michael that,' Rebecca said quietly, and Nicky swung round to her, an odd, stricken look in her eyes. She looked at her friend for a moment, and then her face cleared. She looked more like the old Nicky—cheerful, gossipy, perhaps, but not the kind of person who brooded. Rebecca was startled by the change.

'Oh, I'm *glad*,' Nicky cried impulsively. She caught Rebecca's hands in hers. 'Really, Becky. It's all for the best— you'll realise that later, you know.'

'Have you been worrying about me—is that it?' Rebecca looked at her searchingly. 'You shouldn't be. Don't be. I'm all right. Really ...'

'I hope so ...' Nicky dropped her eyes. 'I hope it's all been—oh, you know—for the best. In the long run ... Anyway.' She looked at her watch. 'I'll have to dash. We'll hash it all over tomorrow, all right? Make a list, all the pros and all the cons, the way we used to at school, do you remember?' She pressed Rebecca's hand, and rushed off, and Rebecca, puzzled by her manner, set off to Lakka. It reminded her of Nicky at school, she thought, as she urged the moped up the hill from Gaios, and tried to keep out of her mind the other memories, of the time she had taken this road in the dark ...

Yes, Nicky at school, when she had been, even then, something of a gossip, a person who could never resist interfering, but also a person good-hearted and well-meaning, who was contrite when her interference led to trouble ... The time when Rebecca's father had died, for instance, and Rebecca had been called out of class to the headmistress's study, to have the news broken to her. She had confided it to Nicky that night, and sworn her to secrecy because she knew the rest of the class was buzzing with rumours and curiosity and she couldn't bear, just then, to have people pity her or question her. And Nicky had sworn, and the very next day, told everyone. She had the best of reasons: it would protect Rebecca, she thought. If the others didn't know, they might say the wrong thing, they might tease Rebecca or upset her. 'I did it for the best, Becky,' she had wailed, when Rebecca, furious, had confronted her.

Rebecca sighed to herself. She had been eleven, Nicky just thirteen: people didn't change, she thought sadly. She was still the same, full of the old faults, too proud, hating people to see she was hurt or cared too much about anything. And Nicky was still the same: well-meaning, but clumsy, obviously wanting to help now, and not certain how to do it. That must be it.

She halted the bike for a moment under the olives, at the turning, and for an instant the two griefs, the old and the new, for her father long dead, and for Cal, so recently with her, mixed and cut her anew. Tears misted her eyes. She had loved and admired her father dearly. *He would have liked Cal*, she thought. And then, blinking the tears angrily away, she let the bike freewheel down the hill to Lakka.

That evening she was still feeling a little shaky, not entirely sure she had her feelings under control. She bathed, and dressed herself carefully for Nico's dinner, putting on a dress she had bought quickly, on impulse, on the way home. She had thought it might distract her and cheer her up, for it was very pretty—made of soft billowing white cotton, it left her neck and arms bare, and was belted at the waist with a knotted silk tie of pale turquoise and coral. She brushed her hair until it shone, letting it fall loose over her shoulders and across her forehead, and added a little dark shadow to her eyes, and a little gloss to her lips. Then she looked at herself in the glass critically: she looked different somehow, she thought, more grown-up—older—she wasn't sure what it was, maybe it was just that no matter how she tried to conceal it she looked sad. She turned away from the glass quickly: she mustn't look sad, not tonight, and above all she mustn't break down or cry or anything stupid, because tonight was special— tonight, for Nico and his family at least, it was a sort of celebration.

Nico had said he would collect her in the old battered car which he sometimes drove, and, sure enough, she heard its hoot, promptly at six, just as he had promised. He was waiting for her when she came downstairs, one arm in a sling, wearing his best suit, his hair slicked down, freshly shaved— as if he were off to a wedding, she thought, with amusement, and a wave of affection.

He stepped back as she shut the door of the house and came towards him, and she saw the glance of admiration he gave her. He took her hand, half bowed over it, and with an old-fashioned courtesy took her arm, and helped her carefully into the car. The passenger seat had been draped with a rug in her honour, she saw, and the bodywork was freshly washed and polished. In the Greek manner the windscreen was bedecked with an exuberance of flowers and coloured photographs of Nico's children, and tonight had been added to these little bunches of green ferns—like the one she had found on her bike's handlebars, and now had carefully pressed in her room.

She turned to Nico with a smile as he climbed in beside her. 'Nico—you look so smart! And so does the car . . . It's lovely.'

'But of course.' He gave her a broad smile. 'Tonight is special. Tonight we celebrate. Tonight we say thank you to our friend—*filos mas*—in the best way we can.' He started the engine. 'You are warm enough? You are ready?'

Rebecca nodded and he accelerated away with a great clanging and rattling. The car boomed up the hill and along the coast road, Nico driving with great concentration and avoiding all the pot-holes. Chickens scattered before them; an old woman at the roadside lifted her hand in salute, and Rebecca turned to him with a smile.

'Who will be there tonight, Nico?' she asked. 'Your family? Agape? Alexis? I should like to see Alexis again, he was very kind to me . . .'

'And you bewitched him.' Nico smiled broadly. 'No— Alexis has gone back to Athens I'm afraid. But he left his address for me to give you. He said please to write, and please to send him a photograph . . .'

'Oh, I will.' Rebecca laughed. 'Well, I'm looking forward to tonight so much. I've been thinking about it all day . . .' She hesitated. 'Will you tell me tonight, Nico—all the things that happened? I should like you to do that . . .' She glanced down at his arm 'You're better?' she went on gently. 'It doesn't hurt too badly? And you can drive very well,' she added, laughing, as Nico completed the complicated manoeuvre of changing gear, which involved taking his one good hand off the steering wheel, dropping it to the gear, and replacing it quickly.

'Oh fine . . .' He dismissed her worries with an airy wave of the hand, and the car swerved. 'Another few weeks in plaster the doctors said, and then, presto, better than ever!'

'I'm glad . . .' Rebecca turned her eyes to the view beyond them. They had reached the turning to Lakka, and the light was just beginning to turn a pale violet on the horizon. Below them the sea was calm and still, hardly shifting, without breakers.

'A good night—' Nico grinned at her. 'For fishing.'

'Ah yes.'

'But that kind of fishing—the special kind, that is over now. I accept it,' he said. He glanced at her. 'It is in the past—all those adventures. My grandchildren can talk about it one day, maybe.'

Rebecca glanced at him, for he spoke with an odd finality, but he merely smiled, and slowed. 'That is why we celebrate tonight,' he said. 'For you. To thank you. And because something is over. Finished.'

Rebecca lowered her eyes. 'Finished,' she echoed dully. 'Yes, I know. It is.'

Nico stopped the car. He turned to her.

'No sadness,' he said gently. 'Not tonight. Tonight is for wine and food and talk and happiness. You know, we Greeks say—every end is a beginning . . .' He paused. 'Now—you will go in, Rebecca? Everything is ready, you are expected. I must just put the car in my shed and lock the door so my mad Demetrios cannot sneak out later and drive off to see his sweetheart. You go in—*ne*?'

He reached across and held open the door for her, and Rebecca climbed down outside his house. The air was still, the scent of the gardenias was sweet in the air, and she paused for a moment, looking around her with pleasure: at the little whitewashed house, at the pergola which leaned under the weight of an old vine, at the flowers and ferns that decorated the courtyard. Nico pulled away, and reversed the car out of sight around a wall, and, smoothing down her dress, Rebecca walked hesitantly to the door. It was to be a surprise then, she thought, as she tapped lightly and received no answer. She would open the door, and there they would be assembled, all Nico's family, and they would laugh, and hold out their arms and draw her inside, and pour her a glass of ouzo or retsina ... She tapped again, and then turned the handle.

The door creaked back, and she stepped inside into the main room of the house. Then she faltered: was there some mistake? The room was empty, half in shadow, lit only by the fading light that entered the small windows.

She stepped forward uncertainly.

'Agape?' she said softly, not understanding. 'Leandros?'

And then she realised that the room was not empty. Someone was sitting there, quietly, in the shadows; someone who stood up now, someone tall, who seemed too big for the little room, someone she had thought never to see again. Someone who did not speak, but who lifted his arms to her ...

'Cal!' She was not conscious of moving, but she must have moved, or he must have done, for the next moment she felt his arms tighten around her and crush her against him. She heard the exhalation of his breath, smelled the dear familiar scent of his skin and his hair.

'My own darling,' he said, his voice a little broken, and held her tight, and kissed her.

For a long while they clung to each other, not speaking, then Rebecca drew back from him with a low cry. Quickly she touched him, his hands, his arms, his face, his hair ...

'You're safe—Oh, Cal. You're safe and you're not hurt at all—Nico said you weren't but I wasn't sure, I thought he might be trying to shield me ... But—oh—Cal, you shouldn't be here. You mustn't stay—you said yourself. It can't be safe yet. You weren't going to come back ...' She broke off, staring at him, the torrent of words suddenly coming to a halt. He regarded her quietly, his eyes never leaving hers.

'Something has gone wrong—is that it? Oh, Cal, say it isn't. And how did you get here? I don't understand, Cal, please ...'

Very gently he lifted a finger and laid it against her lips. 'If you will be quiet for a moment, and stop bombarding me with questions . . .' His voice was a little uneven, and he smiled down at her. 'I'll tell you. It's quite simple. And you're being very obtuse. I came back for you.'

'For me?'

'Of course. I don't intend us to be parted again.' He paused. 'If you agree, that is.'

There was a little silence. Rebecca stared at him. She stepped back a little from his arms; she lifted her hands and then let them fall to her sides. The silence washed over her, beat in her mind like the sea. Cal stood quite still, his eyes never leaving her face.

'I love you, Rebecca,' he said, with quiet force. 'I love you, and I want you to marry me.'

She gave a little incoherent cry, the tension in her body making her tremble. She could not speak, and Cal's mouth set in a stubborn line.

'If you're not sure—perhaps I've put this badly, too suddenly,' he began awkwardly, colour mounting in his cheeks. 'If you would perfer to wait—of course I understand. But I wanted you to know what I felt. I have no doubts, you see. I am utterly certain, or I would not have spoken. More certain than I've ever been about anything in my life. I knew, I think, the first time I met you. And since then . . .'

'But Cal—I love you!' Suddenly she found her voice, and as she spoke she saw his face change, saw it light up, saw all the darkness disappear from her eyes. She turned back to him impulsively and he caught her hands with a low cry. 'I love you,' she said again. 'And I wanted to tell you, but I knew I mustn't, because you had to go away, and you were so resolute about that, and I understood—I thought I understood—but it was terribly hard. And then, the night in the olive grove, when you'd gone, when Alexis was there, I said it then. I said it to him—no, not to him really, to the air, and I was glad. It was a relief to say it. I felt as if I wanted to shout it from the top of a mountain, and . . .' She drew breath, and looked up at him, suspicion coming into her face as she saw the corners of his lips lift in a smile.

'You knew!' she said accusingly. 'Alexis told you—is that it? He told you what I'd said?'

'Yes, he did. I met him in Athens, and he told me. As a matter of fact, with the wisdom of his eighteen years he gave me a lecture. About life and love and men and women and one woman in particular, and how, unless I was a complete fool, which he was gracious enough to say he thought I was not—I ought to pull myself together and do something about it. By that time I had already decided that I would, in any case, though he didn't know that. But I was glad he told me. It spurred me on. We met last night. I left for Paxos in a fishing boat at dawn this morning, and ... Oh, Rebecca.' He drew her to him gently. 'There's so much to explain. Will you let me try?'

There was an old wooden bench in the room, beneath the window, and taking her hands, he drew her to it, and they sat down together. Cal held her hands in his, and pressed them tightly.

'I thought, you see,' he began, 'I thought that I must not be selfish. It was so clear what I felt—and so strong. Even if we had not made love it would have been the same—and after we made love, well, then I nearly gave in. I nearly told you, what I felt, what I wanted for us. All the time, in the caves, in the wood the next morning, when you came up to the Villa Circe, at the dance on the sands—even in the church—Rebecca, the words were there all the time, pounding away in my head—it nearly drove me mad. It took all my willpower not to say them. But ...' He hesitated and looked up at her ruefully. 'You see, I thought you deserved something better—a different kind of man. Someone more like you—with your youth, your optimism, your strength.'

He hesitated, and she saw his eyes darken. 'I don't know, Rebecca it's difficult to explain. Since my stepsister died, since I'd left my church, I'd been filled with such self-hatred, with such a sense of failure. It made me bitter and hard, and I knew what was happening, I could see it, and I hated myself the more ...'

'You blamed yourself for her death,' Rebecca said quietly. 'I could see that—and I could understand it. But you shouldn't, you must see that ...'

'I see it now.' He lowered his eyes. 'You see, for a long time, after Elaine died, I hated myself for going on living. For being strong and healthy—it seemed so cruel, so arbitrary. Why her, and not me? Every time I went out, every time I enjoyed myself, every time I realised that—even if it was just for an evening—I'd forgotten Elaine, and forgotten her death, I felt ashamed. I felt that the only way I could mourn her properly was by—in a sense—denying my own life, closing it down, shutting it up, so it just became a routine, a round. Work, and then more work. No pleasure. No joy. No release—maybe it was the last legacy of those Puritan New England aunts of mine, I don't know. I knew it was mad. I knew I was gradually killing myself off—but I didn't care. It gave me a certain savage pleasure. Until I met you, that is. And I discovered that I was not the half-dead thing I'd thought I was: that I was a man—alive—glad to be alive— that I wanted to plan for the future—that I wanted a future. With you.'

There was a little silence, and Rebecca pressed his hand gently. 'I understand,' she said. 'I think I understand. When my father died—I remember feeling like that.' She hesitated, looking away. 'I remember the first time it hit me—it was about two months after his death, the school holidays, and— oh, I don't know—I was staying with a friend, and we went swimming, and it was a marvellous day, very hot, and we were having such fun, laughing—and suddenly, I thought: I mustn't do this. I shouldn't do this. My father is dead.' She paused. 'But I was only eleven, and there was my family—my mother and my sisters. It passed. I can see it was different for you. But you know, don't you, you must have thought, that the last thing Elaine would have wanted was for you to be miserable, for her death to cast such a shadow on your life. You must know that.'

'I do know it.' He looked into her eyes. 'I also know that of course it wasn't due entirely to Elaine, or her illness. It was my own fault. A writer's fault, if you like. In my work, you see— well, any writer plays god in a sense to his characters—do you see? The people, the events: he controls them. And I suppose I wanted to control my own life in the same way; when I couldn't—when I looked around me and saw a million things that were wrong, that seemed so transparently, so nakedly wrong—I wanted them to be controllable too. Changeable.

He shrugged. 'The worst kind of pride, the kind the Greeks call *hubris*—when men want to imitate gods. I see that now. . . .' He paused, and then stood up with a quick gesture. 'Anyway. The point is I felt I could not burden you with all his. Why should I? I had to free myself first. And then—when I felt free—the night we went to the church, the night of the party, when suddenly everything seemed very simple and very possible—I still couldn't tell you that I loved you, not even then.'

'Why not. Oh, why not?' Rebecca swung round to him.

'Because there was no time—it was all too fraught, too dangerous, I thought you might not believe me.' He paused. 'And because of something Nicky said. When I danced with her.'

'Nicky?' She stood up quickly. 'I might have known it!' She gave a cry of exasperation. 'She will interfere—what did she say?'

'Oh, various things . . .' He looked at her with a wry smile, but she saw a momentary uncertainty had come back into his eyes. 'She read me the riot act, in fact. Briefly but tellingly. She said the reason you were here in the first place was that you were running away from an unhappy love affair in London. That you were in a sense on the rebound, that you couldn't trust your own emotions, and that I had no right to take advantage of you when you were in that state. She was quite frank. She said she'd warned you, and she'd given you chapter and verse of an episode in my life of which I am deeply ashamed—it happened not long after Elaine died—and God knows what version she gave of it. But she said she'd warned you, and you'd refused to listen, and so she was now appealing to me—to my better nature, *if* I had one, which she doubted. She was very fierce—and, well, you had been very reticent about your reasons for leaving London, for leaving your last job, and I suddenly thought she might be right . . .'

'Well, she wasn't right!' Rebecca sprang up angrily, and turned him to face her. 'Cal—listen—believe me. I'll explain all that sometime—it's not important. But there was no love affair. I wasn't in love. I wasn't on the rebound, for God's sake, that's all in Nicky's imagination. And she had no right to say that. Damn it. I know my own mind. I love you.' She

paused, as he began to smile. 'As a matter of fact I've neve
really loved anyone else. So there.'

'Oh dear . . .' He drew her to him softly. 'First love. For m
too. A notoriously unreliable emotion. What shall we do?'

'Prove the cynics wrong, of course.' Rebecca tilted her chin
'What else?'

'I quite agree,' he said dryly. Then he kissed her.

'You know,' he said at last, when they drew apart. 'I'v
been thinking of that, of your kisses, of kissing you, ever sinc
I left you. In the storm—on Grey's boat—in Athens. I'd hav
had to come back, you know, no matter what. An arme
guard wouldn't have prevented me . . .'

'An armed guard?' Rebecca laughed softly. Then he tol
her about the night of the storm, and their escape, and she—
closely and jealously questioned, told him about Alexis an
the success of their deception.

'So the men are safe,' she said at last. 'Quite safe? Is it reall
all over?'

'All over. They have new papers. New lives. Nico ha
accepted that it's all at an end, that we can't try the sam
thing again. And Grey—well, Grey is a great romantic.
think he sees himself a little as Byron, you know, defendin
the nation that gave birth to the idea of liberty . . . an
besides, Grey likes subterfuge and excitement. He will miss al
this, more than anyone. He says he's going to retire—to
cottage in the Lake District, and finish the book he's bee
writing on Plato for the last thirty years. Maybe he will.
don't know. I wouldn't bet on it. He wants us to go and sta
with him, incidentally. He was very taken with you. A woma
of spirit, he said . . .'

Rebecca smiled. 'And Carstairs and his dreadful wife hav
gone,' she said. 'They left today. They've given up—so
suppose it is over. Oh—and I would have forgotten. Hov
strange.' She frowned. 'I met that Greek, the official, Costa
Andropoulos, today, when they were leaving. And he wa
very odd. I thought he was angry to begin with—because he'
failed—and then I wasn't so sure. He seemed to think I woul
see you again. I told him I wouldn't, but he insisted. H
said—if I did, I was to give you a message. I was to say—"A
Greek *first*." And that you'd understand. Do you?'

Cal was listening intently, and at her words a broad smile lifted his lips. 'Is that what he said? He said that?'

'Yes. Oh, and he said you'd had a most interesting conversation, you and he, the night of the party—and that surprised me. I didn't see you speak.'

'It wasn't a long conversation. But it was an odd one.' Cal paused. 'It was when you were dancing with that Sullivan boy. I spoke to him briefly—it was a little like a play. I knew who he was, and pretended I didn't—he did the same. So, we fenced around one another for a bit and then—I wanted to know and something he said gave me the opportunity to ask—he was telling me where he worked, I think. And I said—"Which are you first—a government official, or a Greek?" I wanted to know because, instinctively, I liked him. And I thought if he was a Greek, truly a Greek, he would understand what we were doing, and he would not try overhard to hinder us. He pretended to take it lightly, though I think he understood. He turned it into a joke; he answered me with another question. He said, "But which are you first, Mr Ryder—an adventurer or a lover?"'

'And what did you say?'

'Oh I said, a lover. But that that didn't preclude my also being an adventurer, I hoped—though not of an amorous kind. He laughed. That was the end of the conversation. Until now. But it explains a few things. Perhaps—' Cal shrugged. 'Perhaps he didn't exert himself or his officers with total zeal. Perhaps he obeyed his orders—up to a point. It's a fine distinction—one I think he'd appreciate. And we did get away . . .'

'You mean he wanted you to succeed?' Rebecca stared at him round-eyed and Cal shrugged.

'I wouldn't put it as strongly as that. Perhaps he didn't entirely want us to fail. His message certainly suggests that. It also suggests, to me, that he knew I was coming back. And that makes certain things easier. It means—if you would like—that we could stay here.'

'Stay—on Paxos? You and I?'

'Why not? The alarm is over. Nico swears that he accepts it's all over. As a matter of fact I think Nico would say anything if he thought it would help to keep you here, and if he thought it would facilitate our union. He's been babbling to me of marriage quite unashamedly . . .' He paused, and then drew Rebecca to him. His dark eyes looked down into hers.

'Which reminds me,' he said, with an edge in his voice. 'You haven't yet given me an answer . . .'

'Say "yes" and have done with it?' Rebecca smiled up at him challengingly. His fingers tightened around the nape of her throat, and he began to massage the skin there gently, with fire in his touch.

'That's roughly what I intended. Yes. Otherwise . . .' he paused, watching her, watching the response he awoke in her with this, the gentlest of touches, 'I might have to start persuading you.'

'Then, "yes",' Rebecca said. 'But I might not mind a little persuasion . . .'

And so he gave it her. And time passed, until finally there was an impatient rap at the door, and a great deal of coughing, and an embarrassed but triumphant Nico at last burst in upon them. He announced, when he saw them in each other's arms, that he was glad things were at last taking the course which he, and Leandros, and Agape and indeed practically the whole island had known they should take from the first, and so—by way of celebration—would his two friends now join him for the celebration dinner? It could be a rehearsal, he said, for the wedding feast, the menu for which was already planned, and really, though he understood these things, could they not join him now? Everything was prepared and laid out at Agape's house: there was wine and food. Demetrios would play for them, and later—he felt very happy—they might all sing and dance. And then, after—well, the Villa Circe was all prepared. A fire had been lit, the house was warm; it was waiting for them both to go back to—later.

Rebecca blushed at this, but Nico gave her a broad wink. Once upon a time, he gave her to understand, he had been altogether more formal about such arrangements. But, well, time went by and customs changed. Why, according to his cousin Alexis, in Athens the most extraordinary things came to pass . . .

So Cal and Rebecca went with him, and joined the feast,

and the dancing. And then, very late, when the first light was breaking on the horizon, they said goodbye, and left, and Cal drove her through the olive groves and up the track, to the summit of the hill, and they climbed down out of the Jeep and stood on the terrace together, and looked at the sea.

'Nico said,' Rebecca said at last, resting her head against Cal's shoulder, 'that in Greece they regarded every end as a new beginning . . .'

Cal smiled at her. 'Quite proper,' he said. 'Then shall we begin?'

And putting his arm around her, he led her into the Villa Circe.

Here's how to get this special offer from Harlequin!

SEPTEMBER
TREASURY EDITION
COUPON

As simple as 1…2…3!

1. Each month, save one Treasury Edition coupon from your favorite Romance or Presents novel.
2. In four months you'll have saved four Treasury Edition coupons (<u>only one coupon per month allowed</u>).
3. Then all you have to do is fill out and return the order form provided, along with the four Treasury Edition coupons required and $1.00 for postage and handling.

Mail to: Harlequin Reader Service

In the U.S.A.
2504 West Southern Ave.
Tempe, AZ 85282

In Canada
P.O. Box 2800, Postal Station A
5170 Yonge Street
Willowdale, Ont. M2N 6J3

RT1-B-2

Please send me my FREE copy of the Janet Dailey Treasury Edition. I have enclosed the four Treasury Edition coupons required and $1.00 for postage and handling along with this order form.

(Please Print)

NAME _____

ADDRESS _____

CITY _____

STATE/PROV. _____ ZIP/POSTAL CODE _____

SIGNATURE _____

This offer is limited to one order per household.

SUPPLIES LIMITED

This special Janet Dailey offer expires January 1986.

Coming Next Month in Harlequin Presents!

855 A FOREVER AFFAIR Rosemary Carter
Despite its savage beauty, her husband's African game reserve is no longer home. Was it carved in stone that she could never love another man? Surely a divorce would change that!

856 PROMISE OF THE UNICORN Sara Craven
To collect on a promise, a young woman returns her talisman— the protector of virgins—to its original owner. The power of the little glass unicorn was now with him!

857 AN IRRESISTIBLE FORCE Ann Charlton
A young woman is in danger of being taken over by a subtle irresistible force rather than by open aggression when she takes on an Australian construction king who's trying to buy out her grandmother.

858 INNOCENT PAWN Catherine George
Instead of looking past the money to the man behind it, a mother is prompted by panic to blame her husband when their five-year-old daughter is kidnapped.

859 MALIBU MUSIC Rosemary Hammond
California sunshine and her sister's beach house provide the atmosphere a young woman needs to focus on her future—until her neighbor tries to seduce her.

860 LADY SURRENDER Carole Mortimer
The man who bursts into her apartment can't see why his best friend would throw away his marriage for a woman like her. But soon he can't imagine any man—married or otherwise—*not* falling for her.

861 A MODEL OF DECEPTION Margaret Pargeter
A model takes on an assignment she can't handle when she tries to entice a man into selling his island in the Caribbean. She was supposed to deceive the man, not fall in love.

862 THE HAWK OF VENICE Sally Wentworth
Most people travel to Venice to fall in love. Instead, an au pair girl makes the journey to accuse a respected Venetian count of kidnapping—or of seduction, at least.

Take 4 novels and a surprise gift FREE